MW01115477

10 LIGHT-YEARS TO INSANITY

C. M. DANCHA

Published 2019 by Creativia (www.creativia.org)

Edited by Graham, Fading Street Services

Cover art by Cover Mint

Contact author at michaeldancha@gmail.com.

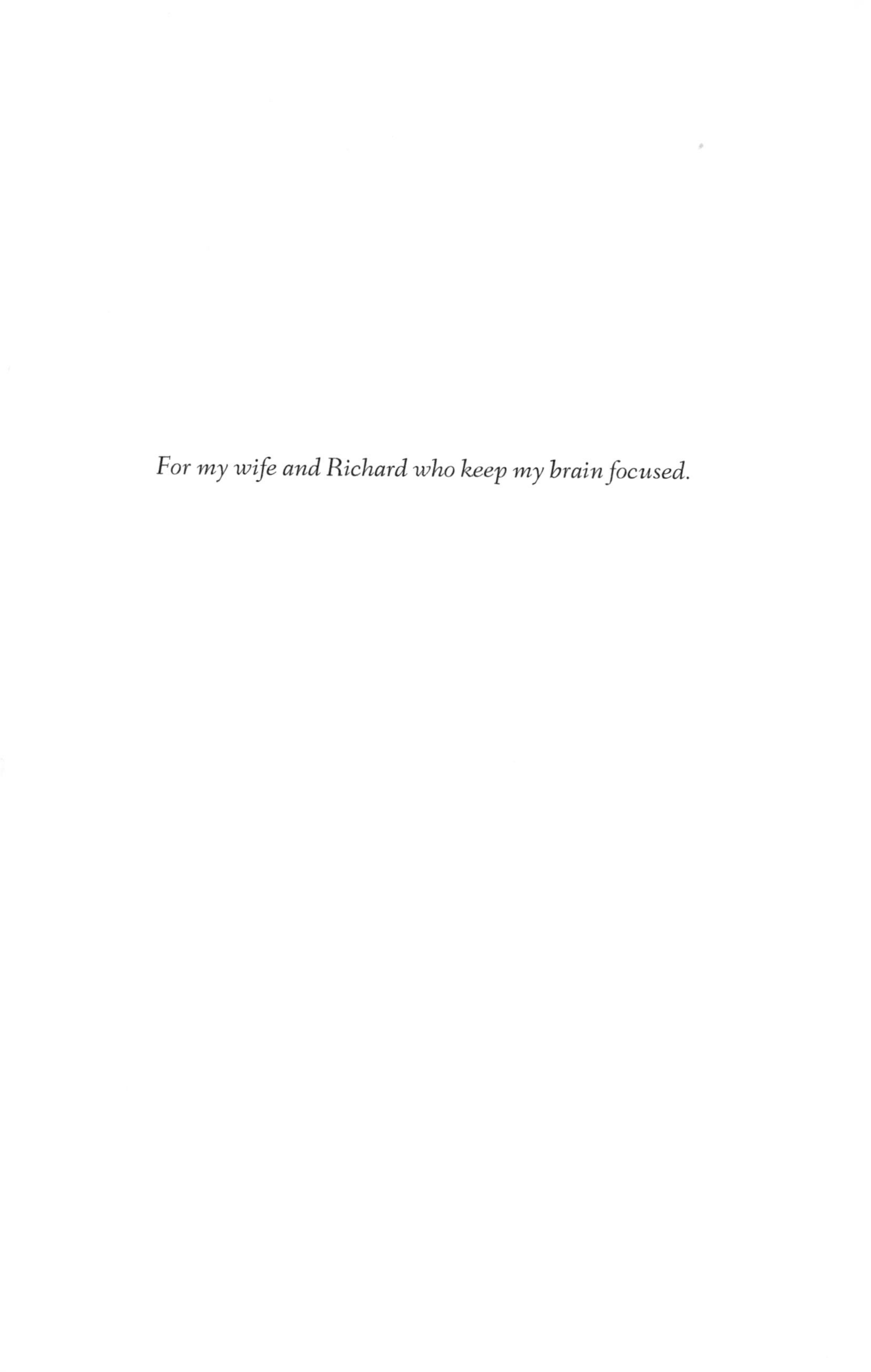

For my wife and Richard who keep my brain focused.

1

Officer Morg sat in the captain's gyro chair[1] trying to look busy and ignore the Earthling sitting next to him.

He mumbled to himself in Yandish. "ʅ⨅ Φ⊑ʅ ⟆ ɯ⏃⍀Φ⊑//ʅʌ σ ⏀ǫɯ ⟆ ʌ'Φ ⟆ ⊑ᒥᒧΦ Φ⊑ɯ ⊑ɯ/// ᒥᒪ≁, ʅ'ⴷ σǫʅʌσ Φǫ ≁ᒥᒪΦ ⊑ʅⴷ ʅʌ Φ⊑ɯ ⍀ɯ⨅ᒥᒪ ⟆ ɯ ʅʌΦɯ....?" "If this Earthling doesn't shut the hell up, I'm going to put him in the refuse interlock and eject him into space. Doesn't he ever shut his voice hole?"

"What did you say, Morg? You know I don't understand Yandish. Turn on your translator[2] so I understand what you're saying."

Morg was more irritated with himself than the Earthling. He had turned off his translator but forgot not to talk to himself. He had reached a breaking point and couldn't help himself. Talking out-loud was the best way he knew to drown out the Earthling's continuous blabbering.

Morg flipped the translator to *voice* mode. "Sorry, Earthling. I must have hit the translator off switch by mistake. What were you saying?"

That's all it took to get the Earthling yapping again. "Ah, ... You know, I don't remember. After a few seconds of reflection and believing he had Morg's attention, the Earthling began to ramble again.

"Morg, did I ever tell you about how I ended up on Yanda? It was about eight years ago when I was nineteen years old. I was minding my business behind ...."

In the past month, Morg had heard this story at least three dozen times. He had it memorized and could repeat it verbatim. Listening to it was almost intolerable. With each retelling of the story, the Earthling made himself more heroic. If this continued, he would be a superhero by the end of their trip. Morg could imagine the final version. The kid would save the universe from a wicked, evil force.

Morg scrambled to think of a way not to listen to the story again. If he could wait until the Earthling got wrapped up in his ridiculous, heroic tale he could flip off his translator. Too bad there wasn't a way to avoid hearing the melodic drone of the Earthling's words and see his animated arm, hand, and eye movements. But at least he wouldn't have to hear the Yandish translation of the story again. If the Earthling got extremely carried away with himself, Morg could mentally sneak away and think of better times on his home planet of Yanda.

".... the old man's place, having a couple tokes on a fantasy stick[3], when out of nowhere this UFO drops out of the sky and sets down. Let me tell you, it freaked me out. I hate to admit it, but I was scared. I had never seen a spacecraft before. I thought aliens from outer space was a bunch of B.S. But there it was, a large elliptical spacecraft pulsating like a throbbing boner." Morg had no idea what a boner was but the Earthling cackled with laughter each time he said the word.

"I turned to run, but before I could take one stride, something grabbed me from behind."

Morg wanted to break in with the smarmy comment of, "Gee, let me guess. Could it have been a harness beam?" but decided not to irritate the little creep sitting next to him.

"The next thing I knew was that I woke up inside a holding pen with about a hundred other humans. There were men and women, but no children. I found this kinda strange, but it made perfect sense when I found out where we were being taken. Sorry, I'm jumping ahead of myself. Anyhow, there were people from virtually every country on Earth in the holding pen. A man who spoke English told me we were on the alien spacecraft. I thought he was nuts and this had to be a gag. I changed my mind when an alien brought in a couple pails of food and body waste containers. My god, he was an ugly son-of-a-bitch. Morg, compared to that alien you are photogenic."

It took every bit of control Morg had not to leap from his gyro chair and throttle the Earthling. He slowly calmed down and thought to himself how he would like to lay into the Earthling. Making fun of anyone's appearance was the last thing the Earthling had a right to do. Talk about ugly. He had traveled the universe as a Yandan Invasion Trooper but never ran into a creature as ugly as the Earthling. Pale white skin, yellow filaments sprouting from the top of his body and beady little eyes. His bone and muscle systems were very underdeveloped which limited his lifting capability to no more than three stralocks[4]. What a wimp.

Also, the coloring of this Earth creature defied the universal laws of nature. On every planet Morg took part in conquering, the male of the species was always adorned in vibrant pastels, primary and secondary colors. From the neon blue and reds of the Tworks to the aqua and rust colored Asislyians. It was always the same. The male was vibrantly colored to draw the attention of predators. This allowed the female to flee and hide. But not on Earth. The male and female were covered with the same dirty off-white to dark-brown outer layer. That was the norm. Any mutations like albinos and ginger-colored Earthlings were shunned by the rest of society. What a drab and monotonous place the planet Earth must be.

"Anyhow, this space vehicle turned out to be a slave transport operated by Crelons. You know who they are, don't you, Morg?" The Earthling didn't wait for Morg to respond. If he had, he would have waited a long time.

As the Earthling jabbered on, Morg sat back and thought about how he got himself into this mess. The memory of being selected to escort the Earthling halfway across the universe was cloudy. It seemed like eons ago even though it had only been a very short time.

He remembered being summoned to the commander's field office on the newly-invaded planet of Goltog. The Yandan invasion force was still encountering stiff resistance from the undermanned and underequipped Goltogian army. One look at the commander was all it took for Morg to know his future wasn't stellar.

"Officer Morg, how have you been? Care for some Cannis?"

The commander's offer to share the expensive and rare drug was another bad sign. It was well known that the commander only offered the drug to soldiers who were being reassigned to a life and death mission or an undertaking no one else wanted. Either way, it rarely ended well.

"Morg, I'm sure you're wondering why I sent for you." Here it comes, the slap in the face for over a hundred years of faithful service.

"I need a dependable agent to take a high priority item to a planet we are considering for colonization."

"May I ask which planet and what is the cargo?"

"It's not important Morg, but if you must know, the planet is Earth and the cargo is one of their kind. I think they are referred to as Earthlings. Your cargo is the offspring of a high-ranking official on Earth."

The last thing Morg expected was to be an escort for a living being. An inanimate object would have been a reasonable piece of cargo. The destination was also a surprise. He had a good working knowledge of the planets within the Yandan Empire. He could recite those already part of the alliance and those targeted for colonization. But he never heard of Earth which meant it had to be many light years away. That meant he would be gone for months, if not years, on this babysitting detail.

"Commander, don't you think this would be a better detail for an agent who has less invasion experience than I do? After all, I have over ten decades of...."

That's as far as Morg got trying to talk his way out of the assignment. The commander shot a menacing glare his direction and the tips of his sensory antennae leaned forward and turned from purple to crimson. Morg knew it was time to shut up and accept the task forced upon him. To avoid any further confrontation with the commander, Morg went to the Cannis dispenser and took a deep snort of the drug. He might as well get something beneficial out of this crappy assignment.

"Commander, it would be my honor to fulfill this assignment. When do I leave?"

"Your transport is being readied as we speak. The Earthling will meet you on Yanda when you dock there."

The Cannis started to cloud his thoughts and euphoria spread through his armored, skeletal body plates. It had been years since he inhaled the rare and expensive drug. It was potent, very potent. It took his mind off the lousy assignment. Being sent on a second-rate detail for months and having his career sliding downward didn't seem so bad now. He'd have plenty of time during the escort detail to figure out who he pissed off. He must have crossed a high-ranking official to get such a crappy detail.

He bowed to the commander and headed to the exit.

"Officer Morg, I forgot to tell you something. I know what you think about this assignment. After all, I was your time and grade once. So, to make sure you get the cargo to its destination alive and well, I will be holding your offspring and mate hostage. They will be released when the Earthling reaches his home planet. For their sake, don't screw this up, Morg."

He wanted to turn and put a pincer through the commander's torso. Unfortunately, that wouldn't achieve a thing other than his own death and the elimination of his entire lineage. Assaulting ranking officers was an automatic death sentence no matter what the circumstances. He must keep his temper and need for revenge in check until it passed or better conditions presented themselves.

As he walked away from the commander's hooch, he debated

whether to proceed immediately to Yanda or return to the front lines for some last-minute killing of Goltogians. The euphoric high from the Cannis gave him a feeling of infallibility and pushed him toward the killing fields. But then, reality crept into his consciousness. If he got hurt or wounded, the penalty would be.... would be too terrible to imagine. It was best not to think about what the commander and Trifect[5] *would do to him, his mate, and offspring.*

Four days later he met the Earthling on Yanda. He quickly understood why he was being blackmailed. The scrawny, pathetic loudmouth was unbearable. He introduced himself as Joe something-or-other. Morg couldn't care less. He decided to call him Earthling or kid. Using the kid's given name would imply a personal relationship and that was the last thing Morg wanted to present to the universe.

Before they lifted off from Yanda, Morg considered killing the Earthling several times. As hard as he tried, he couldn't think of how to make the Earthling's death appear to be an accident. Plus, he couldn't chance being the primary suspect. In the end, it was the need to keep his mate safe which convinced Morg to buck up and fulfill the escort mission.

His memory began to evaporate as he resigned himself to a disgusting future. There was no sense lamenting the past; it was unchangeable.

Morg had to give the Trifect credit. They perfectly anticipated his reaction to being locked in a small space transport with the Earthling for months. What he didn't know was that the Trifect chose him because of his military background and psychological profile. He was the only trained pilot with military invasion experience and enough patience to put up with the Earthling's outrageous personality. All the other Yandan candidates for the mission were deemed unacceptable. They would kill the Earthling within a few short weeks, without regard for the consequences to their offspring and mates. Morg was the only candidate who had a reasonable chance of making it to Earth with his cargo in one piece.

"I thought I was going to lose my mind before we got to Crelon or wherever we were being taken. The humans I was locked up with were a bunch of dullards. All they could do was cry, moan, groan, and worry about what was going to happen. You know me, Morg. I'm an upbeat kind of guy; a man of action. No sense worrying about the future when there's plenty of fun and adventure to be had in the present. Anyhow, by the fourth week with these losers, I couldn't stand to be around them. Thankfully, there was this one bird from Iran or Iraq or some damn place in the Middle East who I got really friendly with, if you know what I mean. You do know what I'm talking about, don't you, Morg? I've never asked you this before, but you do have a reproduction unit, don't you, Morg? Morg, are you listening to me?"

The Earthling's annoying questions interrupted Morg's daydreaming about his situation, offspring, and mate. Damn him. Why did he have to disturb such wonderful thoughts and memory playback?

"What did you say, Earthling?"

"I said, are you listening to me? If you're not going to listen, then I'm going to work on the Shadow Drive system[6]."

Letting the Earthling near the Shadow Drive system was the last thing Morg wanted. He was unqualified to work on it and lacked the basic intelligence and dexterity to understand the system. The last time he worked on it, the transport's propulsion system crashed. They drifted in space for four days until Morg could correct the Earthling's *improvements*.

Morg fought the urge to physically silence the Earthling. "Yes, I'm definitely listening to you. What a wonderful story. Don't stop now. Please continue, Earthling."

"You better listen, Morg. You know what the commander told you about getting me to Earth in one piece and making sure I arrive there happy as hell."

"Yes, yes, I remember. Please continue. Tell me again about that... what did you call her?"

"A bird. A chickee-poo. A plaything. I swear, you are hopeless,

Morg. Have you always been this dense? Let loose a little, buddy. You don't have to be so uptight with me."

It was a good thing the Earthling couldn't read his thoughts. Otherwise, he would find out how close he was to a gruesome, painful death.

"Okay, now try to stay with me, Morg. As I was saying, this bird and I were getting to know each other really good. But you can only screw around so much, right? So, as the days went by, I began to worry about how I was going to get out of this predicament. Somehow, I had to get off this Crelon ship and make my way back to Earth or a friendly planet."

The Earthling paused and looked over at Morg to see if he was listening. Morg could feel his beady little eyes boring into him so he pretended to listen by flushing his breathing gills. From the time he spent on Yanda, the Earthling knew this meant his shipmate was focused and paying attention, so he continued his story.

"Then, one day, I overheard two Crelon guards laughing about how their human cargo was going to be auctioned off on a planet named Treestte 64. I had been eavesdropping on the Crelon guards for weeks learning their language. What I heard wasn't encouraging. I wasn't thrilled about being sold to the highest bidder on an alien planet. But what I heard next blew my mind. Apparently, the inhabitants of Treestte 64 consider humans a delicacy. That's right, those losers eat humans and are willing to pay big for dining on human flesh and bones."

The Earthling took a couple sips from the overhead energy feeder[7] to clear his throat. "Now, I was really starting to worry. How the hell was I going to avoid being a drumstick on a Treestteian's dinner table?"

One look at the Earthling told Morg he had reached the only enjoyable part of the story. The image of the Earthling roasted and served on a Treestteian banquet table was exhilarating. The mere fact that the Earthling still broke out in a sweat when retelling this part of the story made Morg ecstatic. He wanted to let his pleasure pods[8] display their aqua and chartreuse colors of elation but knew this would annoy the Earthling.

"Well, I saw my chance when we got to Treestte 64. Being a clever guy, I noticed right away that the Treestteians loved foul odors. When they came by the holding pens for pre-auction inspections, my fellow inmates with the foulest body odor attracted the most attention. And, let me tell you, after two months on a slave transport without a shower or bath made us very ripe. But there were some who were intolerable. Those were the ones the Treestteians flocked to as though they were celebrities."

Morg looked for a chance to daydream again but could see the Earthling was keeping a close eye on him while he blabbered away.

"I had a couple days before the auction, so I did everything I could think of to clean myself and try to smell fresh. I took at least half of my water ration each day and hand washed. When I ran out of water, I stole and begged for more from the other captives. My girlfriend was an easy target. She couldn't understand why I needed so much water but gave me most of her ration. There was no way I was going to tell her the real reason. I knew one captive might be able to deceive the bidders and auctioneer but two would be unlikely. So, I kept making up stories about why I needed her water. She was a good girl and I should have told her what I was up to, but you know, everything is fair in love and war. Besides, she gave her life for a worthy cause." The Earthling pointed to himself and started to cackle. He amused himself by lackadaisically describing his girlfriend's sacrificial death.

"When auction day came, the auctioneer went through the holding pens sniffing each captive. He wanted to make sure they reeked of body odor. When he came to me, he knew something was wrong. He smelled under my arms, on the backside and from top to bottom. He was not happy that I was nearly odorless. He began to throw a fit but then the auction chimes rang. He mumbled something under his breath and led the other captives to the auction bidding pit. The bidding was hot and furious. The smelliest captives were coveted and commanded the highest prices. The few who still had a few pounds of weight after the long journey on the transport were highly sought after. In fact, a few fights broke out in the auction pits over the fattest and smelliest humans."

As many times as Morg heard this story, he never bothered to ask what happened to the Earthling's girlfriend. For some strange reason, this time he took the opportunity to ask.

"What's that? Oh, a gruesome-looking Treestteian bought her. I waved to her and tried to look heart-broken as she was led away in chains. At one point, she collapsed to the ground weeping and shrieking. I'm sure she was a tasty morsel." The Earthling winked an eye at Morg and grinned. There was no question this gesture had some type of underlying meaning. Morg didn't have a clue what it meant but figured it had to be something loathsome. He refused to demean himself by asking for an explanation.

After years as an Invasion Trooper, Morg had become callous and hard. He wasn't very sentimental. But, in this case, he felt sorrow for the female Earthling that got suckered by the jerk sitting next to him.

"Well, when I got to the auction block the bidders backed away. The Treestteian sense of smell is very sensitive. From fifteen to twenty feet, they could tell I was almost free from body odor. In their minds, my fresh scent indicated that I had a terrible disease."

"The auctioneer opened the bidding and waited. No bids came from the remaining audience. He did everything he could to get a bid, hoping to get rid of me. The bidders started to leave the pit, wanting nothing to do with me. When there were only a few remaining, the Treestteian auctioneer offered to give me away for free. Not one bidder accepted his offer. He finally gave up and put me back in the holding pen, cursing the entire time."

The auctioneer was livid and laid into the Crelon slavers; "Here, you take this diseased human. Get him out of my sight. And, don't ever come back here again with an inferior product."

"The Crelon slavers weren't happy that they had to haul my ass around after leaving Treestte 64. They decided to make my life as miserable as hell. Every day on their transport was a day of slavery. Clean this, pick up that, make and serve food. And, there were some unmentionable things which an important Earthling, like me, shouldn't be forced to do."

Morg thought to himself, "⊬ɯ⍋⊑, ⊬⍜⎍'⍀ɯ...." "Yeah, you're important all right. If it wasn't for your old man, you would be back on Yanda scrubbing trash pits. You're lucky he is the Prefect and General Counsel for Earth's Global Union Assembly. He demanded your safe return to Earth as a condition for finalizing the treaty agreement with Yanda."

Morg couldn't stop the negative thoughts that flooded his mind. He fought to put a positive spin on the situation. "Earthling, if you had been bought on Treestte 64, I wouldn't be sitting here listening to your whiny, obnoxious diatribe. I'd be doing something important like leading an invasion brigade or rubbing with my mate. Oh well, I lasted this long without throttling you. With the help of my ancestors, I'm sure I can last until this mission is finished." Morg was ready to flip off his translator when he heard the kid say, "Finally, the Crelon slavers put in at that pathetic planet you call home. Tell me the truth, Morg. Aren't you embarrassed by Yanda? It's so damn dreary.... and, smelly. By the way, what's with that constant vibration in the air on Yanda? It never stops and no matter where you go, it follows you."

"Earthling, for your information, that vibration is ...."

"I know, I know. It's something you guys do to maintain orbital balance, blah, blah, blah. That's not important. Be quiet for a minute and let me finish my story."

Morg was fuming. He was so mad he couldn't put together a coherent thought. If he had, the Earthling would have heard a few choice Yandan swear words and curses. He was ready to turn off is translator but decided to keep it on. There was a strange desire to hear if the kid said anything else insulting about Yanda.

"Well, I'm sure you want to hear how I got back at the Crelon slavers, so listen closely because I'm not going to repeat this."

"Don't worry, I'm not going to interrupt, you piece ..." Morg caught himself before finishing the sentence. He could wait for a better opportunity to verbally blast the Earthling.

"The Crelons sold me to a Yandan creep who wanted a flunky to do his monotonous labor. I was constantly working, cleaning, and taking care of those Yandan Nortels[9] you all love to smell and eat. As part of the deal, the Yandan offered his residence as a party house. I must admit, those boys, or girls, I guess Crelons are both, know how to throw a party. It went on around the clock for days. I've never seen anything to compare to the addiction, drunkenness, and debauchery the Crelons cooked up. Anyhow, the official departure clearance for the Crelon ship arrived at the Yandan house. I was lucky enough to intercept and read it. I knew exactly when they were cleared to leave Yanda. I had less than six hours to execute my revenge."

The Earthling took another sip from his energy feeder. Out of the corner of his eye, he scowled at Morg making sure the Yandan was paying attention. After all, this was the best part of the entire story and he wanted to make sure his flight buddy heard every word.

"Before the Crelons left for the launch terminal, I put a couple cases of Brofult in their vehicle. As you know, they love that drink. Personally, I think it tastes like crap but the Crelons and you guys love it. Now, here's the kicker. What the Crelons didn't know was that I loaded the Brofult with a laxative. There was enough in each container to turn their insides out."

The Earthling stopped to shake his head and laugh at his cunning deed. "I knew they would hit the Brofult hard as soon as they jumped a light year or so away from Yanda. They did, and I watched it on the transponders I hid on their ship. God, it was hilarious. Seeing the expressions on their faces when they started getting sick and doubling over in excruciating pain was great. And, then they started crapping. It was funnier than hell. There was Crelon crap everywhere and, best of all, there were no slaves on board to clean it up."

Morg sat there and watched the Earthling laugh uproariously for a couple minutes. The kid was certainly his own best fan. Finally, the laughter faded, and he got up from his gyro chair. "Morg, I got to get some shut-eye. Wake me in a couple hours, buddy. If you're lucky, I'll show you that recording from the bridge of the Crelon ship. Oh, and by the way, put in coordinates to stop at Feltte Six. I hear they got some high-flying birds on that planet."

Morg watched in disbelief as the Earthling strutted off the ship's bridge and headed for the sleeping quarters. He was stunned. It took until the Earthling was out of sight before his parting words started to register. With his translator still on, Morg started to mumble under his breath, spitting out each word with increasing anger.

"You want to stop where? What the hell do you think this is, a tour transport? Getting your jerk-ass to Earth is a top-secret mission. But you think it would be fun to stop at a planet known to harbor some of the worst criminals in the universe. Are you insane, Earthling?"

Morg paused to take a deep breath so the anger pods on the top of his head wouldn't blow open. These pods had never blown open except in combat. But here he was in deep space, alone with an inferior creature who had pushed him to his limits. He allowed the Earthling to get under his scales. In war, he could strike back. All he could do now was fume and mumble, "Earthling, if you try to show me that playback of the Crelons crapping all over themselves one more time, I'll... I'll... I'll make you wish that you left Yanda on their ship."

2

"Do you know there's a body in the cargo bay?"

The feeler hair on Morg's backside detected a slight variance in the pressure on the bridge so he turned his gyro chair toward the disturbance. As he suspected, the Earthling was walking his way. He had a large food item stuffed in his voice hole and was trying to chew and talk at the same time. It was bad enough listening to the Earthling's incessant blabbering. But now, he had to watch bits of food eject and fly around the bridge as the kid tried to get the words out. Morg reluctantly turned on his translator.

"Morg, did you hear me? I said, do you know there's a body in the cargo bay?"

Morg stared at the Earthling, attempting to detect whether this was another of his practical jokes. If the Earthling was screwing around, he was doing a damn decent job of hiding the truth.

"What do you mean, there's a body in the cargo bay?"

"My god. You're a military man; a trained killer. You know what death is and you know what a body is, and you know where the cargo bay is. Add them all together and what do you get?"

Morg unstrapped himself from the gyro chair and headed for the cargo bay. He didn't say a word to the Earthling but made himself a promise. If there wasn't something dead in the cargo bay, there would be by the end of the day.

The smell coming from the cargo bay was overwhelming. It was the smell of death. Morg had been in enough battles to know the dead thing on the other side of the door was a Yandan. There was only one creature in the universe that gave off this distinctive acidic and sour odor.

Lying on the floor behind a stack of boxes was Morg's mate. Even in death, she was still attractive and alluring to him. Sticking in her back, lodged between the third and fourth filter gill was a Yandan military slit knife. Whoever killed her knew precisely where to put the knife to cause instant death. Or, the assailant was damn lucky. Morg bet the killer was well versed in the art of assassination.

Morg had conducted hundreds of postmortem investigations looking for clues about the killer, time, and cause of death. This time, he wasn't anxious to examine the crime scene and corpse. There was something sacrilegious about touching, prodding, and examining the shell of a being he knew so well and spent countless hours of intimacy with.

It took two hours to complete his examination of the crime scene and victim. All the physical evidence was collected, categorized, and stored. Body samples and fluids from the victim were ready for the forensics analyzer to determine if there were any irregularities. The only bit of evidence which struck Morg as unusual was a tiny piece of spongy, two-tone, material lying by his mate's head. His first guess was that this material was organic and not synthetic. He wouldn't know if his guess was right until the forensics analyzer spit out its report.

The shell of his deceased mate had decayed significantly and was only a day or two away from falling apart. If that happened, the internal organs and body fluids would flow in every direction like water cascading through a faulty dam. There was already some seepage on the floor around the corpse which he would have to mop up.

It was obvious she had been dead for weeks. He wondered if she died before take-off from Yanda or killed in transit? Normally, the forensics analyzer was able to pinpoint the time of death to within twenty-four hours. But, in this case, the cool temperature and varying atmospheric pressure in the cargo bay caused by the Shadow Drive system would corrupt the time of death estimate by at least a few days, plus or minus.

With all the evidence collected and recordings made of the crime scene, there was no reason to keep her on board. Morg gently lifted her shell onto a gurney and pushed it to the refuse interlock. He put a thermal grenade down her gullet and ejected her into space. This type of grenade didn't need any type of atmosphere to burn. With a two-minute fuse, it would incinerate her insides before blowing the body shell to pieces. Morg thought this would be a fitting ending for his mate who loved space travel and daydreamed about the stars.

On his way back to the bridge, Morg made a mental note to check the ship's recording system. It might reveal whether the assassin slipped up and left a recording of himself boarding the ship with or without his mate. He didn't put much hope in recognizing the killer or watching his mate board the transport. Any assassin who killed with such precision, wouldn't forget to erase or destroy the recordings from a ship's playback system. On newer transports, recorded playbacks were transmitted immediately to the nearest information storage facility in the solar system. But, the playback recordings on this old tug were stored in a compartment accessible to anyone with modest technical skills.

Morg wondered why the disappearance of his mate wasn't communicated to him in deep space. Even though his offspring were irresponsible much of the time, they would eventually report her missing. He walked back to the bridge, thinking about what questions to ask the Earthling about the crime scene. Halfway there, the answer to the communications question popped into his head. The Trifect must have put a *nocomm* on his mission. Nothing could be communicated to or from the transport for the entire time it was in transit to Earth. The last thing the Trifect wanted was for their enemies to eavesdrop and find out who was being escorted to Earth.

Morg couldn't believe his eyes when he entered the bridge. Standing next to the view-window with a painter stick in his hands was the Earthling. He was drawing lewd and lecherous illustrations on the view-window. To highlight the illustrations he included stars, black holes, and other heavenly bodies. Nude Earthlings, Yandans, Crelons, and other assorted species and creatures covered the entire twenty feet of view-window. All were in compromising positions and acts of debauchery. A few of his pictures were death scenes. Morg understood how the kid knew of Earthlings, Yandans and Crelons, but how did he know about these other beings?

The stupidity of mucking up and using the view-window as a full-length mural was almost beyond comprehension. But, on closer examination, Morg had to admit the Earthling's illustrations were quite ingenious and artful. One of the human figures caught his attention. It was a female Earthling who was sitting between two male Earthlings. All were nude. The woman's swept-back hair consisted of the fire red and orange of a neighboring solar system's gases and reflected lights. Her breast nipples were two prominent, rose colored stars. And, between her inner thighs was a large black hole. If these drawings had been created by a prominent artist, they would have been taken seriously. But there was no doubt in Morg's mind that the Earthling was screwing around. This was just another way to amuse himself.

Morg was about ready to interrupt the Earthling's fun and games when the thermal grenade blew. It could be seen off the starboard side of the ship about a quadrant away. Within two seconds, a minor shock wave hit and vibrated through the transport.

The Earthling jumped back from the view-window and spun around to find Morg staring at him.

"What the hell was that?"

"I discharged the corpse with a thermal grenade in it?"

"Really? Who was that dead guy in the cargo bay?"

"It wasn't a guy, it was my mate."

"Are you kidding? That corpse in the cargo bay was your mate? Wow, that's unreal."

Morg waited for some sort of condolence but none came. The closest the Earthling came to saying something pleasant was, "Oh, well. Now both of us have lost a mate."

At first, Morg didn't know what the Earthling was talking about. Then, it hit him. "No, I lost a life-long partner. You lost a three-week fling."

Morg's jab bounced off the Earthling like a wisp of air. Before either of them could say more, the ship's Roboland system announced, "Please return to your gyro chairs and buckle the harness straps. Arrival at Feltte Six will be in eighteen minutes. Docking will be at gate 12W. Upon disembarking, proceed to the Process Area with your credentials. Be advised that inadequate or no credentials will result in a quarantine placed upon the arriving ship. The current crime rating on Feltte Six is 8.3 out of 10. Have a productive stay."

"Morg, are we going to have fun, or what?"

Morg didn't bother to answer or acknowledge the Earthling. All he could think about was the smartass comment about his deceased mate. If that wasn't irritating enough, there was also the question of how the Earthling diverted their flight to Feltte Six without his knowledge. He couldn't believe they were making a stop at one of the most crime-infested planets in the universe.

3

THE DOCKING BAY WAS LIKE ANY OTHER IN THE UNIVERSE except for one minor detail. Everywhere Morg looked, armed guards roamed the area carrying the latest armament. The sheer number of armed personnel reminded Morg of how Yandan invasion brigades set a perimeter on newly invaded planets.

Thermal grenades, laser rifes, full body armor, and barrier shields were prominently displayed. There was no attempt to camouflage the weapons. The authorities wanted each new arrival to know there were limits on Feltte Six. Arriving guests were free to kill each other but shouldn't give one iota of thought to attacking a government enforcer. When that happened, it was an immediate death penalty; no capture, no incarceration, and no judicial review. It was straight to the afterlife if the offender believed in that sort of mysticism.

"Attention, all new arrivals. Please proceed to the Process Area located behind docking slip 7K. Each new arrival can bring one weapon of choice onto Feltte Six. Do not carry this weapon to the Process Area. Provide the Process Agent with a visual of the weapon and its location on your ship. The weapon will be retrieved and loaded onto the glider transport you choose. Those who wish to buy a weapon may do so after clearing the Process Area. You will find that we have a wonderful selection of the latest weaponry. All weapons are guaranteed to be jam-proof, work in harsh environments and tested for accuracy."

Morg was very familiar with glider transports. They were high-speed, conveyance trains which used reflective magnetic current for propulsion. He had ridden on them quite often on Yandan colony planets. What he didn't understand in the announcement was the reference to choosing a glider. How many places could you go on this planet? He figured he would learn soon enough. In the meantime, he debated whether to take his sabre assault rife[1] or leave it in secured storage on the transport. After weighing the pros and cons, he decided it was better to have his favorite weapon at his side. It had kept him safe through many campaigns. With so many unknown dangers on Feltte Six, there were plenty of reasons to have the old friend tag along.

The Process Agent was an import from another planet. Morg guessed he was Krelatian. The short and stout beings were easily identified by the grumpy frowns painted on their blue, oval faces. Krelatians were in high demand throughout the universe because of their ability to treat everyone shabbily. No matter what they were thinking they always projected a cantankerous attitude. It was amazing how many beings admitted to crimes simply because they couldn't handle a Krelatian's stare. To fill the dead air, true and bogus admissions came pouring out.

"Is this the sabre assault rife you want to bring onto Feltte Six?"

Morg nodded to the Process Agent.

"It will be tagged with the same serial number which has been imprinted below an undisclosed area of your body shell. This number will be good for thirty hours. If you plan to stay longer, return here for a serial number update."

Morg turned to walk away and find the Earthling.

"Wait. Are you with the Earthling I processed before you?"

"Unfortunately, yes. Did he insult you or say something stupid?"

"Yes, but don't worry. He won't get off this planet alive. Remember, you are responsible for the disposal of his body. Okay, move along."

Morg wanted to know more but the Krelatian was already processing the next new arrival.

As Morg walked out onto the glider platform he wondered what the Earthling said to the Process Agent. It was either profoundly stupid and insulting. Or, the Krelatian could pick out the soon-to-be-vaporized from among the new arrivals. Morg chose the latter explanation. After processing thousands of new arrivals, the Krelatian developed a sixth sense. It allowed him to pick out the losers after only a one-minute interview. Morg's spirits lifted a bit knowing someone else in the universe shared his bottom-of-the-barrel opinion of the Earthling.

The glider platform was chaos and mayhem. It was jammed with new arrivals from every galaxy in the universe. Wall-to-wall beings bumped into each other as they tried to fight their way to the departing gliders of their choice. The excitement in the air was electric. To Morg, it seemed like these beings were acting like children attempting to board a ride at an amusement park.

As he watched the craziness, he scanned the entire platform for as far as he could see in each direction. In total, there were a dozen glider transport tubes labeled with destinations such as "Detroit 1967", "Mytop 2212" and "Fragsten 2156". Morg was well-versed in the history of the universe. It didn't take him long to realize that these locations had one thing in common. They were all cities and countries from various sectors of the universe known for crime and violence. In short, they were historical shit-holes of the universe.

Within a couple of minutes, the significance of the four-digit number behind the name became clear. The number corresponded to a year when the location experienced a catastrophic event. 1967 was the year of civil rioting in Detroit by its minority population. 2212 was the year the ruling family of Mytop was ousted from power and a decade of violent civil war ensued. And, 2156 was the year crime syndicates took control of Fragsten.

Morg's initial impression of this strange world was right. Feltte Six was nothing more than a giant amusement park which catered to the scum, bottom feeders, and low-lifes of the universe. It offered every vice, crime, and form of violence imaginable. Drugs, sex, blackmail, murder, torture, and despotic power were all available. New arrivals only had to reach out for the evil they desired. Then it was a contest between rival guests who wanted the same vice. Whoever was tougher and shrewder won that vice. The other guest usually didn't leave Feltte Six alive.

There were only two rules in the theme parks. If you killed someone, you were responsible for disposing of the body. You could hire someone to cart the corpse to the incineration station or take it yourself. It didn't matter. The remaining rule was that government enforcers were *untouchables*. They were off-limits to assault, battery, harassment, and back-talk. If they gave an order, it was followed without question. Failure to follow these simple rules resulted in an immediate death sentence carried out by an enforcer squad.

Otherwise, there were no rules governing what was allowed in each theme park. It was the law of the jungle. If you wanted something another being had, you could buy it, steal it, or kill for it. If you chose to murder your opponent, it was best to ambush him in a surprise attack. No one was going to condemn you for not playing fair.

Broadcasted glider departure announcements increased in frequency. New arrivals, from the last couple of spaceships landing on Feltte Six, raced to get to their glider departure gates. Pushing and shoving, fist fights, and countless arguments broke out in all areas of the docking platform. Morg expected to see at any moment the Earthling involved in some type of altercation. He figured it was only a matter of time before the Earthling's obnoxious personality rubbed a mercenary, tough guy, or all-around badass the wrong way.

As each glider departed for its destination, Morg became more concerned that he lost the Earthling. He was beginning to think the Earthling boarded an earlier glider. He might be on his way to one of the cesspools where he would lip-off to the wrong being and get himself vaporized. Morg wouldn't hear anything about the Earthling's death until the government got around to sending him an official death notice. That might take days and would be a courtesy notification because Morg was his arrival mate. The only thing that would speed up the process was if Morg had to dispose of the body. Regardless of the circumstances, the Earthling's death would thrust Morg into an untenable situation. What would he do? He would be a disgraced warrior who lost his mate, family, career, and home planet.

"Paging Morg from Yanda. Officer Morg from Yanda. Please respond. Weapon pick-up for Mr. Morg from the planet...."

Morg's head pivoted to the direction from where his name was called. He was lucky that his ears were shaped like parabolic dishes. This made his hearing very sensitive. His superior sense of hearing more than compensated for average eyesight and smell.

Fifty-yards away, he spotted the Earthling in front of the Detroit 1967 departure dock. He was talking with the Feltte dock employee who paged Morg. In the employee's hand was Morg's assault rife. Even from this distance, Morg could tell the Earthling was trying to con the Feltte departure clerk out of something.

Morg came up behind the Earthling in time to hear the Feltte departure clerk say, "Sir, I can't give you this assault rife. Your embedded serial number doesn't match with the serial number on the rife."

"Aw, come on. The owner of the rife is a friend of mine. I promise to give it to him when I see him at the Detroit 1967 park."

Morg was standing close enough to see the Earthling remove a couple Cannis capsules from his pants pocket and offer them to the clerk. "Here, take these. You've worked hard and deserve a reward. Give me the assault rife, and these are yours."

The dock clerk's eyes opened to twice their normal size when he spotted the Cannis capsules. He couldn't stop staring at them. He knew they were worth a small fortune. At least twice his yearly wage on the black market.

"Okay, but you have to promise not to tell anyone. I could get in big trouble letting you have a rife registered to another being."

The Earthling reached out to take the rife from the clerk, but his hand never touched the weapon. Morg stepped between the two crooks and grabbed the rife and Cannis capsules.

"Son, I suggest you take your dishonest ass out of here, right now. And, so you know, I'm Morg from Yanda and this is my rife. Now get."

The departure clerk was shaking with fear. Not only was Morg a mean-looking SOB but all it would take is one word from the Yandan to get him fired or vaporized. He waved his serial number validator over Morg's left arm in one quick swipe and then turned tail and started running.

Morg slung the assault rife over his shoulder and grabbed the Earthling by his left ear. Squeezing the earlobe between his pincer thumb and forefinger was all it took to get the Earthling squirming and whining. "Morg, stop Morg. That hurts like hell."

Morg didn't care how much the Earthling complained. He was so pissed that he considered exerting more pressure and watching the Earthling either pass out or soil himself.

"Pick up your tote bag, jerk-off."

As the Earthling gingerly bent over to grab the handles on his bag, the platform announcer said, "Last call for Detroit 1967 glider. Board immediately at dock 24L. This is the last glider for Detroit 1967 today. The crime rate in Detroit is 93.3. Have a favorable trip."

"Morg, we have to get on the Detroit glider."

Without letting up on the earlobe pressure, Morg asked, "Why?"

"Because that's the park I signed up for. I don't know a lot about the other parks, but I've read a lot about early Detroit history."

"How did you pay for it, with more Cannis capsules?"

"Morg, the glider doors are closing. Come on, pal. I'll tell you how I paid for it when we get on the glider."

Morg debated whether to board the Detroit glider. If they didn't go to the Detroit park, where the hell would they go? At the last moment, Morg pulled the Earthling by the ear onto the glider. He whimpered the entire way and when Morg tossed him into a double-wide berth, he grabbed his ear to make sure it was still attached to his head.

"Good god, Morg. Was that necessary? You damn near ripped my ear off."

"You're lucky I didn't rip your head off. Let that be a lesson. Stay where I can see you and don't try to backstab me again. Do you understand, Earthling?"

"Yeah, yeah, I get it. Hey, can I have my Cannis capsules back?"

"No. I'm keeping them for now. You be a good boy and I'll think about returning them."

Morg and the Earthling settled in as the glider pulled out the station and rocketed to Mach One speed.

"Welcome to the Detroit 1967 glider. Your estimated time of arrival will be in 157 minutes. This glider will travel at an average speed of 1.4 Mach. All passengers must provide a proof of travel permit. Please place your permit over the video screen on your armrest."

The Earthling followed the instructions to validate his travel permit. He tried to avoid Morg's glare knowing he only purchased one permit for himself.

"I don't suppose you have one of those for me?"

Morg didn't wait for the Earthling to make up a lie about why he didn't buy two permits. He took out one of the Cannis capsules and held it over the video screen. It took five seconds for a response. "A representative of Feltte Six Parks will come and see you within the hour."

"Morg, please don't give all the capsules to these guys. That's all I have."

Morg didn't believe the Earthling but played along with his

charade. "We'll see. If you help me, I may return some of the Cannis."

"What do you mean, Morg? You know I'd do anything for you?"

Morg wanted to call him a liar and slap him on the side of the head but decided to take a less violent approach. "Tell me about finding my mate in the cargo bay. What were you doing in there? Did you see her board the transport? Did you move the body? Did you see anyone else? Did you take anything off the body or pocket anything unusual from the immediate area?"

For the next thirty minutes, the Earthling rambled on and on telling Morg everything he knew about finding the body. His explanations and descriptions were so convoluted and disjointed that Morg interrupted often to ask questions. In the end, Morg didn't know how much of the Earthling's story to believe. At times, his explanations seemed reasonable yet, at other times, they made little or no sense. If they were back on Yanda, Morg could have run the Earthling's responses through a truth box. The box would tell him if the Earthling's explanations were truthful or lies. But, in deep space, Morg had to rely on his interrogation training. This entailed looking for kinetic body movements which might indicate deception. A pulsating carotid artery, dilating eye pupils, and turning away from the interrogator could mean stress and deception by the interrogatee. But the Earthling was impossible to *read*. His hyperactive, nervous behavior and constant twitching blocked any chance Morg had of identifying the body indicators of lying. He would have to rely on the physical evidence analyzer for the time being. When they got to a planet with modern interrogation equipment, he could get the truth from the Earthling.

"Mr. Morg, I'm an employee of the Feltte Six park system. I understand that you don't have a travel permit to Detroit 1967. I'll need to collect payment before we arrive. Otherwise, you won't be able to leave the glider."

Morg found it interesting that the glider employee didn't identify himself. There was only one reasonable explanation why he remained nameless. He knew that Morg would be paying for his passage with high priced drugs rather than Feltte Six currency. He and his cohorts running this glider could pocket the Cannis as payola and immediately improve their standard of living. But they had to do it without their superiors finding out.

"Will this cover the passage?" Morg held out one Cannis capsule for the glider employee to see.

"Well, that will get you to Detroit 1967, but it's not enough for your return trip."

Morg knew how to deal with scumbags. Bid low and then add a little more to get what you want. When Morg held out the second capsule and announced that this was all he had, the glider employee jumped at the deal. He grabbed the two capsules and issued Morg a round-trip passage permit.

"Thank you, Mr. Morg." Morg watched the scumbag virtually dance away. He had made a huge score by obtaining the two Cannis capsules. He couldn't wait to get together with his cohorts and laugh about the chump who gave them a small fortune in exchange for a lousy glider ride. It wasn't often they fell into a financial bonanza like this. For the next year or two, they would live high off this booty.

Morg looked up expecting to see the Earthling close by. He was gone. The little creep had ducked away while Morg was dickering with the dishonest glider employee. He thought to himself, "Just what I want to do. Go on a scavenger hunt for the Earthling."

Morg resigned himself to searching out and corralling the Earthling. He needed a nap, but, of course, his travel companion had to turn everything into a juvenile adventure. He got up and started walking through the glider. He was amazed by how little vibration there was on a glider traveling at over Mach One speed.

"Morg, is that you? You old, Yandan son-of-a-bitch."

Off to his right, sitting in a berth were three of the ugliest and meanest looking beings in the known universe. All wore lightweight body armor from their collarbones to toes. The armor was the best quality available even though it looked like it had seen better days.

Morg recognized them immediately as Athlon mercenaries. They were nearly seven feet tall and weighed close to three hundred pounds. Most of their rust-colored faces were grown over with a heavy beard which was razor sharp. Anyone, other than an Athlon, who touched their facial hair would suffer hundreds of tiny, razor-thin cuts which burned and hurt like hell. It also served a secondary function of hiding the numerous battle scars which crisscrossed their faces.

Morg hadn't intended to meet anyone he knew on this glider trip. But here were three mercenaries he'd hired on many occasions. They were perfect fighters for clearing out pockets of the enemy dug into impregnable positions. It was usually easier and more cost-effective to pay an Athlon mercenary to risk his life than send in a Yandan invasion trooper. If the Athlon was killed only the service fee was lost. If a Yandan assault trooper was killed a huge training investment went to his grave with him.

Morg smiled. He knew these three all too well. They had been under his direct command on several invasions. They were gregarious and ill-mannered, but damn good at what they did. They relished life-and-death situations and made a game of killing the enemy. He never bothered to learn mercenaries' names because their lifespan was so short. But, these three had survived enough battles to receive the nicknames Crex, Blex, and Stex. Morg never bothered to find out the origination of their nicknames. He figured their over-the-top bravado would end in vaporization soon enough.

"Hey, guys. What the hell are you doing on this glider?"

"We're between conflicts. Thought we'd come here and sharpen our skills. You know our motto; a kill per day keeps the grim reaper away."

The three mercenaries laughed hysterically. Their laughter and gaiety were infectious. Morg chuckled along with them even though he no idea what was so funny. He wondered who or what was a grim reaper these three referred to?

"What are you doing here, Morg?"

"Oh, I'm on a special assignment for the Trifect. It's a top-secret mission. I turned it down several times, but they kept begging me and offering a huge bonus to take it. So, I finally agreed and....and, here I am." Morg held out his arms and gestured as though he was the most important agent in the Yandan military and diplomatic corps. He was embarrassed to tell the Athlons about his real assignment. So, he decided to embellish and overinflate the importance of his mission. They would never learn the truth, and if they did, so what? He'd be long gone.

"Well, are you going to tell us what's the mission?" When Crex realized Morg wasn't going to answer his question, he added, "Come on, Morg. You can tell us. Hell, we've fought side-by-side many times and had to protect each other's ass. If you can't trust us, who can you trust?"

Morg knew they were right and deserved an answer. He couldn't tell them the truth, so his mind raced to piece together a grandiose yet believable story. As he opened his mouth to feed them a fake tale, Stex grimaced and said, "Would you look at that? Where do these freaks come from?"

Everyone turned and looked in the direction Stex was staring. Twenty yards away was the Earthling thrashing away in the aisle, entertaining a group of about two dozen new arrivals. Morg stared in disbelief and wondered what the hell he was doing. The Earthling was gyrating his hips, bobbing his head up and down and flailing his arms in the air as though he was swatting imaginary bugs. Had he overdosed on some exotic drug or was this another of his foolish antics meant to con the weak-minded?

"You know, I think I've found my first kill when we get to Detroit."

"No way, Crex, I saw him first."

"Screw you, Stex. It doesn't matter who saw him first. The only thing that matters is who declares him first and that was me."

Blex couldn't stay out of the argument any longer. "You are both crazy. I saw this nutter when we got on the glider and declared him then. I can't help it if you two weren't listening."

"Blex, you're full of ...."

That's as much of the mercenaries' arguing Morg heard. He tuned them out and started to consider his options. If he went over and corralled the Earthling, his mercenary buddies would know he lied about the top-secret mission he was on for the Trifect. On the other hand, he had to protect the Earthling. Somehow, he had to forewarn the goofball that he was targeted for vaporization by three of the most prolific killers in the universe.

He decided to act before the Earthling spotted him and blew his cover story. He walked toward the Earthling hoping the screwball didn't turn around. As he approached, he heard the Earthling say, "Okay, ladies and gentlemen. For your entertainment pleasure, I'm going to take you back several centuries to the real Detroit when it ruled the music world with the Motown Sound. Here's a giant hit from 1968 by soul brother, Marvin Gaye."

The Earthling said *ready-start* which flooded the glider compartment with background music. He bobbed his head up and down and snapped his fingers waiting for the right break in the melody. Using his vap pistol as a make-believe microphone, he lip-synced the words to "I Heard It Through the Grapevine." For all his foolishness, Morg had to give him credit. The kid was definitely putting his heart into the performance.

The sounds coming from the glider audio system seemed familiar to Morg. If he wasn't mistaken it was the same racket which the Earthling played non-stop during the first couple weeks of their voyage. To Morg, it was noise pollution. But, to the kid, it was no different than the continuous drone coming from the Shadow Drive system. He would sing and hum along with the songs without realizing what he was doing. After two weeks, Morg reached his limit and pulled the plug on the audio system. The kid had no idea how to fix the system. No matter how much he protested and tried to explain the importance of music in Earth culture, Morg pretended to be ignorant about repairing the system. Now, here he was a few weeks later dealing with another problem created by Earth music. But this one was much more serious. It could mean life or death.

The Earthling was finishing his performance when Morg grabbed the brachial plexus nerve in his shoulder and spun him around. The Earthling was semi-paralyzed and stopped lip-syncing immediately.

Through a clenched jaw and only loud enough for the Earthling to hear, Morg said, "Look at me as though you are infuriated. There are three Athlon killers behind me who have picked you out as a target when we get to the Detroit park. You've made such a spectacle of yourself they think you'd be an easy target. When we get to the park, disappear and I'll try to delay them. I recommend you stay well hidden. These guys are the best and love killing. I'll see you back at the transport within twenty hours. Now, take a poke at me as though you are pissed."

Morg caught the Earthling's round-house swing, put him in an arm lock and threw him in an empty seat. He shouted loud enough for everyone to hear, "Now stay there and shut up. I'm tired of your bellowing like a stuck Tralock[2]." It was easy giving a convincing performance for the mercenaries due to the growing animosity between he and Morg.

When Morg turned away and started back to his compartment, the Earthling made a vile hand gesture at him. Under his breath, he whispered, "That damn Morg. Why is he always interfering with my fun? I don't care about three mercenaries. They don't scare me."

"Nice job, Morg. What did the little shit say? And, what was he doing?"

"I didn't let him say a thing." Morg paused for a moment wondering if he should add anything more. No, that was enough explanation for the three mercenaries who weren't known as deep thinkers.

"What was the other thing you asked? Oh, yeah. The kid was singing, or I should say, he was pretending to sing." Morg could see the confused look on the mercenaries faces so he tried to explain.

"Singing is when wind and string instruments are used to make funny noises and a being, like that kid, bellows words along with the noises. I don't understand the concept, but millions of beings find it comforting and entertaining."

"What were the words about?"

"Crex, I have no damn idea. It was something about grapevines, honey, and losing your mind. It made no sense to me at all."

Morg and the three mercenaries sat down and spent the remaining twenty trip minutes reliving and telling exaggerated stories about battles they fought. The entire time, Morg played through in his mind how he was going to delay the mercenaries when the glider stopped. He had to make it seem believable. The Earthling needed a huge head start to disappear and stay alive within the Detroit park.

"Ladies and gentlemen, our arrival time at Detroit 1967 will be in three minutes and twenty seconds. We ask that you remain seated until the glider slows down to a safe cruising speed. The crime rate in the Detroit park is now 94.5. Have a productive stay and remember, you are responsible for the corpses you create."

As the glider pulled in to its terminal bay, the mercenaries were once again arguing about who had first dibs on killing the Earthling. This gave Morg just enough time to put himself between the Earthling and the mercenaries. When the glider doors opened, the Earthling sprinted out. Morg began a performance creating as much delay and interference as possible. First, he pretended to fall over. Then he dropped his assault rife and spent a few moments examining it to make sure it wasn't damaged. Lastly, he ran into and knocked over another new arrival, apologizing profusely as he dusted him off.

By the time Morg and his killer buddies got onto the docking platform, the Earthling was long gone. He had grabbed his bag and vap pistol and disappeared like a wisp of smoke.

"Well, where the hell is that little dick-weed?"

"Blex, he either knew we were gunning for him or has an important appointment."

Being the unofficial leader of the killing squad, Crex took

command and started to organize the hunt for the Earthling. "Okay, guys. This park is too damn big to hunt this guy down together, so we'll have to separate. Morg, are you in?"

The Yandan didn't have a choice. He had to stay involved. It was the only chance he had to protect the living cargo he was assigned to deliver to Earth.

"Sure. Count me in. I'll tell you what. If I find the little shit before you guys, I'll let you know where he is, and you can compete for the kill."

"Thanks, Morg. We owe you. Come on over here and we'll divide up the park."

The three mercenaries and Morg walked over to the holographic map of Detroit 1967. A quarter of the park was allocated to each assassin. Morg got the west side of Detroit which was roughly a ten by twelve-mile area.

"Okay, everyone set your transponders to channel 34Easy. Report in every hour and if you run into problems, say something. It's better to get help and share the kill than end up vaporized due to false bravado. Oh, I shouldn't have to say this, but if one of you vaps this little weasel, let the rest of us know."

Crex, Stex, and Blex grabbed their gear and loaded it into black and white cabs. Everything in the park was a replica of what Detroit looked and sounded like in 1967. From the antique automobiles to tenement buildings to party stores and pot-hole riddled streets.

Morg waited until the mercenaries were out of sight before starting to second guess where the Earthling might have gone. What excuse had he used to divert the transport to Feltte Six? It was something about birds; high-flying birds. What are high-flying birds? Then it hit home. The Earthling used the same term when referring to his girlfriend on the Crelon slave ship. He wanted to *rub* with a female species. Or in human language, he wanted to share his reproductive unit with a female.

Morg approached the cab supervisor who was responsible for

assigning new arrivals to taxis. "Hey buddy, I'm looking for an Earthling who is about this tall and has...."

"Sorry, don't have time to talk with you. Get in line if you want transportation, otherwise, don't bug me."

Morg got the supervisor's attention by applying the same nerve pinch he used on the Earthling. "Listen, asshole. I'm looking for an Earthling and you're going to help me unless you want to be permanently disabled."

The cab supervisor tried to squirm away, but it was no use. Excruciating pain shot from his shoulder up and down the left side of his body. He couldn't move and could barely say, "Okay, okay. Let go and I'll do anything you want."

"Good god was that necessary?" One look at Morg answered that question.

After Morg described the Earthling, the cab supervisor rubbed his chin thinking back through the last dozen or so new arrivals he assigned to taxis. He decided not to BS the Yandan; he was much too dangerous to screw around with.

"Yeah, yeah, I do remember the Earthling. The kid couldn't stop yapping. I gave him to cab 66 because he wanted to go to the brothels downtown and on the east side of the park. The driver of 66 specializes in sexual desires and fantasies."

"Okay, so how do I get ahold of cab 66?"

"Let me see if I can track him down." The cab supervisor walked over to a holographic locator board and searched for number 66. "Here he is. Looks like he's on the move."

"Call him and ask where he's going."

After a short exchange, the cab supervisor reported, "He's coming back here. Already dropped off the Earthling."

"Okay, tell him to report to you when he gets back. He has an important fare waiting."

Fifteen minutes later, Morg was in cab 66 driving toward east Detroit.

"Where we going, chief?"

Morg looked over at the dark-brown, humanoid driver who had the whitest teeth he had ever seen. The clothes the cab driver wore were also something he never saw anywhere in the universe. The driver's shirt was a shiny, black satin material with large, billowy collars that flapped up and down as he walked. His pants glistened three or four distinct colors when the shark skin material reflected the sunlight. Beneath his spit-polished black, patent shoes the driver wore see-through nylon socks. Morg hoped the driver was as helpful as he was fashionable.

"Jimmy Washington. Is that your real name?"

"No, man. You don't want to know my real name. It's too hard to pronounce. Everyone who works in the park is assigned an alias. Jimmy Washington was a common name in the real Detroit, 1967. Pretty cool, huh? Anyhow, name your destination."

"Take me to where you took the young Earthling from your last fare."

"You mean the kid who blabs on and on and is in love with himself? The one with a foot fetish?"

Half of what Jimmy said definitely described the Earthling. "Yeah, I think that's our boy. On the way there, tell me everything you remember the Earthling saying. It's worth a healthy tip if your info helps me find him."

It turned out that Jimmy had an incredible memory. He repeated verbatim the entire conversation he had with the Earthling. The story rolled as casually out of his voice hole as his carefree driving. He weaved in and out of traffic, making sure he didn't hit any of the passed-out drunks, burning trash fires and abandoned cars littering the road.

It wasn't easy listening to Jimmy. Morg's attention was constantly drawn to the acts of violence and lewd behavior occurring in and around the buildings along the highway. He was glad he chose to sit in the front seat rather than the back seat. From this position, he could see everything that was happening on both sides of the street.

At one stop light, four combatants ran across the intersection firing laser assisted, vap pistols at each other. Two miles further, a gang of thugs broke out a store's front window and looted everything they could carry away. Another mob fire-bombed a grocery store. Numerous sex acts were being performed in the alleys or in plain view on the sidewalks. Morg lost count of the fistfights.

"This really is a shit-hole, isn't it?"

"Well, we do have some problems; that's for sure."

Morg looked at the cab driver not knowing if he was making a joke or being serious. "So, what the hell is a foot fetish?"

"He gets off on looking at and caressing feet. Don't ask me to explain it. I don't get it either. Anyhow, I'll take you to the first foot fetish parlor I dropped him off at and then tell you how to get to the other ones I'm sure he visited."

"I'll tell you what. Will this buy your services for the entire day?" Morg held out another Cannis capsule he lifted from the kid's pants pocket when applying the nerve pinch. A capsule the kid claimed not to have.

Before Jimmy could answer, Morg caught a glimpse of a familiar face. It was Crex coming out of a pawn store holding someone by his hair.

"Oh, shit."

"What's the matter?"

Morg watched Crex throw his quarry to the ground and then stomp on his gut. "Ah... ah. Nothing. Nothing is wrong. Thought I saw someone I knew."

Jimmy waited until he knew Morg was listening again. "Yeah, that can happen here. Listen man, that capsule will cover my expenses, just fine. All I have to do is tell mama I won't be home for a day or so."

Morg hadn't planned on seeing the mercenaries. The odds of running into one of them was about ten thousand to one. It was a damn good thing Crex wasn't paying attention to the traffic passing by. If Crex had spotted him, tracking down the Earthling would have been futile. The last thing he wanted to do was lead the mercenaries to the valuable cargo he must keep alive.

When the taxi reached the downtown perimeter, Jimmy switched over to tour guide. "Morg, let me point out some of the more interesting attractions of Detroit 67. That large building over there is the Strohs' brewery. It's a million-square-foot factory which makes beer and ice cream. A lot of our visitors like to slurp up the lager beer after a tough day of crime and corruption."

"That's an odd combination; beer and ice cream. What's that about?"

"There was a thirteen-year period called Prohibition. Alcoholic beverages were outlawed during this time. To stay in business, the Strohs company diversified and started making other products like ice cream. It was so damn good that after Prohibition, the company kept making it. It still sells good. It's a big hit with our addict guests who have a sweet tooth."

"Do you see that building over there, Morg? The one that looks like an ancient coliseum. That's Briggs Stadium. That's where the Tigers play baseball. The first guy to score a run in this stadium was Shoeless Joe Jackson. That was 1912, I believe. A few years later, Shoeless Joe was banned from the game for throwing the World Series. Man, that guy could play."

Morg had no idea what Jimmy was talking about. Tigers, runs, and some being who didn't wear shoes. It sounded like a nonsensical work of fiction.

"Too bad you're not going to be here for more than a day. The Red Wings are playing Toronto this weekend at the Olympia. Being an invasion trooper, you'd love the violence. When those two teams get it on there is one brawl after another. Even the fans get into it and start fighting in the stands. Oh, I forgot the best part. The fans throw octopuses onto the ice."

Morg looked at Jimmy and wondered if he had made a good decision hiring him as an escort. Some of the things he described were bizarre. But it was too late to make changes. It was Jimmy for the next twenty plus hours.

"Okay, man, here we are. Up those stairs and ask for Henrietta. I'll wait for you here."

Morg cautiously strutted into the foot fetish parlor and asked for the Madam.

"Madam Henrietta, my name is Morg. Jimmy, the cab driver, recommended I talk to you."

A big smile crossed the Madam's face which was overly-caked with makeup. Morg couldn't help wondering what she might look like without the heavy spread of red lipstick, rouge, pasty blush, and eyeliner.

"Oh, that Jimmy. I love that guy. What can I do for you, sailor?"

Morg looked behind himself to see if there was a sailor, whatever the hell that was.

"No, Madam. My name is Morg, not sailor."

When Henrietta stopped chuckling, Morg asked, "Madam, I'm looking for a male Earthling about this tall with yellow filaments, I mean hair, and ...."

That's as far as Morg got with his description. The broad smile on Henrietta's face turned upside down into a frown. "I hope you're going to kill that little prick. I threw his ass out of here about a half-hour ago. Do you know what he did to....?"

Morg graciously backed out of the parlor. He couldn't agree with her enough. He reassured her that he would kill the Earthling as soon as he could find him.

As Morg walked down the front steps, his transponder went off. A holographic image of Crex appeared in his peripheral vision. "Morg, have you heard from Blex lately? I can't find him and Stex hasn't heard from him either. He isn't answering his hailing signal."

"No, I haven't heard from him. But I wouldn't worry. Blex can take care of himself."

"Yeah, I guess so. I'm probably overreacting, but you know, after being in combat with someone for years you kinda form a sixth sense and can tell when he's in trouble."

"Don't worry, Crex. Keep sending him a hailing signal and I'll keep an eye out for him."

"Hey, Morg. Have you turned up any clues on our prey?"

"Not one. Seems like the little shit vanished into thin air." Morg signed off, thankful that Crex didn't ask where he was. He didn't like lying to a combat buddy but finding the Earthling and keeping him away from the mercenaries was more important than anything else.

"Hey, Yandan, want to buy some Cannis capsules?"

Morg looked down to find a youngster, no more than ten years old, standing next to the cab. "No thanks, pal. Maybe later. But, have you seen an Earthling...?"

When the other street urchins in the area saw Morg talking to the youngster selling Cannis capsules, they hurried over smelling an easy mark. They all wanted to get in on the action and sell their drugs, stolen merchandise, and various sex and criminal activities to the Yandan. It didn't matter to them that most of the products, including the Cannis capsules, were fake. They pushed and shoved and yelled their sales pitches at the same time. It didn't matter to Morg because he had no idea what most of the street urchins were talking about.

"Okay, you punks. Get out of here. Leave the Yandan alone. Get, before I give you a good beat-down."

It was Jimmy the cab driver coming to Morg's rescue before the local riff-raff swindle him out of everything he owned. The street urchins reluctantly backed off swearing and making lewd gestures at the cab driver. They had lost their meal ticket for the day.

"Man, they are a pain in the ass."

"You got to give them credit, Jimmy. They are persistent."

"Yeah, so are flies to shit. No offense, Morg."

"None taken." Morg threw a couple Feltte Six credits out the window to the urchins as Jimmy pulled into traffic.

"Did Henrietta help you?"

"Not really. The human was there but she kicked his ass to the curb after he got out of hand."

"What did he do?"

"She told me, but I don't want to repeat it. Too bizarre to describe. Let's move on to the next place you think he might have gone."

For the next four hours, Jimmy Washington and Morg went to every sex parlor specializing in foot fetishes. The reception Morg got was the same at each parlor. "Yeah, he was here. We kicked him out and I hope someone vaps him."

Morg was at a loss. Why would anyone pull the same crap at every sex parlor and expect different results? It didn't make a lot of sense. It was almost as if the Earthling wanted to create a commotion at each parlor. Was it intentional? If so, how did it benefit him?

Between the second and third hours, Crex let Morg know that Stex was missing. It was the same scenario as Blex. He wouldn't acknowledge the hailing signals and then his transponder went dead. Morg conceded that it was too much of a coincidence. There was no way two seasoned mercenaries, who survived more battles than probably anyone else in the universe, would come up missing. They simply vanished within an hour of each other, as though they never existed.

After visiting the last foot fetish brothel, Morg put in his hourly signal to Crex. His signal kicked back indicating that Crex's transponder was either out of range or not working. The Detroit 1967 park was only forty miles square. There was little chance that the transponder was out of range.

Morg tried to think of every possible explanation for three seasoned mercenaries disappearing into thin air. Only one explanation withstood the test of deductive reasoning. Someone had targeted Crex, Blex, and Stex as bountiful prey and harvested them. But who would have enough bravado and expertise to pull it off? He hated to think what might have happened to his combat buddies, but at least he no longer had to worry about them taking out the Earthling. This left only a few thousand other lunatics, assassins, and military agents who might get irritated enough to vap the Earthling.

"Jimmy, I'm bushed. Is there somewhere we can go to relax? I don't think we're going to find the Earthling."

"No problem. I know the perfect place to unwind."

Five minutes later, Jimmy pulled up in front of a three-story brownstone on Gratiot Avenue. Behind the front door was one of the largest humanoids Morg had ever seen. This guy was at least seven-feet tall and as wide and muscular as a silver-back ape.

"Hey, Jimmy. What's happenin' bro?"

"You are, Lucius. I know it's a little early, but are you open?"

"For you, we're open anytime. Have fun. You know the way."

Morg followed Jimmy through a series of hidden sliding doors. When they passed through the last door, they found themselves on an elevator. It dropped at an alarming rate through a maze of subterranean tunnels and shafts. When it stopped, they were in a tunnel which dead-ended in both directions. Jimmy walked up to the stone wall and pulled open a camouflaged door leading into an unlicensed blind pig[3]. Morg had a good sense of direction but now he was lost. If he had to get back to street level by himself, he would never find his way.

The interior of the blind pig was lavish but dimly lit. Morg guessed the room could hold up to two hundred beings. All the booths, chairs and tables were handcrafted from the finest woods and leather. The walls were littered with original oil paintings. Morg knew just enough about art to know these paintings were valuable. In fact, he recognized a few which disappeared centuries before. Was it possible that these lost treasures ended up in a party room beneath an amusement park?

"Howdy, gents. What's your pleasure?"

Standing at their table was a Landan waitress. Considering the quality of everything else in the room, it didn't surprise Morg that she was Landan. These women were known for their dependability, secrecy and, above all else, beauty.

"Hi, Luna. Why don't you bring us a Cannis dispenser and something to drink? You pick it."

"Oh, Jimmy. I'm sorry, I didn't recognize you in this low light."

Luna bent over and gave Jimmy a smooch on his cheek. Morg had to admit to a pang of jealousy watching this gorgeous woman kissing Jimmy. For the first time in a couple days, he thought about his mate and how much he missed her.

Three hours later, Jimmy and Morg were wasted. The Cannis dispenser released a mild, vaporized form of the drug. It was less concentrated than capsules but just as effective over a couple hours. The blind pig filled up with customers, all seeking relief and relaxation. Even in his drug-induced stupor, Morg realized this establishment was for park workers. Cab drivers, waitresses, stoolies, and vendors selling every type of vice and service congregated in the blind pig to relax. They needed downtime after a tough day of dealing with the new arrival of creeps, jerks, assassins, and thugs. There was only so much lust, debauchery, crime, and evil the workers could put up with each day.

"Jimmy, is there a communications station in here? I need to contact my offspring."

"Yeah, sure. Luna, will you show my friend where the CS is? Thanks, dear."

Jimmy watched Morg stagger away and smiled to himself. For a Yandan, Morg was a decent guy. He was going to ask Morg why he hadn't used the ship's communication system, but the answer was obvious. He either forgot or the transport was under a communications quarantine which meant that Morg was on a top-secret mission.

The oldest of Morg's six offspring answered the communications contact on the second pulse. He was a spitting image of Morg. The same hard facial features, scale coloring, and gill placement. Morg couldn't get over the quality of the transmission. The offspring looked like he was next door rather than a few light years away.

"Hello, offspring. How are you?"

"I'm fine. In fact, all of us are great. Where are you?"

"I'm on another invasion mission. Have to keep invading more planets so Yanda will prosper." Morg hesitated for a moment and then said, "Offspring, I have some difficult news for you. Your female life-giver...."

"She's dead, right?"

Morg was dumbfounded. He sat at the CS wondering if he heard the offspring correctly. "What did you say?"

"We were notified a couple days ago that your mate has been classified as non-functioning."

"Explain."

"Apparently, a deep-space sweeper was collecting debris about two light years from Yanda and picked up a section of scales." As the offspring explained, a couple of his siblings wandered into the transmission background. "They were brought back to Yanda and identified as your mate. Actually, we're glad you contacted us. We were wondering if we can split up her possessions and sell the stuff we don't need?"

As the oldest offspring continued to talk, and the others asked a relentless number of questions. Morg heard very little of what they said. He didn't know whether to be outraged, disappointed or accepting of the things the offspring said and questioned. No warm greeting. Not one word of sorrow. Not one question about why their female life-giver was in deep space. No questions about how she died. And, no indication they missed either of their life-givers. All they wanted to know was if they could steal her possessions. Morg broke the communication and wandered back to his table. He was in dire need of more Cannis.

"Bad news, Morg?"

"I guess not, Jimmy. I should have seen this coming."

"Sorry. Hey, you never did tell me why you're looking for the Earthling."

"The best explanation I can give you is that I'm his babysitter. My job is to make sure he doesn't get in trouble or killed. I realize now that I'll never find him in this park, so all I can hope for is that he doesn't get killed in the next sixteen hours. Our passes are good for only a little over a day so that might help him stay alive."

"Man, I don't know. I only spent twenty-five minutes with him, and he irritated me so much I wanted to blow off his head."

"He does have that effect on everyone he meets. Believe me, I've thought about doing the same thing several times."

By three o'clock in the morning, Morg was so inebriated Jimmy had to carry him out of the blind pig. For a sixty-two-year-old who weighed only 176 pounds, he possessed incredible strength within his wiry frame. He hid it well under his flamboyant clothes.

There was no sense taking Morg to a sleazy hotel to sleep off the drugs. Jimmy decided to take him to the departure platform and load him onto the next glider returning to the arrival docking bays. It was more than a two-hour trip back to the docking bays. If Jimmy gave Morg a Cannis stabilizer injection before the glider left, he would be reasonably sober when he got to his ship. Other than that, all Jimmy had to do is to lock Morg's assault rife onto his battle armor, so no one could steal it.

Jimmy wasn't in the best shape to drive but whoever heard of a cab driver hiring another cab driver? As he headed down Gratiot and then Grand River avenues, he thought he saw a holographic billboard posting with the Earthling's picture on it. Jimmy did a double-take, but by the time he peered over his shoulder for another look, the billboard had switched to the next posting. He had to be seeing things. Billboards broadcasts were used for news and crime updates.

Jimmy locked Morg into a glider berth, gave him the anti-Cannis injection and left a note inside the discharge sleeve of his assault rife. It read, "Thanks, Morg, for your company. You were a great customer. I had a good time and if you are ever on Feltte Six again, look me up. Sorry, we couldn't find the brat you are babysitting. Here is my private contact number. Jimmy W."

He watched Morg's glider speed up and then rocket out of the departure gate. He was confident that no one would mess with Morg during the glider trip even though he was sound asleep. After spending a couple days at a crime theme park, visitors were exhausted and thankful to be alive. All they wanted to do was leave Feltte Six and go back to their normal, boring lives. Surviving Feltte Six was a status symbol and made each survivor a minor celebrity on their home planet.

Jimmy Washington needed to get home, take a hot dip in the cleansing bath, and get some well-deserved sleep. He hoped his girlfriend would leave him alone for a day or more, so he could recuperate. If she pestered him, he would show her the Cannis capsule from Morg. That's all it should take for her to back off and realize the next year or two would be financially care-free. They might be able to take a well-deserved holiday somewhere in the galaxy.

A mile before turning off Gratiot Avenue into his neighborhood, Jimmy's daydreaming about spending his new-found wealth evaporated when he saw another holographic billboard. This time his eyes weren't playing tricks. A full-face picture of the Earthling was prominently displayed on the billboard with the words, "Wanted for Questioning".

Jimmy started talking to himself. "Shit, I knew that punk was going to get me in trouble. It's just a matter of time before the authorities come knocking at my door, wanting to know what I know about that sleazeball." Jimmy pounded his fist on the steering wheel as he cursed and yelled, "Damn, damn, damn."

4

THE FORCE OF THE TRANSPORT'S ENGINES KICKING INTO shadow drive was enough to throw Morg onto the floor from his gyro bed. In a matter of ten seconds, he went from a deep sleep recovering from the effects of Cannis inebriation to a rude awakening with a small knot on his head.

Morg grabbed the nearest stable fixture and got to his feet. He could tell from the hum of the shadow drive system that the ship was moving at a fast clip into intermediate space. But who was at the main controls and where were they going?

He was still woozy from the all-night Cannis party. But, getting to the bridge and finding out what the hell was going on cleared his head.

As he entered the bridge area the aroma of female fragrance was the first thing he noticed. He believed the correct term, used on most planets, was perfume. He spotted a female humanoid with long red hair and a low-cut blouse off the shoulders, sitting in the captain's gyro chair. From the back, he couldn't see her face. But he could tell from the way she worked the controls she had experience flying a transport.

Whoever was at the controls threw the ship into four successive hyper-banks. The G-Force from each tossed Morg back and forth across the bridge. With each turn, he was able to grab onto anchored pieces of equipment long enough to avoid severe injury. Even though Morg's expertise was ground-force invasions, he had enough military flight experience to know the reason for these evasive maneuvers. It was to outrun and avoid being shot down by an enemy ship.

When the transport leveled out in straight-line flight, Morg jumped up and ran to the empty gyro chair at the helm. He strapped in and started checking the ship's dashboard for red warning signals. Everything was in the safe green zone. Engine performance, speed, and atmospheric conditions onboard were operating within allowable specifications. His eyes shifted to the exterior video screens. He couldn't see anything other than the twinkle of stars amid the blackness of space. There wasn't any danger lurking close to the transport, so why had the redhead pilot put the ship through such severe evasive maneuvers?

Morg turned his gyro chair toward the redhead just as several thermal missiles flew past the transport and exploded in its path. Before Morg could react, the redhead put the transport into a free-fall followed by hard right and left banks and steep climbs.

"Man, that was close."

Morg knew that voice. He didn't have to look at the redhead humanoid in the captain's gyro chair to know who it was. As much as he wanted to look, something told him not to, at least, not until they outran or hid from their pursuers. The first priority was to stay alive. Then he would deal with the juvenile delinquent.

"Yandan transport E647. Disengage shadow drive and stand down for boarding by Feltte Six authorities."

"What did you do, Earthling?" When the Earthling didn't respond immediately, Morg shouted, "I said, what the hell did you do on that planet?"

"I didn't do anything, Morg. Come on, man. How much trouble could I get into in less than twenty hours?"

"I don't want to imagine. Get your hands off the controls; I'm taking over."

"You aren't stopping, are you? I'm telling you, they have me confused with someone else."

Morg knew the Earthling was guilty as sin. He was an expert in detecting physical reactions which indicated deception. It was required training for Yandan Invasion Officers. Getting accurate information from captured enemy combatants was critical. It usually meant the difference between victory and death. The change in the Earthling's voice pitch alone screamed lie, lie, lie. The kid was a good liar in some situations, but not this one. Every pore in his body oozed deceit.

"Earthling, you're so full of crap. Do you think I was born yesterday? I know you got tossed out of several foot fetish brothels and the Madams wanted you killed."

"So, you were following...." That was as much as Morg heard. He ignored everything else the Earthling said and put the transport into a standard evasive weave pattern. He needed to buy time and figure out what to do.

Less than a minute later, the Feltte Six commander hailed the Yandan ship again. "Yandan transport E647. You are hereby commanded to disengage your shadow drive and stand-down. Any further attempt to flee will be met with a harsh military response. If you value your lives, ship, and cargo, you will stop at once."

Well, there it was, the final ultimatum. Either stop and turn the Earthling over to the Feltte Six authorities or continue to run and hope their pilots were lousy gunners. There was no sense jumping to hyper-drive because the pursuers would do the same and follow Morg's flight signature.

Morg checked the control panel and counted five Feltte Six ships in pursuit. They were in an inverted "V" pursuit pattern with three ships behind the Yandan transport and one on each side. Whatever the kid did on Feltte Six must have been quite grievous. He must have really pissed off someone to have five Interceptors tail them this far into space. They were now well outside the Feltte Six space boundary.

Morg was running out of time. He had to make a decision and hope it was right. He could tell that the Feltte Six interceptor commander was irritated. The tone of his "stop now" command was beyond harsh. Morg knew if he surrendered the Earthling there was little to no chance of seeing the kid again.

There was only one thing in Morg's favor. Their transport was a disguised cargo hauler. The Trifect did everything possible to make the transport look unappealing to pirates and monitoring systems. It supposedly had an out-of-date shadow drive system, obsolete equipment, and no military hardware. It was old, slow, and ugly. Anyone encountering the transport in space would take it for a hauler on its last legs. In fact, most junk haulers were in better condition than the Yandan transport.

What no one other than Morg knew, was that the Trifect equipped the transport with the latest defensive battle armament. It was the best in the universe. The newest technology and a hundred percent automated. All Morg had to do was verbally instruct the defense system to annihilate the pursuing Interceptors and that would be the end of the chase.

The situation he now found himself in was ideal for getting rid of the kid, but what would be the consequences? The Trifect would consider him derelict in his mission. His offspring would be destroyed and his assets on Yanda confiscated. The penalties for failing to deliver the kid to Earth were extreme. But destroying five Interceptors belonging to a friendly alliance planet wouldn't go over very well, either. More than likely, he would be considered a criminal with a bounty put on his head. Then it would be up to the Trifect to somehow protect him from Feltte Six prosecution. But, would they or would they allow him to be a sacrificial lamb?

As Morg debated with himself, red warning signals lit up the control panel. The Feltte Six Interceptors had primed their launch systems and were seconds away from firing thermal missiles.

He couldn't wait any longer. "Defense system destroy pursuing Interceptors."

There was a slight kick in the transport's forward momentum as Thermax projectiles launched and vaporized the Interceptors, one by one. The Thermax projectiles were ten times more accurate and deadlier than the standard thermal missiles. They were completely stealth, undetectable, and couldn't be deflected by defensive shields. In a way, Morg felt sorry for the Feltte Six crews. They never knew what hit them.

"Way to go, Morg. My man. That was so unbelievably badass. "

That was as much of the Earthling Morg wanted to hear. He turned off his translator and spoke in a commanding voice deserving of a war hero. "System, lock destination to Earth."

Morg lay back in his gyro chair and sighed in relief. For the time being, they were safe and could resume their flight plan to Earth. He figured they had roughly one to two light years in travel time before Feltte Six authorities figured out what happened to their Interceptors. They would raise hell and submit an official protest to the Yandan High Council. Of course, the High Council would play along and act outraged. They would condemn the pilot of the transport who attacked and destroyed ships belonging to an alliance planet. But their biggest problem would be explaining how a run-down transport sported the most advanced weaponry in the universe. Morg was sure the Trifect hadn't bothered to tell the High Council about arming the transport to the max. Why should they? The real power on Yanda rested with the Trifect. The High Council was nothing more than a figurehead of Yandan might and superiority. Between the Council and Trifect, they would have to come up with one hell of a cover story to appease the Feltte Six authorities.

Morg turned ninety degrees in his gyro chair. He finally gathered enough interest to see what the Earthling was up to. After one look, he wished that he had set the controls to autopilot and gone to his quarters to relax. He needed rest and a cleansing. Not to mention ignoring the nut case who was dancing around the bridge in grand celebration.

The Earthling was still wearing a shoulder-length, red wig which looked as though it hadn't been brushed in several years. His face was almost unrecognizable. Heavy red lipstick was painted in perfect proportion from corner to corner of his mouth. It drastically contrasted with the caked-on, dark ebony makeup and perfectly plucked and dyed black eyebrows.

Morg didn't know whether to laugh or scream in anguish at the costume the Earthling wore. Besides the low-cut, off-the-shoulders blouse, the Earthling wore a very tight mid-thigh skirt. Fishnet stockings and elevated shoes completed the wardrobe. For some vague reason, Morg knew the shoes were called spiked high-heels. Every bit of the Earthling's skin was dyed the same dark ebony shade as his face.

The Earthling was swaying this and that way. He moved his hips, head, and shoulders to the vibration Morg could feel resonating throughout the bridge. It was the same vibration Morg banned the Earthling from playing weeks before. It was that damn thing Earthlings called music. Somehow the kid had figured out how to repair the ship's audio system.

He turned on his translator and got an ear full of blasting, base-pounding harmony. It reverberated throughout the bridge. The vibrations engulfed Morg. He folded over the membrane covering his ear cavities to avoid damage to his audio receptors.

The kid was in his own little world. He was so busy dancing and singing along with the recording that Morg thought he may have finally lost his mind. Between verses, he kicked each of his high-heel shoes into the air at Morg and laughed provocatively. If that wasn't enough, his hand gesture for Morg to join him on the make-believe stage was over the top.

"Thank you, ladies and gentlemen. That tune was R-E-S-P-E-C-T, written and sung by the famous Aretha Franklin a couple thousand years ago." The Earthling flipped a few strands of red hair out of his face in perfect female fashion and continued his act. "This next tune is dedicated to my good friend from Yanda who just saved my ass from the Feltte Six authorities. Morg, old buddy, this one is for you."

Morg had reached his limit. The lunacy had gone far enough. He now regretted not giving up the kid to the Feltte Six authorities. He got out of his gyro chair, walked over to the Earthling, and swiped the red wig off the kid's head.

The Earthling winced in pain and felt the top of his head. He made sure his real hair was still there and he wasn't bleeding. "Dammit Morg, that hurt. The damn wig was pinned to my hair." The kid continued to swear as Morg dragged him over to the co-captain's gyro chair and threw him in it.

"Stay there and don't touch a thing. I'm going to the rest bay. If I come back here and find anything out of order, I swear I'll lock you in the cargo bay for the rest of the trip." Morg took two steps toward the rest bay and stopped. He turned and said, "By the way, when I get up, we're going to have a long talk about what you did on Feltte Six. And, take off that outfit. You look like a damn fool."

The Earthling's eyes grew to the size of saucers. Morg had obviously hit a raw nerve. Even through the painted on makeup, Morg could see fear and apprehension spread across the kid's face. He wondered how the kid would have reacted if he mentioned the three missing mercenaries. That subject was also on his list of discussion topics.

An hour later, Morg sat in a cleansing bath thinking about his mate, offspring, Jimmy Washington, and the time he spent on Feltte Six. He had to admit that he had fun in the Cannis blind pig with Jimmy. Too bad the fun times were overshadowed by the nonsense, stupidity, and probable crimes committed by the Earthling.

Morg started to relax and was close to sleep when an alarming thought raced through his head. The Feltte Six authorities knew the transport's identifier code and most likely its flight signature. They hailed the transport by its identifier code, E647. There was no reason to believe they hadn't communicated the transport's flight signature to their command headquarters.

Morg started talking to himself. It was a bad habit but one he couldn't break when he was under stress. "Shit. I'm sure Feltte Six has sent a Look-For bulletin to every planet and monitoring station within four light years. Dammit, we either have to get rid of the transport, hide or...."

A loud, thunderous burst coming from the bridge ended his discussion with himself.

"Son-of-a-bitch. Now what? I swear I'm going to...."

5

Morg sprinted to the bridge wearing only a towel around his midsection. Before he rounded the last corner, he smelled the pungent odor of arcing electricity and heard a strange hissing noise. The blue-grey smoke billowing from the bridge area was thick and seemed to be intensifying. He couldn't see a thing. If the Earthling was still in the area, he must be passed out from smoke inhalation and on his way to death by suffocation.

"Earthling. Earthling, can you hear me?"

Morg waited but heard nothing other than the continuous hissing. The sound reminded him of relief valves on Yandan invasion ships. It was one of the sounds associated with landing and stabilizing the ship so military cargo could unload.

The two filter gills on either side of his neck worked perfectly. Toxic fumes and smoke were scrubbed by the gills, leaving only the correct combination of clean gases to enter his body. He wished his eyes were as proficient, so he could see through the smoke and haze.

There was nothing Morg could do other than wander through the smoke hoping to stumble over the Earthling.

"Earthling. Say or do something if you can hear me."

The Earthling let Morg search hopelessly for a few minutes before he removed the tiny ventilators from each nostril and put them in his bra. He prayed they wouldn't fall out when Morg carried him to safety. He started tapping on the floor knowing the Yandan's acute hearing would pick up the sound immediately. He smiled to himself and started to moan and groan and threw in a couple weak coughs. He considered calling out to the Yandan but didn't want to push his luck. Morg wasn't very bright most of the time but he would probably pick up on theatrical overacting.

He was having great fun playing the role of a despondent victim buried beneath an avalanche of toxic fumes. This was almost as fun as what he did on Feltte Six.

As he calculated, Morg found him in less than ten seconds. Through the smog, the Yandan's scaly and gnarled feet, with eight toes each, appeared. All he had to do was hold his breath another twenty seconds to prevent any more toxic gases from entering his lungs.

Morg bent over and picked up the limp Earthling with one hand. He carried him to the rest area and put him in a gyro cot. He needed to get back to the bridge and deal with the fire before any more damage occurred. He checked for a pulse by placing a hand appendage on the Earthling's carotid artery located in his neck. The kid was still breathing. His pulse was weak but still throbbing at regular intervals. There was a part of Morg hoping not to find a pulse. Morg took one last look at the Earthling before heading to the bridge. He found it strange that the kid's complexion appeared to be normal. He didn't know a lot about the humanoid anatomy, but this didn't seem logical. Suffocation should cause some type of change to the skin color. A humanoid with fair skin and lack of pigmentation, like the kid, should show a bluish or salmon-pink color when starved of oxygen.

The Earthling cracked open one of his eyes and watched the Yandan hurry from the rest area. He was tempted to get up and get a drink but thought it too risky. The Yandan may return unexpectedly.

He rolled on his side and decided to get some well-deserved sleep. Creating chaos and mayhem was hard work even if it was fun and exciting.

Morg checked the ship's emergency control panel before going back to the bridge. The Kalon fire suppressant system was still discharging at ten percent efficiency. That explained the hissing sound Morg heard. But, why hadn't the smoke and Kalon gas dissipated? A quick check of the ventilation system provided the answer. For some unexplained reason, the venting system was jammed. With the vents open the microorganisms could devour the toxic waste and return pure oxygen, hydrogen, and nitrogen to the ship's interior. But closed vents prevented the pollutants from getting to the cleansing microorganisms.

Morg did a manual bypass reset and stood motionless waiting to hear if the venting system started to operate. Within ten seconds, he heard the vents open and the fans start to rotate. It would take less than five minutes before most of the smoke and gases dissipated and the bridge was ready for inspection.

Morg stood outside the bridge and watched the hazy clouds of smoke slowly clear. He wondered if there was a gasnometer stored someplace on the ship. With this piece of equipment, he could measure the toxicity throughout the bridge. He was particularly interested to know what the reading was at floor level. How long could the Earthling have lain on the floor breathing toxic fumes before passing out and dying? Unfortunately, it was too late to start looking for this piece of equipment.

Rather than go directly to the scene of the fire, Morg made concentric circles around the bridge starting on the outer walls and then working in toward the control panel. This was another tactic he learned during his years as a Yandan Invasion trooper. At any investigative scene, Yandan officers were taught to start on the perimeter looking for clues. Then they worked inward toward the crime scene or body.

Nothing stood out or looked out of place. The Earthling's high-heel shoes were against the far wall and his red wig was on the floor about fifteen feet behind the control panel. Otherwise, there was nothing that caught Morg's attention. If anything, the area looked too normal, almost staged.

All suffocation and strangling crimes Morg investigated had one thing in common. The victims always left behind some type of evidence showing they struggled to find the air needed to survive. They flopped around like a fish out of water knocking over furniture and fixtures. They spilled drinks or left behind some other type of evidence. But that wasn't the case on the bridge. Nothing was knocked off the control panel and there wasn't a thing left behind from the Earthling's cross-dressing outfit. Morg thought how odd it was that the Earthling hadn't ripped off his necklace or some other piece of jewelry as he struggled to breathe.

Another thing which bothered Morg was why hadn't the Earthling escaped from the bridge when the Kalon system went off? He must have had enough time to run out of the area to safety. Why did he stay on the bridge to be overwhelmed by the fumes?

With these questions still swirling in his head, Morg wandered over to the captain's gyro chair and sat down. He was lost in thought for the next couple minutes, mulling over possible explanations for the kid's reaction to the fire. When he finally looked at the control panel, the first thing he noticed was that the communications sub-panel was in terrible condition. The entire control panel was in bad shape, but the sub-panel was fried. The housing was deformed due to intense heat and the interior components which made the system work were a giant lump of worthless silica.

Since leaving Yanda, the ship was in a communications quarantine, so no one could determine their destination, cargo, or mission. Now, the transport was incapable of communicating with any other ship, outpost, or planet. If they had an emergency like the shadow drive system failed, no one would come to their rescue. They would drift alone in the cold depths of deep space until another ship or sweeper stumbled upon them. And, when the other ship's crew boarded the Yandan transport all they would find was two shriveled-up bodies.

Morg tried to think of a way to establish some type of communications with the outside world. At minimum, a simple SOS transponder would work. He considered bastardizing components from other systems within the ship. But, not one combination he could think of solved the problem. He finally gave up and headed to the rest bay to question the Earthling. There were a lot of unanswered questions which needed explaining and the kid was the only one who knew the answers.

"Earthling, wake up." Morg shook the kid repeatedly until he thought a dousing with water was needed. The kid was awake but pretended to be asleep. At times, he enjoyed irritating the Yandan.

The Earthling rolled on his back and opened his eyes. "Morg. My buddy. What's going on?"

"You and I need to have a talk."

"Sure, dude. I'm at your disposal. What do you want to know?"

"How did that fire start on the bridge?"

"You know, I've been asking myself the same question." The Earthling paused for a few seconds to prop himself up in the gyro cot. He acted as though he was in deep thought trying to figure out what started the fire.

"Morg, I was just sitting there, daydreaming about some birds I've known, when flames erupted from the control panel. Within seconds, the fire was out of control and the room filled with smoke. That's the last thing I remember until you woke me up.

Morg looked in the Earthling's eyes and watched his physical movements to detect whether the Earthling was lying or not. He didn't pick up on any physical indicators, but the Earthling's voice fluctuations gave a hint of deceit.

The Earthling knew he was being scrutinized so he made a superhuman effort to keep his eyes straight ahead and not turn his body away from the Yandan. He knew all the tricks in the book Morg was using to detect dishonest answers. The worst thing he could do, was turn away and give Morg a reason to believe he was trying to run away from stressful questions.

"Why didn't you try to put the fire out?"

"I didn't have anything plus I thought the Kalon system would go off." The Earthling took another pause to look like he was thinking about something important. He added with a half-smile, "I guess I could have taken off my dress and tried to beat the fire out."

Morg looked quizzically at him. He didn't understand human sarcasm.

"Sorry, I didn't mean to make light of the situation. Can you fix the communications sub-panel?"

Morg sluffed off the kid's remark about beating out the fire with his dress. He thought, "How strange the Earthling would ask about the communications sub-panel when it hadn't been mentioned. How did the kid know it was inoperable?" There was no sense calling him out on this because the Earthling was too smart to get tripped up on a minor detail. He was now convinced the kid was holding back something. His story might not be a total lie, but it was at least a collection of half-truths.

Morg yapped on and on about the condition of the communications sub-panel and what it meant to their survival. The kid took this time to wonder if his cock-and-bull story was convincing. It would have to do because there was no way he was going to tell the Yandan about arcing the circuits in the sub-panel to start the fire. If the Yandan ever discovered that, he would flip out and beat him relentlessly to find out why. The last thing he wanted to do was tell Morg about the top-secret, crypto message received from the Trifect commanding them to return to Yanda. That would lead to the revelation he was fluent in Yandish as well as every other alien language he encountered. His ability to learn alien languages allowed him to read the Trifect's crypto message and respond with, "Message received, acknowledged; returning to Yanda. Signed, Officer Morg". Nothing was going to stop his voyage to Earth. If that meant he had to destroy the communications sub-panel, lie to Morg and the

Trifect, and kill a few beings along the way, that's what he would do.

"Earthling, snap out of it. Did you hear what I asked?"

"Huh, what did you say, Morg?" The alien's words finally broke through the Earthling's daydreaming about the evil he created since leaving Yanda. He would postpone savoring the fond memories of outfoxing and killing the three Athlon mercenaries until later.

"I said, what's with the women's clothes?"

"Oh, that. I went to a party on Feltte Six where everyone dressed like the opposite sex. For me, it was easy. But, for some of the guests it was comical. Especially, the beings who are both sexes. Pretty damn funny, if you know what I mean." The Earthling ended with a light chuckle.

The Earthling's explanation was so spontaneous and said with such conviction Morg believed every word. Morg realized that anything the kid said about his sexual fantasies and deviant behavior was absolutely true. However bizarre or ridiculous, it didn't seem to matter to the kid. He was proud of parading around in female clothes, attending cross-dressing parties and paying for deviant sex act like a foot-fetish.

Thinking about the Earthling's odd sexual behavior sent a chill through Morg's endo-nerve system. He knew such behavior existed, but this was the first being he ever met who enjoyed discussing it. He wondered if all Earthlings were this weird.

"Why didn't you change out of the women's clothes after the party?"

"I don't know. I kinda liked the way the clothes fit, and they made me feel sexy."

The Earthling didn't like how this conversation was trending. This was another lie. He actually hated wearing the tight-fitting skirt and looking like a penguin as he tried to maneuver in high-heels. But, Morg mustn't find out the truth. He kept the women's clothes on after the party, so he could slip onto the transport without raising suspicion. The Feltte Six authorities had his entry picture and were looking for a thin, six-foot two-inch male with blonde hair. They gave little attention to the redhead, female Earthling who was slim as a rail and slightly attractive in makeup.

With every lie he told the alien, there was more chance of tripping over himself before reaching Earth. He needed to get the Yandan focused on something else, and quick. He came up with a conniving and manipulative idea as Morg began to ask his next question.

"Officer Morg. Before you ask another question, I have to be honest and tell you the other reason I kept on the women's clothes." The Earthling looked down modestly, batted his eyelids which still had long lashes, and said, "I thought you might like to see me in women's clothes."

The Earthling's ruby red lips formed a sensuous smile as Morg leaped from the gyro chair and ran from the rest area. The kid wondered if the auto-record system captured Morg's facial expression before he fled. He hoped so. This would be as much fun watching on replay as the Crelons crapping non-stop on themselves and their ship.

6

"Where the hell is my son?" This was the third time Conway asked, and he was tired of getting the run-around.

"We think he's somewhere near Feltte Six, Prefect Conway. From the reports we've received, his transport left Feltte Six about five hours ago."

"Where the hell is Feltte Six?"

"It's one of our protectorate planets about three light years from Yanda."

"So, you think he's somewhere close to Feltte Six? Is he there or not?"

"The Trifect member sitting in the middle, power position at the conference table responded. "We have no reason to believe he isn't at this position, Prefect Conway." The Lead Trifect knew he made a mistake as soon as the words left his mouth. The double-negative response made him sound like a lame-brain politician who was trying to peddle an outrageous lie.

The Earthling's father looked in disbelief at the three-member Trifect panel. The first thought that raced through his mind was, "These guys control most of the known universe and we're going into business with them? Are you kidding? They're nitwits." There was a part of him that wanted to pull out of the trade pact with the Yandans right then and there. He held himself in check, knowing such a premature move would spoil his plans and put his son in danger. He needed to play along with these incompetent oafs a while longer; at least until his son touched down on Earth.

"Let me see if I have this right." Conway paused to collect his thoughts and form a strategy for his next line of questioning. He loved this type of confrontational arguing. It reminded him of his days on the debate team at the university. "If you have his location correct, my son is still seven light years from Earth. Is that correct?"

The three members of the Yandan Trifect quaked as they passed non-verbal signals back and forth to each other under the conference table. Lucky for them, Prefect Conway could not see their hand and feet signals on the visualizer[1] screen. He could only see from their green and orange abdomens up. They were petrified that the kid's old man would find out they ordered the transport back to Yanda. If he discovered this screwup, the trade pact between the two planets would very likely be terminated or put on indefinite hold.

Again, the member of the Trifect sitting in the power position responded. "Yes, that's correct." He hung his head sheepishly knowing what was next from Conway. He looked at the visualizer screen and saw that the kid's father was ready to explode. Even on the visualizer which muted colors, he could tell that Conway's face was as red as an Orkaet Sweat Beast.

Conway lifted out of his chair and screamed, "Are you kidding me? He's due here in three weeks. Now, one of you tell me how he is going to cover seven light years in three weeks."

When none of the Trifect offered an answer, old man Conway exploded again. "You Yandans are pathetic. I think our Global Union Assembly needs to re-examine the proposed Carbon and Sulfur Emissions Trade Agreement (CASETA) you want us to sign."

That threat reached out and grabbed each Trifect member by his reproduction glands. They started to squirm and talk at once. The

Lead Trifect won out and began to babble an official response. He was hoping against hope to stifle the Prefect's threat to back out of the trade agreement.

"Prefect Conway. There's no reason to re-evaluate the CASETA trade pact between our two great planets. We've made such meaningful progress in a very short period of time. It would be a shame to negate all the work our envoys have already accomplished. I understand your concern for your son but, rest assured, he's in the hands of our most trusted military officer. His name is Officer Morg and I can guarantee you that he will keep your son safe and sound. As soon as...."

Conway cut off the Lead Trifect's endless rambling. It was nothing more than the same feel-good, sales pitch he used a thousand times during negotiations. "He'd better be safe and sound, Trifect."

"You have our assurance, Prefect Conway, that your son, ah, ah, ... your son is safe and ..."

The Trifect spokesman had made two blunders. He couldn't remember the name of Conway's son and he walked into Conway's trap. The Mentat,[2] standing out of sight, signaled Conway that the Yandans were either lying or withholding information. Conway gave him a slight nod to confirm what he already suspected.

"Good! If you guarantee my son's safety, then let's contact him right now. Signal the transport he's on and get him on a three-way communication."

The Trifect found themselves in a corner. No matter what Conway said, they couldn't allow his son or Officer Morg to appear on a three-way communication. If they did, it was inevitable the kid or Morg would spill the beans about being ordered back to Yanda.

"Sir, we can't do that. Your son's ship is on a communication lockdown. It's the only way we could ensure his safety during the flight. If an enemy intercepted a communication, they could either destroy the transport or hijack it and hold your son for ransom."

"Gentlemen, you will have my son contact me within forty-eight hours. I don't care how you do it, just do it. If I don't hear from him, then our trade pact is canceled." Conway watched each Yandan's scaly face turn grim with disappointment. He pushed the disconnect button on the communications panel, leaned back in his chair and laughed hysterically. When he caught his breath, he looked over at the Mentat and asked, "Well, how did I do? Was I convincing?"

The Mentat, who was trained to be an objective reader of minds and emotions, gave his boss, Prefect Conway, a slight grin and thought, "What a jerk. No wonder this man and his son are hated."

Ten light years away, the three members of the Trifect were scrambling, trying to figure out how to salvage the CASETA Agreement and meet Conway's demand to talk with his son. They sat at the conference table playing with drinking cups, peeling labels from Brofult containers, and mumbling to themselves. Each member was lost in deep thought. They sought a solution which satisfied Conway and the Feltte Six authorities. And, it couldn't jeopardize the agreement to buy toxic natural resources from Earth.

The Lead Trifect got up from the conference table and walked over to the Cannis dispenser. He was hoping several snorts from the dispenser would take the edge off the serious task at hand. Perhaps a drug-induced, mellow state of mind would lead to a simple solution which solved all their problems.

This time the Cannis didn't work.

"Brothers, I don't think there is one solution that fixes everything. In fact, I can't come up with a good lie that solves everything."

"So, what do we do."

The Lead Trifect took one last snort from the dispenser and walked back to the conference table. "Here's the way I see it. Yanda is in dire need of another dependable source of sulfuric acids and carbon dioxide toxins. We need those chemicals to add to our atmosphere, so all Yandans can remain healthy. That makes signing the CASETA Agreement the most important thing. It far outweighs every other consideration." The Lead Trifect paused long enough to make sure his two brothers on the military panel understood his assessment.

"There are two ways to get these chemicals. We can sign the CASETA Agreement with Earth or invade their planet and take the chemicals. Brothers, we can't afford to fight another conflict now. We're involved now in three wars and we simply don't have the soldiers, equipment, supplies or money to go to war with Earth. The bottom line is that we have to get the CASETA Agreement signed as quickly as possible."

"I agree, Sir, but how do we handle the Feltte Six authorities? They want Conway's son taken into custody and charged with the crimes he committed on their planet. Yet, Conway demands his son be delivered to Earth posthaste."

"We buy off the Feltte Six authorities. We pay them for the five Interceptors and flight crews they lost. Plus, we kick in some punitive damage payments for other incidentals which are pissing them off. That's all; we call it a day. It will cost a lot but it's a hell of a lot cheaper than invading Earth."

The other two members of the Trifect nodded their heads as they processed the proposed solution.

"Sir, do you think they'll go for a deal like that?"

"Are you kidding, brother? Their planet's economy is based on crime. The place is infested with every type of vice and perversion known in the universe. Taking bribes and payola is a way of life on Feltte Six. Everyone is a crook, including the planet's ruling council."

The Lead Trifect waited to see if there was any opposition or further discussion needed on his proposal. When none came, he began to dish out assignments.

"Okay, I want you two to signal the transport and establish a communications line with Morg. Use the crypto band to communicate so he knows it's an emergency and has to answer. Come and get me when you've reached him. If he sees all three of us, he'll know for sure his new orders are legitimate."

"Sir, if we can't find you when we establish the connection, can we go ahead and give him the new order?"

The Lead Trifect considered the pros and cons of the question before answering. "I would rather you find me, but if you have no choice, go ahead."

"Sir, we want to get this right, so tell us precisely what we can tell Morg."

"First, Officer Morg is to disregard the directive to return to Yanda. He is to reprogram the flight simulators to proceed to the original destination of Earth. Also, Officer Morg is to push his shadow drive system to the max. He is not authorized to make any more stops anywhere. I don't care what emergency or excuse he has, no more stops. He must cover over seven light years in three weeks which we know is impossible. Bottom line is that he has to do the impossible for the security and safety of his home planet, Yanda."

"Sir, we will carry out your orders. Will you be staying on Yanda or visiting the war zones?"

"I'll be in my office, brothers. I need to figure out a way to buy off the Feltte Six governors without giving away the entire wealth of Yanda.

Jimmy Washington slumped over in his chair gasping for air and trying to stay conscious. In some remote recesses of his mind, he could hear a familiar female voice screaming.

"Why don't you leave him alone? Can't you see that he can't take any more? He's told you everything he knows."

"Hey, shut up wench unless you want some of this." The largest of the four Feltte Six, uniformed enforcers wound up and delivered a round-house fist to Jimmy's jaw. The force sent him and his chair across the room.

Jimmy's lady screamed and ran to his side. She cradled his bleeding head in her lap to protect him from more torture and see if he still had a pulse.

"He's sixty-two years old, for god's sake. You're going to kill him. Please stop."

"He should have thought about that before he helped two criminals escape."

"Jimmy has never broken any laws." With snot dripping from her nose and tears pouring down her cheeks, she forced out through clenched teeth, "Check your files, he's got a perfect record. He's been a loyal Sixer."

"Missy, don't you dare refer to this traitor as a Sixer. That term is reserved for born-and-bred Feltte Six nationals who are true patriots, like us."

The four enforcers stood slightly straighter, showing off their badges and medals for bravery and heroism.

"Well, aren't you shining examples of Feltte Six bravery and morality. It takes real guts to beat up and torture an old man. I hope you poor excuses for Sixers ..."

That's as far as Jimmy's young girlfriend got before the enforcers had enough of her sassy back-talk. One of them picked her off the floor by the hair and dragged her into the adjacent bedroom to have his way with her. It took two hours before the four enforcers were satisfied. They finally left Jimmy's house when she gave them the Cannis capsule Jimmy got from Morg. Without this payola, she was sure they would kill her and Jimmy.

"Sir, you better come down to the communications chamber."

"Have you made contact with Officer Morg?"

"No, sir."

"Then, what's the problem?"

"The transport is.... has vanished."

"What? I'll be right there."

The Lead Trifect left his office and waddled through the palace hallways to the communications chamber. Yandan were not known for being fleet of foot. Their eight-toed feet with sharp spurs protruding from each heel prevented a full stride. Otherwise, their legs were perfect for running. Large, muscular thighs plus long and tight calves were an ideal combination for speed. The only way a Yandan could take advantage of his well-developed legs for running was to have the spurs surgically removed. The trade-off was that he wouldn't have them to use in hand-to-hand combat. Also, they grew back in six months, requiring another costly surgery.

The palace was huge and getting to the communications chamber took over thirty minutes. As he saluted to underlings and swerved to avoid hitting others, the Lead Trifect wondered, "What the hell do all these Yandans do?" There were thousands of them filtering in and out of offices and scurrying though the hallways. Certainly, many of them were the rear echelon for military operations. They made sure the soldiers had the equipment and provisions needed to kill the enemy and stay alive. They were an absolute necessity considering Yanda's business was war. A sizable number of the others ran the government's assistance programs. The average, non-military Yandan was a ward of the State relying on the government for all the basic necessities of life. That accounted for many of these beings, but he couldn't shake the question. "Does it really take this many Yandans to run the planet?"

As he turned the last corner into the communication chamber, he made a mental note to look into this question. It was about time to have a committee evaluate the government's payroll budget. It needed to answer some simple questions. Was there a duplication or triplication of work by different government departments? Had some jobs outlived their need or usefulness? Were new jobs created for good or frivolous reasons? He suspected that too many employees was one reason why the planet had a tough time making ends meet.

There were five Yandans in the communication chamber. The other two Trifect stood in a corner whispering to each other. They had sheepish and dour expressions on their faces. The three communications experts sat at the control panels pretending to play with the digital dials. All of them tried to avoid the Lead Trifect's piercing stare. It didn't take a genius to know he wasn't going to like the impending conversation topic.

"Brothers, what the hell is going on?"

"Sir, we can't locate Morg's transport. It simply disappeared. No one from their ship will respond and the auto response from its control panel isn't working."

"What about their flight signature. Can we pick that up?"

"We've tried, sir, but nothing so far."

"Have any of our outposts or alliance planets reported contact or sighting the transport?"

"The last sighting was when the Feltte Six Interceptors made contact with the transport. That was before Morg vaporized them."

"Have you hailed Morg on his private comm channel?"

"Yes, sir. He's not answering. To be honest, we're not sure he took his private comm channel on this mission."

The Lead Trifect rolled his eyes and responded, "Wonderful. That's just great." He was running out of questions and ideas. "Is there any evidence of an explosion near the last reported sighting of the transport?"

At first, the other two Trifect didn't understand the implications of his question. One of the communications specialists butted in and offered an answer. "I checked on that, sir. The transport did not explode nor was it vaporized. Except for the five Feltte Six Interceptors, there hasn't been an explosion in that sector for many years."

"Did you contact Morg's offspring and mate to determine if they heard from him?"

One of the Trifect slumped in his chair and let his head fall an inch or two from his chest. The Lead Trifect hit a sensitive subject, one his peers didn't want to answer. "We haven't done that yet, sir, but .... but..."

The Lead Trifect was getting irritated. He couldn't wait for his underling to get to the point. "But, what, Trifect?"

"We found out that the remains of Morg's mate were picked up by a sweeper approximately two light years from Yanda. We're not sure what to make of that. We haven't had the time to look into it further."

The Lead Trifect glared at his co-council mates. He didn't know whether to criticize them for poor leadership or classify this as a gross error due to an over-stacked bureaucracy.

"Did the sweeper pick up the remains in the approximate area of the transport's flight pattern?"

"Yes, sir."

The Lead Trifect turned and paced the room, thinking about what he learned so far. With his back still to the other Yandans in the room, he began talking to himself. "So, Morg's mate was on board the transport when it left Yanda. Was she alive or dead at departure and what the hell was she doing on the ship?" After a couple more steps, he began talking to himself again. The other two Yandans moved closer so they could eavesdrop on his thoughts.

"Maybe, Morg hid her on the ship as a stowaway." After thinking about this possibility for a few seconds, he continued. "No, that doesn't make sense. If he went to the trouble of sneaking her onboard, why did she end up dead? Something very odd is happening on that transport. I wonder where it is now and who is in charge? I knew things were going too smooth and it was about time for some shit to come crashing down on me. I got the Feltte Six authorities calmed down about Conway's kid and paid them for the Interceptors and crews. Now, this happens."

The Lead Trifect shook his head back-and-forth and started to chuckle to himself. He couldn't help thinking about the stupidity of the entire situation.

"Brothers, if the transport is still flying, where do you think it is?"

"Sir, we think it's headed for Yanda. After all, Morg did acknowledge our command to return to Yanda, so we have no reason to believe it's going anywhere else."

"How do you know it was Morg?"

"Well, he acknowledged the command with his personal security code."

"Brothers let me tell you what I think. The transport isn't heading to Yanda. I don't know where it's going, but it definitely isn't coming here. Oh, before I forget, make sure you cancel the Feltte Six Look-For bulletin on the transport. No, wait a minute. Keep the Look-For bulletin active. With a little luck, someone might spot our transport and report it."

The Lead Trifect turned and started to strut toward the door.

"Sir, what are we going to tell Prefect Conway?"

The Lead Trifect was out the door and headed down the hallway when his answer echoed into the communications chamber.

"I have no damn idea, brothers. FIND MORG."

7

"Morg, we have to cut back the shadow drive to twenty percent."

"Why? That's the initial phase for docking. I don't see anywhere to dock."

"Look at the navigation screen. Do you see anything?"

At first, Morg saw nothing but open space; certainly no place they could dock the transport. He was ready to tell the kid he was making a mistake slowing down when in his peripheral vision he saw a glimmering, outlined image on the screen.

"What's this?" Morg pointed at the screen with one of his pincer fingers which was long and slender with four knuckles.

"It's a cloaking star. It's called Ziptowtheon. That's where we are going to dock."

Morg looked over at the Earthling in the co-pilot's gyro chair. He wondered for the first time, "Who exactly is this Earthling? He's not the immature simpleton I have mistaken him for. He knows too much about almost everything. Every time he acts like a flake, he turns around and displays an incredible amount of knowledge. Knowledge which a moron wouldn't have stored away. I thought he was lucky when he pulled off one of his escapades by dressing as a woman to escape from Feltte Six. But that wasn't luck. It was a finely conceived and executed bit of espionage to slip through the grasp of the Feltte Six authorities."

Morg continued to watch the Earthling. He thought about other incidents where the kid pretended to be a dunce who stumble-bummed his way through elaborate solutions. Then, the most obvious example of the kid's hidden talents struck Morg square in the head. Where did the kid learn to fly a transport? Morg refused to believe the kid's explanation. There was no way he learned to pilot space vehicles from playing holographic entertainment games. He might be bright but no one in the universe could become a qualified pilot from only computer-generated simulations.

"What is a cloaking star and how did you know about this one?"

"Morg, you know what a ship with cloaking is. This is the same thing except it's a small planet."

"How is that possible? The energy needed to cloak an entire planet is ... is, inconceivable. I know Krytonium can cloak a large object for a couple hours, but nonstop indefinitely is impossible."

"Morg, I'm not sure how they do it, but they've figured out some power source which keeps the cloaking up around-the-clock."

"So, how do you know about this place?"

The Earthling turned toward Morg and winked. "I have my ways, good buddy."

There was another one of the kid's facial expressions which had a hidden connotation. Morg ignored these expressions thinking they weren't important. However, his opinion was changing, and it was time to learn what these signals meant.

"Well, how did you make arrangements to dock here without a working communications system?"

"I contacted Ziptowtheon before the communications panel fire. I knew the Feltte Six authorities were after us, so we had to find a place to hide while we considered our options."

Morg turned in his chair and looked straight out through the viewing portal. Not only did the kid's answers fit together well but they were much too slippery. He had an answer for everything. Even though he believed the kid this time, he couldn't help thinking his answers were only a small piece of a larger explanation. There had to be more than what the kid was telling.

Morg needed a solid hour or two, without interruption, to interrogate the kid. His list of questions was growing daily. It had reached such an enormous number he was having difficulty keeping them stored in his memory in a logical sequence. He wanted to know more about his mate's death, the fire, dressing like a drag queen and pursuit by Feltte Six Interceptors. To this list, he now added another series of questions about the cloaking star of Ziptowtheon. Who were its leaders and what was their relationship to the Earthling?

He thought it might be an appropriate time to start his questioning. With the kid preoccupied with docking procedures, he might slip up and tell the entire truth or more than he should.

"Earthling, can you tell me why the Feltte Six interceptors were...?"

That's as far as he got when the ship's Roboland system cut him off. The docking announcement started. "Please return to your gyro chairs and buckle the harness straps. Arrival at Ziptowe...Ziptooth... Ziptown." The Roboland system paused for ten seconds before continuing with the landing instructions. "I'm sorry, I cannot pronounce the name of the destination planet. Our next destination will be in twelve minutes. Docking has been approved at gate two. You will be met by a representative of .... ah, of the planet."

The kid broke out laughing. "Did you catch that, Morg. The computer couldn't pronounce Ziptowtheon. Now, that's funny."

Morg understood the concept of comedy but saw no humor in a computer's inability to pronounce a word. It was another example of how little he understood the Earthling.

Ten minutes later, the shadow drive system slowed to two percent in preparation for a safe approach into Ziptowtheon's docking bay hangar. Morg could see the planet's image intensify on the navigation screen but still could not spot the planet through the bridge viewing portal.

"Prepare for lock-on. Ten, nine, eight, seven...." Six seconds later, a shimmering harness beam appeared out of nowhere and locked onto the transport. Within two minutes it pulled the transport to rest in bay two.

The Earthling was up and out of his gyro chair before Morg could yell, "Don't disappear on me, Earthling. I want to know where you are..."

As Morg performed last-minute shut-down procedures, he spotted the Earthling through the viewing portal. The kid was already out of the ship and hustling toward a group of beings standing thirty meters away near the hangar entrance door. From this distance, Morg couldn't make out what planets were represented by the members of the reception group.

Morg started to leave the bridge but froze in place to watch the kid bow and shake hands with the reception committee members. Two of the group's members embraced the kid and gave him a hearty hug as though they were long-lost relatives. This was more than a traditional, friendly welcome to Ziptowtheon. All these beings knew each other. Morg wondered, "How could that be?"

By the time Morg got out of the transport and walked to the group, the back-slapping, laughter, and camaraderie had stopped. The four members of the reception group had serious looks on their faces as they listened to the Earthling.

"Oh, hi, Morg. Everyone, this is my good friend, Morg, from the planet Yanda. He is escorting me back to Earth. Morg, this is...."

Morg tuned out the Earthling as he introduced each member of the reception committee. He had no interest in their names. He wanted to know where these beings came from. That would tell more about the cloaking star and their connection to the Earthling than names which were probably fictitious.

Morg played along as though he was pleased to meet these beings. All the while, he was analyzing their appearance, manner of speaking and behavior. One of the four was definitely from Earth. He had a much darker complexion and hair than the kid, but his language and speech patterns were similar.

Another member of the group was a Crelon. There was no mistaking Crelons with their bulbous foreheads and muscular forearms. What Morg couldn't determine was whether this Crelon was a slaver or made his living in some other borderline, illicit profession.

The third member of the group was Yandan. Morg closely examined his fellow planetarian. He looked for any clues which might identify his breeding and family hierarchy. The Yandan kept quiet, knowing he was being scrutinized by Morg.

Morg didn't have any idea what planet the fourth member of the group was from. He had been throughout the universe but never ran across a being like this one. The coloring of the being's outer covering changed continuously. One minute he or she was violet and then it changed to a neon yellow or green. At first, Morg thought the color change was a reaction to its surroundings like a chameleon. A closer evaluation proved this to be a false assumption. Other than the odd coloring and a third leg, this creature was unremarkable.

"Morg, I'm making arrangements to have the transport completely refurbished. Each of these fine fellows is an expert in...."

Morg looked at the Earthling as though he had lost his mind.

"Excuse me, fellow beings. The Earthling and I have to talk." Morg grabbed the kid's arm and yanked him far enough away from the group so they couldn't hear what was being said.

"Have you gone insane? How are we going to pay for refurbishing the transport? And, even if we could pay for it, we haven't got the time to waste. I'll trade the transport in for another ship, and we'll be gone within a couple of hours."

"Sorry, my friend. We can't do that."

"Why not?"

"Because there are no ships for sale or trade on this planet. It's so small, there are only three ships and you're looking at them." The

Earthling swept the docking hangar with a wave of his hand so Morg would look at the other ships.

"Is this another of your jokes, Earthling? These ships are junk compared to the transport. Are you telling me that their owners wouldn't take a Yandan transport in on trade for their dilapidated antiques?"

"You just met the owners of these three ships and, believe me, they don't want anything to do with our ship. The transport is *hot* and there's a Look-For bulletin out on it. Everyone within five light years is watching for it. These guys are willing to do a refurbish for us. But, they sure as hell don't want to take the chance of drawing attention to their planet by having a Yandan transport sitting here."

"Well, aren't there other ships docked off-planet or can't they have a trade-in ship brought from a near-by planet?"

"Morg, why do you think they went to the bother and expense of cloaking this planet non-stop? They don't want anyone to know they are here. Having ships close by would do nothing other than draw unwanted attention."

Morg caught himself before he asked why the Ziptowtheons wanted complete secrecy. He was sure the kid would make up another lie. A lie that sounded halfway plausible yet raised more questions. He didn't have the time to verbally joust with the kid. They needed to get back into space and complete the mission to Earth.

"How are we going to pay for this?"

"Don't worry, I've made a deal with these guys. The ship will be done within two days." Before Morg could comprehend this latest bit of information, the Earthling re-joined his reception committee buddies. What the hell did he mean by making a deal with these guys?

Morg gave up. There was nothing he could do other than go along with the kid's plans. He re-entered the transport to retrieve his assault rife and a few personal items, so they weren't stolen. He flung the duffle bag and rife over his shoulder and headed to the exit. He had to fight his way past the mob of technicians, fabricators and repairmen entering and crawling inside, over and under the transport.

"Officer Morg, I'm JoJo and I've been assigned to escort you around Ziptowtheon. Where can I take you, sir?"

Morg looked down and saw a tiny being of no more than three feet in height and covered entirely in lavender fur. The creature had an impish face highlighted by a pug nose and pouting lips. There was a perpetual smile imprinted on its face even when it talked. Its eyes were abnormally large and covered nearly half the face.

Morg had no idea what this dwarfed creature was, where it came from and if it was mature or juvenile. He guessed it might be female from its name and high-pitched voice. But he didn't know for sure. This little being might be a male or a hermaphrodite with both sex organs.

"JoJo, I'd like to go to my room and get a few hours of sleep. I could also use a deep-steam cleansing and some food. Can you arrange...."

Before Morg finished his question, JoJo grabbed the duffle bag and waddled toward the docking hangar door. Morg stood there admiring the little creature's incredible strength. The duffle bag weighed over two hundred pounds. He was also captivated by his walk. How did he accomplish such forceful strides on legs which were no more than fifteen-inches in length?

JoJo led Morg to a wheel-less, two-seat tram which was powered by reverse magnetics. The little imp was just tall enough to reach the handles to open the wing doors. With an effortless toss, JoJo pitched Morg's duffle bag to the storage bin on top of the tram.

When the doors shut, music flooded the inside of the cabin. It was quite a bit different than the blaring, hard-beat songs the Earthling played and danced to. This was soothing and easy on Morg's sensitive ears. It was enjoyable to listen to. Morg found himself more relaxed and restful than he had been since leaving Yanda. He made a mental note to get some of this music after the mission to Earth was completed.

A pleasant female voice flooded the tram cabin. "What destination do you prefer, Comrade JoJo?"

"The Gracie, please."

"What's the Gracie, JoJo?"

"It's an accommodation building used by special guests to Ziptowtheon. While you are sleeping, Officer Morg, is there anything you would like me to do?"

Rather than answer JoJo's question, Morg thought about how he described the Gracie. "Why am I considered a special guest to Ziptowtheon, JoJo?"

JoJo turned his fury head toward Morg and with a sparkle in his eyes and a broad smile, he shrugged his shoulders. "Damn if I know. You look like a regular Yandan, to me."

Morg didn't know what to make of JoJo's comment. Was the little creature fooling around or a willing pawn who did and said no more than what it was told to say? Whichever it was, there was little hope of getting more information out of the little fellow or gal.

"JoJo, while I'm resting would you reserve a spot for me at a communication center? I have a few contacts to make. Also, think about where I can get a good plate of Trimite intestines."

8

"Hi, pops. What's shaking?"

The kid sat in front of the communication screen and watched his father's face turn crimson. The old man hated being called pops. He had told his son often to drop all references to their father-son relationship. He was to refer to him by his government title of Earth Prefect.

"How many times have I told you to call me Prefect? Is that so hard to remember?"

The kid started to reply but was cut off by his father. "You know, you're going to blow our entire plan if you don't quit screwing around. I see half the damn universe is looking for you." The old man flashed a Wanted Dead or Alive posting on the screen and continued to rant. "If you don't recognize this, it's a Wanted Bulletin for your stupid ass from Feltte Six. What the hell did you do there?"

"Pops, I mean Prefect, it wasn't my fault. Some professional mercenaries were trying to kill me, so I decided to get them before they got me."

"BS Feltte Six authorities don't give a rat's behind about who kills who. You must have done something more hideous than kill a couple guests to their planet."

"No, I'm telling you the truth. That's all I did."

The old man looked out of the corner of his eye at the Mentat standing outside the limits of the communication screen. A simple thumb down from the Mentat told the story. The kid was lying about the extent of his crimes on Feltte Six. The old man laughed to himself and thought how lucky the kid was to be several light years away. If he had been in the same room, a good, old-fashioned beating would have revealed the truth.

"Where are you now?"

"We just passed the Rings of Baccus. Morg landed us on a rogue planet to get some repairs done to the ship."

"Knock off the terrestrial positioning lesson. Do you think I have the universe memorized? Tell me how many light years you are from Earth. And, by the way, do you know the people on the rogue planet, and can they keep their mouths shut?"

"I don't know anyone on this planet, but we're paying them a lot for their silence. I think we're about five light years out from Earth."

In his peripheral vision, the old man saw the Mentat give two thumbs down. Lies number two and three.

The old man wondered why the kid would go to such an extreme to hide their present location. There must be something about this rogue planet he didn't want his father to know.

The old man didn't say anything for a couple minutes to see how the kid would react. Would his son add any more information or make body movements which might betray what he was hiding? The kid remained stoic and stared ahead at his father. The old man gave the kid credit. He was a trained and accomplished liar.

"For your information, I read the Yandans the riot act about finding you. I told them if they didn't have you contact me, it could mean the end of the CASETA agreement. So, whatever you do, don't communicate with anyone on Yanda."

"That's brilliant, pops, I mean, Prefect. We have the Yandans exactly where we want them. If we break the CASETA agreement, it will hasten the downfall of Yanda and its empire."

"I agree. When they can't produce you, it will give me a good reason to move against the Agreement. I should be able to convince the few Assembly member hold-outs to vote against the Agreement. There's not much they can complain about when I show them how unreliable and untrustworthy the Yandans are."

The old man paused and thought a moment before continuing. "Son, to be on the safe side, you better take out the beings you're dealing with on the rogue planet. Get rid of them before you leave so they don't report you to the Yandans."

"Ah...yeah, that's a good idea. I'll do that."

The Mentat flashed another thumb down for lie number four.

"What about that Yandan you're with? Will he be communicating with his superiors, the Trifect? What did you call him? Morg something-or-other. What a doofus name."

As much as the kid despised his father, he laughed when he called the alien a doofus. "You're right. The alien is a doofus. Don't worry about him, I've got him right where I want him. He's totally confused and hasn't a clue about what I'm up to..."

As the kid rambled on, the old man thought, "Yeah, I don't have a clue about what you're up to, either."

"...and besides, the alien is on a communications quarantine. He's under strict orders not to contact the Trifect or anyone else on Yanda. Oh, one other thing. I destroyed the transport's communications sub-panel."

The old man shook his head up and down as a silent confirmation of what the kid did. Finally, he said, "That's good. That's really good. Then there's no way for the alien to reach anyone from the ship?"

The kid liked the old man's praise even though it was long overdue. Even after twenty years of belittlement and ridicule, it felt good.

The kid intentionally forgot to give the old man details about the transport refurbishment. He would only worry and give orders if he knew about the new equipment. It was best he did not know about the new communications sub-panel and the redundant, eavesdropping bugs.

"Right, he won't be able to contact anyone while we're in flight."

Once again, the Mentat gave a thumb down. The old man admired his son's ability to hide the truth. He was truly a chip-off-the-old-block. Yet he couldn't help wondering if the kid ever told the truth about anything. Or, did he reserve his outrageous lying strictly for his father?

The old man reached his limit. It was time to give the kid a wake-up call and bring him back to reality. He needed to know he was dealing with the master of deceit, double-dealing, and espionage.

"Son, I have a surprise for you. I needed another personal assistant, so I hired a former friend of yours." The old man looked off-screen and held out an inviting hand. "Darling, come over here so Joseph can see you."

The kid hadn't heard the old man use his full, Christian name in years. If he had been thinking quick, he would have turned off the communicator immediately. Every rotten trick the old man played on the kid throughout his childhood and teenage years started with the name, Joseph.

Into the screen walked a petite, blonde woman in her late-twenties. Her hairstyle and business clothes were very conservative. Neither could hide her outer beauty. She had a simple yet alluring face. Her skin was flawless like porcelain and adorned with huge blue-green eyes that possessed whoever she looked at. Every move she made was unintentionally graceful. She was shy and meek at the same time she was forceful and domineering. And, she was the only human the kid ever loved.

"Son, you remember Beth, don't you?"

The kid's face flushed, and his normal, egotistic overconfidence drained from his body. He went numb each time he saw the love of his life. He thought an extended period away from Earth would make him forget this lovely creature. He was wrong. He was in love with her this day as much as he was when he left Earth as a pawn in his father's scheme to rule the universe.

"Hello, Joe. How are you?"

The kid didn't respond immediately. He was too busy examining every minuscule feature of her face and hair on her head.

"Joe, did you hear me?"

"Yes... ah, yeah, I heard you, Beth. I'm fine. How about you?"

"I've been good, Joe. Your father was kind enough to give me a job. The extra income is going to help my family a lot."

"That's .... that's great, Beth. What exactly are you doing for him?"

Before she could answer, the old man interrupted with, "Joe, she just started. She'll do whatever I need her to do. Just the way you carry out my orders, Joseph."

The kid wanted to jump through the screen and strangle the old man. The snicker on the old man's face was shameful and the message was clear. Stay in line son and follow my instructions or your sweetheart is going to have an accident.

The rest of their conversation was a blur to the kid. The old man babbled on and on about what he wanted the kid to do, or else. And, the kid kept thinking, "I can't wait to slit your throat, old man."

9

"JoJo, you can stay in the tram. I'll only be a few minutes."

"No worries, Officer Morg. Take as much time as you need." The lavender fur-ball was under instructions to keep a close eye on the Yandan. He was to watch and record everything he did. But, following him into a communications center reeked of obvious snooping. If the Yandan stayed too long in the center, JoJo could wander in and see what he was up to. He could also stay on the tram and rely on his friends to get the number Morg contacted. And, if he wanted to listen to the Yandan's conversation a threat or payola would produce the recording. That is if the center's antiquated system worked properly.

Morg entered a private cubicle and took out the note with Jimmy Washington's private contact number on it. On the third pulse, a young, attractive woman with tan skin, black hair, and alluring eyes, answered.

"Miss, my name is Morg. I'm a friend of Jimmy Washington's. He drove me around...."

"Oh, thank God. I'm so happy you called, Officer Morg. I've been trying to figure out how to get ahold of you for days. Jimmy is...is...." That's all the woman could say before she broke down sobbing. Even with her eye makeup running and hair tossed every which way, there was something very appealing about her. She was the perfect match for a taxi cab driver who was as debonair as any being from wealth, fame, or royalty.

It took over two minutes for the woman to compose herself. "Forgive me, Officer Morg. I'm so sorry. You didn't call to watch me wail like an old woman at a funeral."

Morg started to worry when she mentioned funeral. Was Jimmy dead?

"That's okay, miss. But, please tell me if Jimmy is alive."

"Yes, Office Morg, he's still alive, but not in good shape. Let me take you to his bedside. He's been asking for you." The young woman took the miniature transceiver to another room where Jimmy was sprawled on a bed. He was bandaged from head to toe. Many of the bandages were soaked in the blood and fluids which oozed from a badly beaten human body.

The girlfriend moved the transceiver close to Jimmy's face so Morg could hear his weak voice and read his lips. Jimmy was a mess. Both eyes were swollen almost shut and there were several large bumps on his cheeks and forehead. His lips were split in numerous spots. The dried-over scabs threatened to re-open whenever he spoke.

"Jimmy, what happened?"

"Beat up by...by...."

Jimmy's voice faded out before Morg could understand what he said. The girlfriend guessed his last words hadn't broadcast, so she completed the sentence. "Officer Morg, he said that he was beat up by enforcement agents."

"Why? What did he do to deserve such a beating?"

The girlfriend leaned over Jimmy's face and put her ear to his mouth. She listened for a couple minutes before relaying his answer to Morg.

"He said the agents wanted to know everything about you and

the young Earthling. They demanded to know where the two of you went and why the Earthling didn't leave with you. They wanted to know where he's hiding on Feltte Six. Oh, they also wanted to know who the redhead, female human was that got on your transport before departure."

Morg wasn't sure he heard the girlfriend correctly. Did she say the agents wanted to know where the Earthling was hiding on Feltte Six? He started to ask her to repeat that part of the answer when it hit him. The agents hadn't put two and two together. They didn't realize the kid was the redhead they saw get on the transport. The kid outfoxed the Feltte Six authorities by dressing in drag. They thought he was still hiding out on their planet. At least, that's what they believed when they beat the hell out of Jimmy. Since then, they may have figured it out.

"Jimmy doesn't know anything about a redhead, Officer Morg. What were those agents talking about?"

"Miss, what's your name?"

"Samantha, Sam for short."

"Sam did the agents say if they were coming back to question Jimmy again?"

"They were supposed to be back this morning, but never showed up."

"That's a good sign they aren't coming back. Something has happened to make them back off, so I don't think you'll need to know who the redhead is. If they do show, keep playing dumb about the redhead and deny knowing where the Earthling is hiding. Believe me, it's best you don't know who the redhead is." It would have been easy for Morg to explain the connection to Sam. But, if she tried to convince the agents that the redhead and kid were one in the same person, it would be disastrous. It would only lead to more unanswerable questions and needless beatings.

"What else did they want to know, Sam?"

"They asked Jimmy and me all sorts of questions. We had no idea what the hell they were talking about. They wanted to know where you were going after departure and what was your cargo. They made a big deal out of some type of connection between you and three mercenaries. Like I said, we didn't have any idea what they were talking about. Do you, Officer Morg?"

"Yeah, unfortunately, I do. But, right now, it's not important. The only thing that is important is getting Jimmy healthy again. Do you have a safe house you can move Jimmy to?"

"I can't think of any, Officer Morg. We don't have any relatives here and I wouldn't trust our so-called friends."

Morg thought a moment and then said, "Sam, get ahold of Luna at the blind pig on Gratiot Avenue. She's a Landan waitress working there, and I know she's a close friend of Jimmy's. I'm sure she'll help you."

"Thank you, officer Morg."

Morg saw Sam start to tear up again, so he quickly asked another question to divert her attention.

"Is there anything else I should know?"

Sam stared off into space for a minute, collecting her emotions, before answering. "Yes, there was one thing I overheard which I thought was kinda strange. One agent said the Earthling was wanted for non-disposal of corpses and killing a couple foot-fetish prostitutes. He also set fire to the brothels they worked in. Another agent mentioned that the Earthling was suspected of killing an enforcement agent. The agent was patrolling the brothel neighborhood when he was ambushed."

All Morg could say was, "No wonder they came after us and beat up Jimmy."

Any doubts Morg had about the Earthling's sanity were cast aside. He was riding across the universe in a small space vehicle, no larger than a Yandan abode, with a psychotic killer. Morg had dealt with many killers during his career, but none so crafty as the kid. He wondered if it would be better to slit the kid's throat now and eject him into space? But, once again, he came to the same decision. The kid had to stay alive for the safety and security of Yanda and his offspring. And, there was the nagging belief the kid was withholding information about the murder of his mate.

Out of the corner of his eye, Morg saw JoJo enter the communications center and waddle over to the manager's office. From the way, the manager responded when he saw the little guy, there was no doubt they knew each other. Morg turned his head so that his left ear was directly lined up with the manager's office. With his parabolic dish-like ear, Morg could pick up most of what was being said.

"Tookie, do you see that Yandan over there?"

Morg used the mirror-like finish on the communications panel to see the manager look his way.

"Yeah, JoJo. What's up?"

"How many comms has he made?"

The manager looked at this master panel and responded. "He's only made one communication, JoJo. He's been talking with someone with a private comm number."

"What does that mean, Tookie?"

"Basically, it's a number that can't be found. When the communication is sent it's diverted, scrubbed, and scrambled hundreds of times. It only takes a few seconds but the comm is untraceable. The being on the other end could be anywhere in the universe. A private comm number is very expensive."

"Great, that's just wonderful. Are you recording his comm, Tookie?"

The manager knew JoJo wielded a certain amount of political power on Ziptowtheon, so he was careful in the way he answered. "Yes, the comm is being recorded, but I can't guarantee a quality recording. Our system is very old and long overdue for an equipment update. I've been asking for the funding...."

JoJo was in no mood to hear excuses. "Yeah, yeah. Tookie, I don't want to hear about your problems. Just make sure the recording doesn't get lost. Understand?"

"I will do as you instruct, Comrade JoJo."

Morg knew he wouldn't be able to make a direct comm to Yanda.

The last thing he wanted to do was leave a recording of his contact with Yanda so a Ziptowtheon agent could decode and listen to it. He thought fast and came up with a way to mislead JoJo and whoever he was spying for.

"Sam, I know this is a lot to ask, but can you do me a favor?"

It only took one slight nod of Jimmy's head for her to respond. "Anything, Officer Morg."

"Good. Turn on the transceiver's recorder so all you have to do is send my message directly to the private comm number I'm going to give you."

For the next minute, Morg spoke a coded message into Sam's recorder. It was in an ancient dialect of Yandan which very few Yandans were aware of. Its use was by military commanders when absolute secrecy was needed during combat. There was no reason to worry about intercepted messages because the ancient language confused the enemy. They had no idea what the hell was being said. But, anyone familiar with this ancient language would understand Morg's message. "Trifect, Morg reporting. We are approximately six light years from Earth. Temporarily delayed. The transport is being refurbished at coordinates 2323565-505-897. Cargo intact. Will proceed without further delay to Earth."

"Sam, send this message to private comm number 8789999-9. Do you understand?"

"Yes, Officer Morg."

"Good, good. You take care of Jimmy and go underground until he regains his health. I'll check back in with you when I can."

Rather than say goodbye and risk Sam breaking down and start sobbing again, Morg disconnected the communication. He had made some mistakes when talking with her like mentioning Gratiot Avenue and Jimmy's entire name. With these clues and a couple others, JoJo and his boss could figure out to who and where Morg communicated. He couldn't undo those mistakes. He considered returning to the communications center later to destroy or steal his comm recording. But that would give JoJo and his boss more reason to find out where the comm went and what was the true translation of the secondary message. He could only hope the old recording equipment in the communications center malfunctioned. There was a slim possibility JoJo's boss wouldn't see any merit in backtracking to Morg's contact person.

Morg prepared to leave the private cubicle. He went very slow, pretending to drop something on the ground. When JoJo saw that he scampered out of the communications center and returned to the tram as though he never left it. Morg chuckled to himself watching the cute imp in the reflective panel. It was too bad the little, lavender fur-ball was a devious double-agent.

10

"First Comrade Joe, I don't understand why you've changed your mind. Twenty-two hours ago, when you docked on Ziptowtheon, everything was fine. Our original plan to invade Yanda and her alliance planets was still a go. Now, a few hours before you take off, the plan is off. What the hell is going on?"

The Earthling looked around the conference table at his primary co-conspirators. They were the same four beings who met him the previous day in the docking bay. The difference was they were jovial and agreeable then. Now, they were irritated with what First Comrade Joe, their leader, was proposing.

"Gentlemen, the overthrow of the Yandan empire isn't off indefinitely. It's still a go situation but I think it's better to delay our invasion. We need more time to prepare. For example, I'm not convinced our contingency planning is flawless. I also want to make sure we haven't underestimated the Yandan response to our invasion. You must remember the Yandans have been in continuous wars for hundreds of years. They have seen it all; every type of warfare and every weapon in existence. They are masters of espionage, counter-intelligence, misdirection, torture, and psychological warfare. They wrote the book on terrorism and counter-terrorism. Gentlemen, they are more than a formidable foe and I want to make sure we aren't jumping the gun and ..."

The Crelon interrupted the Earthling's explanation. "First Comrade. It's true the Yandans are professional warriors, but they have never seen our secret weapon. They haven't confronted an enemy who can cloak an entire planet. We can sneak up on them, launch our attack and overwhelm them before they know what hit them. With a little more time and preparation, we'll have twenty cloaked planets. Each has a full complement of men and armament ready to invade. There is no way they can stop us. The longer we delay the more chance they'll learn what we are up to and checkmate our superiority. First Comrade, we must move forward with the original plan. We can't afford to wait any longer."

The Crelon was the leader of the opposition to delay the invasion. The Earthling could tell from body language around the table that two other co-conspirators were in agreement with the Crelon. The sad thing was that the Earthling knew the Crelon was right. But he couldn't tell the group his real reason for delaying the invasion. Specifically, he needed time to figure out how to save Beth from his old man. He needed time to get to Earth and rescue her.

The kid's brain was calculating at a million bits per second. He must convince his co-conspirators that delaying the invasion was the right thing to do. He could pull rank on them, but he didn't want to. He had seen how many enemies his old man created by disregarding the wishes and ideas of his supporters. There was no quicker way to turn a loyalist into an enemy than tossing aside his ideas and suggestions.

The Earthling opened his mouth to present a counter-argument even though he had no idea what to say. "Gentlemen let me add..."

The door to the executive meeting room opened with authority and in waddled JoJo. It was exactly what Comrade Joe needed to break the tension in the room.

"First Comrade Joe. I'm sorry for the interruption, but you

wanted to know immediately if Officer Morg made any communications."

"Yes, JoJo. Come in and tell us who Morg communicated with."

The furry dwarf strutted into the room like a conquering hero and hopped up on one of the executive chairs. He started his summary of Morg's communication like a seasoned politician. "Gentlemen, Officer Morg made one communication to a private comm number. Private comm numbers are untraceable so we have no idea who he talked with or what planet that communication went to. We do know there were two beings on the receiving end of the communication. We have their names and some clues about landmarks on their planet. Their names are Samantha and Jimmy. I don't think it will be long before we can identify the planet where these two beings live."

"What are some of the clues, JoJo?"

"There was mention in the communication of foot fetish murders, a redhead Earthling woman and someone hiding on their planet. As I said earlier, we have the names of a few landmarks so I'm sure we'll be able to identify the planet very soon."

"Very interesting." The Earthling stared up at the ceiling. He pretended to be dissecting JoJo's report. His reaction was all for show. He knew exactly which planet Morg's communication went to. And, he understood the references to foot fetish murders, a redhead and other tidbits of information. It was a sheer miracle that Feltte Six wasn't mentioned by name.

The Earthling knew it wouldn't be hard track down the beings who received Morg's communication. The harder task would be establishing why Morg called these specific beings. What was his connection to these beings? As far as the Earthling knew, Morg didn't know anyone on Feltte Six.

"Was there anything else interesting in the communication, JoJo?"

"Yes, First Comrade Joe. Near the end of the communication, Officer Morg asked the female to pass along a secret message to another private comm number."

This time, the Earthling wasn't acting when he responded with "Very interesting. Do you know anything about this message, JoJo?"

"I'm sorry, sir. As I said before, there is no way to identify a private comm number. It would take weeks to cross-verify all the possible private numbers to isolate the actual number contacted. Also, we ran the message through our language decryption system and came up with zero. Whatever language Morg used is nothing our system has ever heard before. Who he sent the comm to and what it said is a mystery, First Comrade Joe."

"JoJo, we need to find out who Officer Morg sent the encrypted message to and what was in it. I don't care how many men you use and how you do it. Get me that information. Your first priority is that secret message Morg sent. Everything else is a secondary priority. Do you understand, JoJo?"

JoJo jumped down from the chair, snapped to attention and replied. "Yes sir, First Comrade Joe. I'll work on it around the clock. I promise to get the answers."

Morg watched the little imp strut out of the executive room like a newly crowned king. He was so serious about his new assignment it was hard holding back the laughter. The chance JoJo would find out where the secret comm went and what it said was next to zero. It did make the Earthling wonder what Morg was up to and how much he knew or suspected. There was little doubt the message went to someone on Yanda, but what did it say?

This new bit of information from the lavender fur-ball was exactly the ammunition the Earthling needed. Now, he could push through his suggestion to delay the Yanda invasion.

"First Comrade Joe, the information JoJo delivered is not good. We can assume Officer Morg is communicating with someone on Yanda and he is telling them about us. So, we need to push our invasion plans ahead, without delay. Time is our enemy, now."

The Earthling jumped to his feet and slammed his fists on the executive table. He leaned forward and stared with indignation at the Crelon. He held the Crelon in his angry glare for more than two minutes before he said a word. The Crelon was correct in his assessment but he had to make him look like a fool.

"Crelon, this is precisely why we shouldn't go ahead with the invasion. If we do as you suggest we'll get wiped out. It's going to take us several weeks to move our cloaked planets into position and complete invasion preparations. What do you think the Yandans will be doing during those weeks if they know about our cloaking weapon?" When the Crelon and his two allies didn't respond immediately, the Earthling screamed. "They'll be figuring out a way to find our cloaked planets, even if they resort to sending out suicide ships to crash into our planets. And, you know that when we start moving the planets toward Yanda there is a shadow trail left behind. If the Yandans are paying attention, they'll see those shadow trails. They aren't dummies. They'll wonder what is causing them and start investigating."

The Earthling's argument made sense even though he hated delaying the invasion. His co-conspirators were more than half convinced an invasion delay was mandatory. It was time to throw the final pieces of his argument on the table and squash the faction who wanted to invade Yanda as planned.

The Earthling sat back in his chair and began a lecture. It reminded him of the scoldings he got for being a disobedient child. "Gentlemen, think about it. Officer Morg knows about our cloaked planet but he has no reason to suspect what we are using it for. Why should he think there's going to be an invasion of Yanda and communicate that to the Trifect? But, let's assume he does tell the Trifect and they believe him. Why would they suspect there is an armada of cloaked planets preparing to move toward Yanda for an invasion? We need to be concerned about Officer Morg's secret communication but not overreact to what might be in it."

The room went silent until one of the co-conspirators got enough courage to ask, "Should we kill Officer Morg?"

"No, we don't want to do anything to raise suspicion with the Trifect on Yanda. I've loaded the transport with hundreds of listening and video bugs as part of the refurbishment. It will be easy to keep close tabs on everything Morg is thinking and doing. He shouldn't be able to sleep without me knowing what's going through that scaly head of his."

The co-conspirators smiled or half-heartedly chuckled at the Earthling's sarcastic remark. The kid knew he had won over everyone in the room when the Crelon asked, "First Comrade Joe, what are your orders?"

There was a slight groan in the room when the Earthling said, "We're going to slow down our invasion plans." After a dramatic pause, he added, "We're going to slow down our plans because Earth is speeding up her plans."

The Earthling could see positive energy returning to the room even though everyone was confused. The co-conspirators sat up in their chairs and leaned forward to hear more.

"You guys keep forgetting that my old man is Prefect Conway and he's plotting to destroy the Yandans. He is hell-bent on taking complete control of the universe. The fool tells me everything because he thinks I'm his right-hand man. If he only knew about our planet cloaking technology and how I plan to unleash it on Earth." The kid chuckled to himself and was temporarily lost in thoughts of destroying his old man.

"Anyhow, I talked to him yesterday and he's planning to veto the CASETA Agreement which will throw Yanda into a tailspin."

The Earthling looked around the room. He could tell from the expressions on his co-conspirator's faces they didn't understand the implications of what he said. He would have to spell it out, so they understood why their plans needed to change.

"Here's what will happen when the CASETA Agreement gets trashed. The Yandans need the toxic molecules from Earth to survive. If they can't buy them through the Agreement, they will either invade Earth or die a slow, planetary death. Unfortunately for them, they can't afford to fight another war now. They simply don't have enough troopers and resources. They are going to be between a rock and a hard place, as the old Earth saying goes. While the Yandans are trying to figure out what to do, my old man will be solidifying an alliance with the Floridians who also need Earth's toxic gases."

"So, what do you think the Yandans will do, First Comrade?"

"I think they'll shut down or cut back dramatically on the wars they are fighting. After that, they will throw their military and financial might behind an invasion of Earth. By the time they are ready to invade, the Florid-Earth alliance will be so strong that Yanda will have a hell of a fight on their hands. My old man, on the other hand, thinks they will continue to negotiate for an amicable solution. This extended negotiating for CASETA will go on until it's too late. Yanda will realize it's a lost cause and scramble to find toxic gases elsewhere in the universe. Yanda will never forgive Earth for pulling out of CASETA. They'll do everything they can to destroy Earth and Florid."

The Earthling let his evaluation sink in for a couple of minutes before continuing. "It doesn't matter if my old man is right or if I'm right. Either way, things are going to get really ugly for Yanda, Earth, and Florid. They will obliterate each other and all we need to do is wait. Wait until the dust and ashes have settled and then move in and take over the entire universe."

Everyone in the room now had a devious smile on his face. But, behind the Earthling's smile, there was the nagging thought he may have signed his own death warrant. He lied to his peers and made a decision which went against every gut-wrenching instinct in his body. A decision which was as unnatural for him as wearing a skirt, blouse, high-heels and pretending to be a sultry redhead. And, it was done for the love of a woman. A woman who he hadn't seen in years but couldn't get out of his head and soul.

11

"Lead Trifect, there is a field Commander here to see you. He says it's very important that he talks with you immediately."

"What's his name?"

There was a slight pause before the Lead Trifect's assistant turned back to the halo-screen and responded. "His name is Commander Fritase, and he was the field commander at the battle for Goltog."

The Lead Trifect could hear his assistant talking with someone off-screen. The interruption annoyed the Lead Trifect. He was ready to break the halo-screen connection when the assistant revised his earlier statement. "Correction, Lead Trifect. The Commander was Officer Morg's superior at the battle ...."

That's all the assistant had to say to get the Lead Trifect's attention. He jumped up from his desk and made a bee-line to the outer waiting area to meet the Commander.

"Commander Fritase, it's an honor to meet you. I've heard a lot of great things about you through the years." Both Yandans knew the Lead Trifect was lying. He didn't have a clue about the Commander's prior military service, but the introduction was welcoming and respectful.

"Thank you, sir. I wouldn't have barged in on you like this, but something tells me that what I have to show you is very important."

"Well, come into my office, Yandi, and let's take a look."

Commander Fritase almost broke out laughing. It had been decades since anyone called him a Yandi which was a word of fellowship for young, male Yandans. What made it more ironic and comical was that the Lead Trifect was at least two decades younger than the Commander.

The Lead Trifect considered offering Fritase a snort from his Cannis dispenser but decided to wait. It was never a good idea to be inebriated when discussing important matters. There would be time to get high after their discussion if the meeting went well.

After each Yandan sat down, Commander Fritase removed a mobile transcorder from his satchel. He spoke into it to unlock its voice recognition security feature.

"Hello, Commander Fritase. How may I help you?"

"Display non-comm message received this morning at zero-nine-ten."

A holographic beam of light leaped from the transcorder and created a worded message board which hovered three feet above the office floor. In a language the Lead Trifect never saw before, a variety of red symbols appeared on the message board. All were outlined by a bold, white background.

Commander Fritase walked over to the floating message board and began explaining what the symbols meant.

"Lead Trifect, these symbols might look somewhat familiar. Actually, they are an ancient dialect of Yandish. Troop commanders, like myself, use this dialect to communicate military orders to field officers. An enemy who intercepts a message in this ancient language is not only confused by it but is incapable of decoding it. There's only one way for the enemy to understand this language. That's to capture one of our officers and torture him into decoding the intercepted message. Over the past couple of decades, we've lost about a dozen field officers. They committed suicide the instant they were captured by the enemy. Any Yandan officer fluent in this language is cranially pre-programmed to commit suicide when captured. This is one-half of the fail-safe measure pertaining to this language. We also limit the number of officers who can speak and read this language to no more than one hundred. This battle-front language has remained the most effective military weapon in our arsenal for centuries."

"Very interesting, Commander, but what does this have to do with what you want to show me?"

"Only this, Lead Trifect. This morning I received the following message from someone, somewhere in the universe." The Commander turned back to the message board and said, "Transcorder, highlight as I speak."

As the Commander spoke, each combination of symbols which corresponded to his words, turned a bright, neon red.

"Trifect, Morg reporting. We are approximately six light years from Earth. Temporarily delayed. The transport is being refurbished at coordinates 2323565-505-897. Cargo intact. Will proceed without further delay to Earth."

When the Commander finished, the Lead Trifect sat in his chair staring at the holographic message board. He wondered if there were hidden messages within this communique. Or, was it as straightforward as the Commander made it seem?

"Commander, did I hear you correctly? You have no idea who sent this message or where it came from?"

"That's correct, Lead Trifect. I have no way of backtracking to the sender's name or location. But I do know this. The message was sent to my private comm number which very few Yandans know." The Commander anticipated the Lead Trifect's next question and added, "And, I did give my private number to Officer Morg before he left Yanda."

"Does this sound like the type of message Officer Morg would send?"

"Yes, sir. Short, concise and to the point. This is the way a seasoned battlefield officer communicates."

"Interesting. Very interesting. Commander, can you spare a few more minutes? I'd like you to tell the other two members of the Trifect what you've told me."

It took twenty minutes before the other two members of the Trifect got across the Central Government Campus to the Lead Trifect's office. While they waited, Commander Fritase and the Lead Trifect discussed ways to track down the source of Morg's communication. They considered every possible technical trick to backtrack to the source. They concluded there was a slim chance of finding out who sent the communication. It would take weeks, if not months, to complete the investigation. Before the discussion ended, the Lead Trifect decided that identifying the source wasn't worth the time and effort. It was enough to know the Commander was confident the communication came from Morg.

After a brief introduction, Commander Fritase repeated his explanation of the Morg communique. As he lectured and answered a few questions from the other two Trifect, the Lead Trifect studied the stellar charts. He wanted to see precisely which quadrant harbored coordinates 2323565-505-897.

When the Commander finished, the Lead Trifect asked, "Commander, would you repeat those coordinates for me, again?" Without taking his eyes off the stellar charts he checked and rechecked the numbers. After the third time of having the Commander repeat the coordinates, one of the Trifect spoke up.

"Is there something wrong, Lead Trifect?"

"I'm not sure.... not sure at all." The Lead Trifect rubbed and massaged the breathing gill on the left side of his neck. This was a long-time habit he developed as a Yandi.

Finally, he turned and announced, "There's nothing there. Nothing but open space."

The other three Yandans gathered in front of the stellar chart to make their own assessments. It wasn't long before everyone in the room had puzzled looks on their faces. They wondered what rational explanation could explain this odd discrepancy.

"Commander, have you ever known Officer Morg to make a calculation error like this before?"

"Never, Lead Trifect. Officer Morg has been reading stellar charts for decades. Running planetary coordinate calculations is second-nature for an officer with Morg's experience." The Commander got closer to the stellar chart and fixed his gaze on the coordinates which Morg claimed was a planet.

"This is interesting. There's not a planet within a half light year of the coordinates Morg provided." The Commander turned and faced the Trifect. "Gentlemen, you may think I'm crazy, but I think Morg's coordinates are right. I can't explain why there isn't anything on the chart, but I don't think he made a mistake. There's something there even though we can't see it."

"I agree, Commander. And, there's something else that bothers me about this communique. There's no mention by Morg that he is returning to Yanda as we instructed him to do. In fact, he states the opposite; he's proceeding to Earth. Now, I'm sure he didn't get our top-secret, crypto message even though someone claiming to be Morg acknowledged receipt of it. Someone else is making the decisions on that ship or, ... or, something is very, very wrong."

The Lead Trifect walked around his desk and sat on its edge. "It's time we find out what the hell is going on with the transport and our Earthling cargo. Commander, I want you to suit up and take a pursuit interceptor out to these coordinates. I want to know what or who is there. And, after you do that, you are to chase down and intercept the transport, wherever it is in the universe. Do you understand?"

The Commander considered challenging the Trifect's decision for a millisecond. But he could tell by the expression on his face there was no room for discussion. Who would lead his invasion troops while he was gone? He wasn't a time qualified pilot for the new pursuit interceptors. Why not send a more qualified pilot? He was three months away from retirement and now he was being sent on a wild-goose chase to the far reaches of the universe. How would he explain this assignment to his mate? Crap, crap, and double crap.

Anger and rage boiled up within the Commander, but he knew it was hopeless to argue. He bowed to the Lead Trifect and said, "Yes, Lead Trifect, I understand. I will follow your directives."

The tram ride to the launch hanger which housed the new pursuit interceptors took a half-hour. Commander Fritase swore and grumbled during the entire ride.

12

"Are you ready to go?"

Morg knew the Earthling said something but he was too engrossed to know what. He was captivated from the moment he walked into the docking bay complex. There, in bay number two was the transport. At least it looked somewhat like the ship they left Yanda in several weeks before.

At first, he thought a new ship arrived within the past twenty-four hours and docked in bay number two. A quick survey of the docking area quashed that thought. The three antiquated ships which were in the docking bay when they arrived were still parked in their original stalls. The remaining ship had to be the transport even though it looked quite a bit different than the vessel they arrived in.

The entire exterior of the transport was changed to look like a cruiser. The gaudy aerial fins and stabilizer wings were removed and replaced with sleek aerodynamic extensions. The dreary blue-black color of the transport was now a burnished copper tint. It reflected exterior light and monitoring signals to help cloak the ship. The transport's identifier number of E647 had been stripped and replaced with TED88987. The ship which arrived twenty-four hours earlier looking like a boxcar was now a sleek bird of prey.

"Earthling, this is incredible. This is our transport, isn't it?" Morg didn't wait for an answer. His head was filling with so many other questions he had to get them out before he forgot what they were.

"Is its flight response the same after these modifications? Is the flight signature the same? Has the shadow drive system been changed or updated? Is the maximum speed the same or greater?" Questions poured out of Morg. He didn't give the Earthling a chance to answer any of them. He finally stopped the questioning with, "This is unbelievable."

The Earthling was genuinely amused by Morg's reaction to the refurbished transport. It was refreshing seeing the Yandan get excited over a simple thing like a ship overhaul. He never would have guessed Morg could act with juvenile enthusiasm.

The kid washed the grin from his face. "Morg, do you want to stay here all day and admire your new ride, or do you want to head for Earth?"

Morg watched the Earthling stroll away toward the transport's loading door. He grabbed his duffle bag but had a tough time taking the first step to follow the kid. He still couldn't get over the ship's transformation. He wondered how they could do such an incredible makeover in a day? He walked up to the transport's hull and rapped on it. With each rap, there was a *thunk*. This ship was definitely not a dream.

The inside of the transport looked the same as when they left Yanda. It smelled new, but nothing looked different to Morg. On closer inspection, he realized the burned-out communications subpanel was replaced with a new one.

The Earthling watched Morg as he walked around the bridge examining every wall, support column, screw, and fusion joint. He didn't want to give the impression of surveilling the Yandan even if he was. He sat back and hoped the Yandan wouldn't find the eavesdropping equipment. At his request, several hundred surveillance bugs were hidden throughout the interior. Morg wouldn't be able to say, do or think anything without the Earthling knowing about it. This was the first test to determine how well the technicians disguised and hid the bugs.

"Morg, let's get going, pal. We have a lot of light years to navigate."

Morg kept his back to the kid. Something felt different about the bridge, but he couldn't figure out what it was. If his intuition was correct, the alteration would surface in due time. And, when it did, he could hopefully use this new information to his advantage.

Morg slid into his captain's gyro chair and began a preflight check. Normally, this would be a quick two- to three-minute, automated task. But, with all the new modifications to the transport, Morg wasn't taking any chances. Who knew if any of the hundreds of technicians working on the transport made a mistake? It was best to find their screwups now while in the docking bay rather than end up marooned in deep space.

Twenty minutes later, Morg was satisfied the transport's systems were operating correctly. He and the kid strapped into their gyro chairs and began a slow egress from the bay.

"Morg, put on the cloaking feature until we clear Ziptowtheon's outer boundary."

"We have cloaking?"

"Yes, sir. It's that green switch, right there."

Morg looked in the direction the kid was pointing. As he leaned forward to flip the switch, Morg wondered what other features the kid put into the transport. He could have directed the Ziptowtheon technicians to add numerous modifications. And, not one of them needed Morg's approval.

Thirty minutes later, the transport cleared Ziptowtheon's outer boundary. There was no evidence of any other ships in the quadrant so Morg decided to shut down the cloaking feature. He wanted to put the transport through some simple evasive maneuvers. Also, he wanted to know if the transport responded and handled the same as it did before refurbishment. It was still one of the slowest vessels in the Yandan fleet but that wasn't a good reason to ignore its capabilities and limitations. In fact, its speed limitation was an essential reason to know beforehand what the ship could and could not do in a combat situation.

As soon as Morg put the transport through several evasive maneuvers he planned to have a long talk with the kid. He wanted to question him about everything from his friendliness with the Ziptowtheon officials to his mate's body in the cargo bay. There was little chance the kid would answer truthfully but he might slip up and get caught in a lie. That's all it would take; just one, small, intentional lie. With that, Morg could pry open the door to the total truth.

As if the kid knew what Morg was thinking, he got out of his co-captain's gyro chair and started to leave the bridge.

"Hey, where you going? Don't you want to see what this ship can do?"

"I'd like to stay and help, but I need to get some sleep. I was up all night. Plus, I don't feel well. You can handle it, Morg. I have complete confidence in you."

The Earthling sauntered from the bridge, smiling to himself about outfoxing the Yandan once again. It was true he had been up all night and didn't feel well. Of course, that was a logical consequence of snorting and inhaling copious amounts of Cannis.

It had been one hell of a party with his co-conspirators and Ziptowtheon officials. The drugs flowed, and sexual partners were available and willing to please for a small pittance. And, as First Comrade Joe was serviced by a foot fetish prostitute, he wondered about Beth. What was she doing to keep her job while sidestepping his old man's sexual advances?

13

The transport was a light year out of Ziptowtheon. The kid was still locked in his private quarters recovering from an illness. At least that's what he wanted Morg to believe. Actually, he was listening to Motown music and fiddling around with the new video and audio eavesdropping systems. At his request, the surveillance system was hidden around the transport during refurbishment. Learning to operate the audio and video bugs was easy because they all functioned in the same way. If you knew how to control the lens aperture on one video bug, then you knew how to do it on all. Likewise, common operating procedures applied to all audio bugs. But, the difficulty with these new systems was memorizing the location of each bug. He couldn't record their locations because the Yandan might stumble upon the list. The only safe and secure method was to store the location information in his brain.

He spent four hours committing to memory the location of nearly two hundred bugs. His recall was at approximately ninety percent accuracy. It was a hunt-and-peck process which reminded him of the ancient Earth game Mah Jong. His grandmother, who was an expert player, forced him to play the game for hours. She goaded him with,

"One day, you'll be glad I made you learn how to play this. It will make your memory sharp as a tack." Now, twenty years later, her prophecy was coming true. He could finally thank her for putting him through extended misery as a child.

He was memorizing the location of the last few bugs when the system indicated a communication was placed from the bridge. He could see it went to a private comm number somewhere in the universe. He tapped into the system the closest audio and visual bugs to where the communication originated. The quality picked up and relayed by the bugs was fantastic. He could hear Morg's shallow breathing as he spoke in English to someone light years away.

"Sam, this is Morg. How are you and Jimmy?" The Earthling smiled to himself and almost broke out laughing. How convenient, he thought. The recipients of the communication were identified immediately by Morg. These were the same humans Morg spoke to from the communications center on Ziptowtheon.

"Hello, Officer Morg. We are very well, thank you. Jimmy's friend has taken good care of us. She's a saint."

Morg wasn't sure what a saint was but could tell from the sincerity in Sam's voice it must be something good.

"Has anyone come looking for you?"

"Not that we know of, Officer Morg."

"Good. Very good. Well, I wanted to check in with you and make sure that Jimmy..."

Sam hurriedly cut off Morg. She knew from their last communication that Morg could end a comm without warning. She wasn't going to let him do that again. "Officer Morg. Don't break the connection. I have a bit of news for you which might be important."

"Sure, Sam. Go ahead."

"Word on the street is that a couple Feltte Six enforcement agents are coming after you and your passenger, whoever that is. They want revenge for the killing of their fellow enforcement agent at the foot-fetish brothel."

"Who told you that, Sam?"

"Luna has heard this rumor quite often in the blind pig. She's heard it from many different sources, so she thinks it's legit info."

Morg didn't know what to think or say. He expected Feltte Six to put out a Look-For-Wanted posting with a huge reward for the capture and return of the Yandan transport. That was logical, considering he wiped out half their space force and crews. But, would they double down and send a couple agents after the Yandan and Earthling for the murder of one agent? That wasn't logical. No matter how Morg twisted and turned the facts, it didn't add up to the course of action the Feltte Six authorities were taking. It would be much easier for them to let the bounty hunters of the universe take care of the transport and its crew. Something else was at play in this tragic sub-plot and Morg needed to know what it was. It could mean the difference between a safe and uneventful flight to Earth or one filled with constant *hound-dog*, shoot-outs.

"Sam, in the last week or so, have there been any reports of Feltte Six Interceptors lost or destroyed in space?"

"Not that I can think of, Officer Morg. Nursing Jimmy back to health only takes so much time each day so I've had a lot of time to catch up on listening to the news."

"That's very strange, Sam. You should..."

"Oh, wait a minute. About a week ago, Luna said a Wanted posting and reward went up around Feltte Six. It wanted information leading to the capture of Yandan ship E64, something-or-other. I saw the same thing in a news flash. The reward was astronomical, but I don't remember anything about lost or destroyed interceptors."

"Interesting? How much was the reward?"

"I don't remember because I only saw the news flash one time. That's it. One time and then not another word about it. Normally, with a big reward, you hear the flash over and over. However, this was one time and then nothing. I thought it was weird at the time, but if you only hear something like that once, you forget about it fast."

Morg expected Sam to ask if the posting by the Feltte Six authorities pertained to his ship. When she didn't, Morg figured she was either afraid to ask or decided it was none of her business.

"Yeah, I know what you mean, Sam." Morg was too busy processing Sam's information about the Wanted posting to make more small talk. The fact that the posting appeared once and then disappeared was very strange. He could only come up with one reasonable explanation. Someone paid off the Feltte Six authorities to drop the issue. Nothing else made sense and fit all the facts.

As Sam rambled on, Morg kept trying to poke holes in his theory. The cost of buying Feltte Six silence would be huge. There were very few governments or ruling families in the universe with that much purchasing power. Considering the situation, his home planet of Yanda was the likely candidate. But, would they shell out that much *hush-money*? Was the Earthling worth that much? Morg could imagine the turmoil amongst the Trifect when making this decision. He thanked his ancestors he wasn't anywhere near Headquarters when this was debated. He didn't want to think about what the Trifect must think of him now. They gave him the simple assignment of getting the Earthling back to his home planet and it exploded into a fiscal nightmare. And, it was all due to a goof-ball from Earth who created havoc and chaos everywhere he went.

"Sam, thanks for the intel. I'll contact you in a week or..."

"Officer Morg, did you hear what I said?"

"Huh? I'm sorry, Sam. I was thinking about something else. What did you say?"

"There were other beings asking about you and your shipmate. They came into the blind pig a few days ago and started asking questions. Officer Morg, they wanted to know specifically about you. They offered Cannis capsules to anyone providing information which led to your whereabouts."

"Do you know anything about them?"

"Well, I didn't see them, but Luna said they were three of the ugliest looking females she has ever seen. She thought they were Athlon women; about six and a half-foot tall and weighing close to

260 pounds. They had the typical Athlon rust-colored complexion with dark peach-fuzz covering their faces. And, the really strange thing was that they were wearing body armor."

It wasn't unusual for Athlons to gravitate toward high-risk, high-reward professions. Dangerous jobs, where the pay was extremely high, were fine with them. Mercenary, bounty hunter, munitions deactivator were perfect fits for the thrill-seeking Athlons. But, Morg never heard of female Athlons seeking out these dangerous jobs. In fact, it was customary for female Athlons to stay at home to raise the young and run the household. In the entire universe, it was hard to find a planet where the family structure was more traditional.

"Sam are you sure they were female?"

"That's what Luna...". Sam stopped in mid-sentence when distracted by something outside of the transceiver's field of vision. "Wait a minute, Officer Morg. Luna just came in."

"Luna, come over here. Officer Morg is on the trans."

Thirty seconds later, Morg was looking at two of the most beautiful women in the universe. Both had crystal clear complexions and perfectly formed mouths. Their chiseled, high cheekbones and petite, narrow noses reminded Morg of the goddesses revered in ancient cultures. Yet, their differences added as much to their beauty as the similarities. One had raven black hair, eyelashes, and eyes. The other had hair, eyelashes, and eyes which were almost void of color. If an artist had to paint this woman, he would have used a soft, eggshell color.

"Officer Morg, how nice to see you again. If I remember correctly, you weren't feeling any pain the last time I saw you in the blind pig."

Public displays of emotion weren't common for Yandans, but Luna's description of Morg's evening in the blind pig was spot on. Her comment made him bashful, shy, and embarrassed all at once. He knew the temporal gills on his neck had faded from their normal forest green to mild pink. There wasn't anything he could do about it. This is what happened when Yandans were complimented or swooned over by the opposite sex.

Morg gave a typical Yandan smile which was barely noticeable. "Luna, I didn't have a chance to thank you for watching over Jimmy and me that night. And, thanks for taking in Jimmy and Sam. You saved their lives."

"No problem. What can I do for you?"

"Sam said that you waited on some rough-looking Athlon women one night who were seeking information about me. Is that true?"

"That's what happened. I wish you could have seen these Athlon women, Officer Morg. They were mean, foul, and smelled terrible. They scared the hell out of me."

"And, they asked about me?"

"Only you, Officer Morg. No one else. And, they seemed to know a lot about you. In fact, they had a halovision of you. They were showing it around the blind pig looking for anyone who knew you."

Morg was stunned. Where the hell did these Athlon women get a halovision from? In his entire life, there were no more than three halovisions taken of him. Yandan soldiers, especially officers, were under strict rules to avoid halovisions. It was for their own safety. Too many Yandan officers were targeted and assassinated because their halovisions were available to the enemy. Morg forced himself back to the conversation. He could think about the halovision dilemma later.

"Interesting. What else can you tell me about them, Luna?"

Luna looked up and to her right thinking back to that night in the blind pig.

"There were two other things, Officer. These Athlon women were wearing body armor, which I thought was very strange. And, I overheard them say several times, Crex or Blex or something like that."

Morg stared, bleary-eyed, at the two women. It would have been easy looking at these beautiful creatures for hours, but they were the furthest thing from his mind. He was stunned when Luna mentioned the halovision. Now, he was numb. But, for the first time during the conversation, things were starting to fall into place.

When he recovered his faculties, he said, "Ladies, thank you for this information. You have been very helpful. Be careful and take care of Jimmy."

Morg broke the communication, sat back in his gyro-chair, and started to piece together what he learned. Two hours later he concluded there were at least five beings after him and the Earthling. Two were rogue enforcement agents from Feltte Six. They didn't give a damn about the rulers of the planet taking bribes to forget the loss of five interceptors and their crews. The enforcers were out to kill Morg and the kid and were not going to take orders from anyone above. They wanted revenge for the loss of their mate, and nothing was going to stop them.

He wasn't sure, but he pegged the other three assassins on his trail as the daughters of Crex, Blex, and Stex. It had been over twenty years, but he vaguely remembered the mercenaries talking about their daughters. By happenstance, the girls were born within three months of each other. One night at a battle victory party, they laughed and made jokes for hours about the birthing coincidence. That was also the same party where Morg allowed himself to be halo-visioned along with his three mercenary buddies.

Putting this mystery together had taken a lot of mental exertion. He needed to get some sleep and rebuild his energy level. The five assassins scouring the universe for them would be testing his energy level in the very near future. If there was one thing he learned from decades of combat, it was to be well-rested before battle. Let the enemy be fatigued. Good decisions before and during battle belonged to the combatant who was energized and thinking clearly.

Morg set the ship's autopilot and lumbered off to his sleeping quarter. Maybe a dream would reveal how to avoid being killed by any one of these assassins.

The kid was dumbfounded by what he learned from Morg's communication with the two women. For the first time, he was momentarily sorry for the deaths he caused on Feltte Six. The sorrow didn't last long. After all, the purpose of the amusement park planet was to provide an outlet for killing or taking part in any desired vice.

He hadn't done anything wrong other than pick victims who were *untouchables* or had vengeful relatives. He got up and prepared to go out to the bridge and look at the stars. He had been cooped up too long in his quarters avoiding Morg's prying interrogation. He wasn't going to worry about the crazy assassins. Between Morg and himself, the assassins would be neutralized. In fact, it would be fun having something to do during the remainder of the flight.

As he shut down the eavesdropping system, a cutesy computerized voice asked, "First Comrade Joe, which option do you prefer? Would you like to turn off the system or continue monitoring the subject, Officer Morg, on autocue?"

The kid mumbled under his breath, "Shit. What a dummy I've been." He now realized the time he put into memorizing the location of each bug was wasted time. There was no need to manually track a subject. The system could track any subject automatically. All he had to do was name the subject.

The Earthling waited until he heard the sawing vibrations of the Yandan's sleep before leaving his private quarters. He whispered into the eavesdropping system, "Autocue, subject Morg". He then tiptoed out to the bridge for some stargazing and strategic planning. The main subject to think about was the overthrow of his father and the Yandan empire without getting himself and Beth killed.

14

Commander Fritase arrived at Ziptowtheon in record time. *The Shooting Star* 38 was the fastest ship in the Yandan space fleet. It was also an experimental ship in its last stages of development. The Lead Trifect intentionally forgot to tell Fritase his trip would be the Shooting Star's first long-range voyage.

This new ship was the brainchild of Yandan physicists who figured out how to move a warship through space faster than the speed of light. They did this by folding over the absence of light two, three, or even four times. The 38 was then pulled through space at a rate far beyond the rate achieved by using only one band of disappearing light. The speed of this new ship was remarkable and the fact it arrived at its destination in one piece was astounding. And, so far, the test pilots survived the extreme speed. Not one disintegrated or was turned inside-out.

Before leaving Yanda, the Commander was given a hasty training session on how to fly the 38. There wasn't much to do when traversing long distances over one light year. Sit back, enter the destination coordinates and prepare for one hell of a ride. In a day or two, the 38 covered the same distance it took a transport to travel in weeks.

That's precisely what the Commander did. The coordinates provided by Officer Morg, through an unidentified party, were 2323565-505-897. Fritase needed to get close enough to these coordinates to observe any activity, yet, far enough away to be transparent to prying spy systems.

He sat stationary at coordinates 2323565-506-899, roughly one quadrant away from the location provided by Morg. He was playing a game of cat-and-mouse waiting to observe any unusual activity. No other ships, way-stations, satellite beacons, or buoys were within his range. If Morg's transport was receiving an overhaul here, it must be by a mobile crew. But where were they?

Other than life support and nominal energy systems, the 38 was lifeless and undetectable. Without transmitting its signature warning beacon, there was a chance another ship could collide with it. The Commander decided to take this chance and remain hidden.

Verbal communication to Yanda and any type of audio noise on the 38 was prohibited unless there was an emergency. Dead silence was a necessity. When the Commander moved through the ship, it was done with deliberate forethought. He wore special clothing and shoes to deaden the noise created by moving his bulky and scaly body.

He stared aimlessly out the observation window for hours. He was wide awake because he slept most of the voyage. Other than a few shooting stars, the view was stunning, yet boring. Thankfully, he didn't have to rely entirely on visual sight. The 38 was equipped with a highly-sensitive recognition system which detected the slightest movement within two quadrants. Any moving object was shown as a caricature on a large visualizer screen projected three yards from the pilot's gyro chair.

Hour after hour went by without any suspicious activity. The Commander's mind began to wander. He recalled fond memories of his mate and day-dreamed of their future retirement together. When those thoughts faded, he replayed every battle he led invasion troops into. He knew it would be hard giving up the action and excitement of leading superbly trained troops to victory and death.

As the Commander daydreamed and fantasized, the rebellion leaders met on Ziptowtheon. They were going over last-minute details of their plan to deal with the newly arrived warship. They weren't certain whose ship it was but had a good idea it was either Yandan or from an allied planet in the empire. Luckily, their listening orbs heard it arrive like a thundering herd of Treslonian Muck Buffalos. The ripple-vibrations caused by it coming to a screeching stop alerted Ziptowtheon to the uninvited guest.

The Crelon was the unofficial leader of the rebellion group. He took over when First Comrade Joe was gone, collecting intelligence, and devising schemes. "Comrades, it appears that First Comrade Joe was right. The arrival of this unidentified ship means that someone is suspicious and has decided to check out our location. It's likely the spy ship belongs to the Yandans or one of their allies."

The Yandan co-conspirator joined the discussion. "We should have killed the Yandan invasion trooper when he arrived with the First Comrade. I grew up on Yanda and I can pick out the fanatics who believe Yanda does no wrong. That one, Morg or whatever his name is, fits the bill perfectly. He is a crazed loyalist. I'll say it again, we should have killed him."

"That's what I thought at first but killing him would have brought more attention to us. Plus, we would be giving up a valuable source of inside information. With the First Comrade monitoring everything the Yandan does, we'll learn valuable intelligence about what the Trifect is planning. I'm sure the scrambled message Morg sent out to a private comm number was why the First Comrade anticipated the arrival of a spy ship."

The Crelon paused to let the other three co-conspirators digest his opening thoughts. "I don't think we need to overreact. Even if Morg told the Trifect about a continuously cloaked planet, who would believe him? And, on top of that, why would the Trifect think a cloaked planet was part of an invasion force? There is no reason for them to believe we are sneaking up on their main bases intending to overthrow their empire." The Crelon chuckled under his breath and added, "Ya know, the whole thing even sounds preposterous to me and I'm one of the leaders of this rebellion. No, fellow comrades, we have to keep our heads and follow First Comrade Joe's plans."

The Earthling co-conspirator entered the conversation. "How did the Yandan ship get here so fast?"

"I don't know. Maybe they had an interceptor close by on routine maneuvers. It's hard to say. We won't know until we execute our plan. So, let's go over the plan one more time to make sure everything is in place."

Within twenty minutes, the four co-conspirators were satisfied they understood First Comrade Joe's plan and were ready to move forward.

The Crelon leaned over the meeting table and spoke into the transceiver. "Please send in Comrades JoJo and Tookie."

JoJo was the first through the door. He bounced into the room with such enthusiasm the Crelon wished First Comrade Joe had picked someone else for the highly sensitive and dangerous mission. It wasn't easy finding revolutionaries like JoJo who were willing to give their soul and body to overthrowing the Yandan empire.

The little lavender fur-ball strutted up to the meeting desk, saluted and bowed to each member of the rebellion council. "Comrade JoJo at your service, sirs."

Before the Crelon could welcome the little guy, all eyes in the room shifted to Tookie, the Communications Center supervisor who complained about every little detail of his job and life. Rather than enter the room with conviction, Tookie slinked in trying to avoid everyone's gaze and attention. His face betrayed his intention. He planned to talk his way out of this assignment, whatever it was. He never volunteered for anything and didn't have an ounce of heroism, like JoJo. He avoided conflict at all cost. He was perfectly happy following strong leaders who were willing to sacrifice themselves. If there was ever a time in his life he wished to be invisible, it was at this moment.

"Comrade Tookie, please have a seat next to Comrade JoJo."

The Crelon didn't bother to introduce Tookie to the members of the co-conspirators group. Because the mission was very secretive, it was best Tookie not know the identities of anyone other than JoJo.

"Gentlemen let's get right to your mission. You will be flying an exact replica of the Yandan transport First Comrade Joe and his fellow traveler arrived in. Everything about this replica has been retrofitted to look and perform exactly like their transport. The shadow drive system has been fine-tuned to produce a flight signature almost identical to the original transport. And, it's re-labeled with the E647 identifier code. Your mission is to leave Ziptowtheon, set in a flight pattern for Earth and pretend to be First Comrade Joe's transport."

"Sir, may I ask why we are posing as a decoy?"

"Good question, Comrade JoJo. The answer is simple. There is a spy ship sitting in a nearby quadrant which we believe will follow and intercept you outside of Ziptowtheon airspace. We want to know who it is and why they are here. Any other questions?"

Tookie raised his hand to ask a question, but the Crelon ignored him and rambled on with the rest of the mission plan. "At first, ignore the spy ship's demand to stop. After he threatens three or four times to vaporize you, stop the transport and allow him to board. Once he's on board, pull your ship away so he can't escape using the bridging ramp. Then, overpower him and return to Ziptowtheon with both ships."

That's all it took for Tookie to come unglued. "Sir, how are we going to overpower this being who is military trained? Look at us. Do we look threatening? I'm not sure the two of us could take on and subdue a cockroach."

Tookie was in a state of shock. He couldn't believe he was so belligerent to a high-ranking council member. Next to him, JoJo was trying to control his temper and not throttle Tookie for being a self-centered wimp.

"Comrade Tookie give us some credit. We've equipped your decoy transport with knockout gas. It will render the intruder unconscious until you get back to Ziptowtheon. All Comrade JoJo must do is toggle the blue switch on the bridge control panel and the intruder will go down like he's been hit with a vap pistol. Just make sure you have ventilators in your nose."

"Sir, if he's a Yandan, won't his filter gills keep him safe from the knockout gas?"

"Not this time, Tookie. The knockout gas is an ultra-high concentration which Yandan filter gills can't process quick enough. Enough of the gas will bypass the filters and take the Yandan down. Plus, the gas is stationary which means it hangs in one place as it dissipates. Very little of it will move throughout the cabin and bridge. This is another reason why you have nothing to fear."

"He's telling you the truth, comrades." The Yandan co-conspirator decided to add the last bit of sales pitch to make the fabricated knockout gas story believable. "They tried the gas on me, and it worked exactly like my fellow comrade described. You have nothing to worry about if you wear your ventilators and activate the gas when the intruder reaches a designated location in the boarding hallway."

The Crelon could tell Tookie was still wary of the mission but JoJo was so excited he could barely control himself.

"When do we leave?"

"Comrades, they are waiting for you at the docking bay. Good luck and we'll see you back here in short order."

15

Commander Fritase almost fell out of his gyro chair when a Yandan transport appeared out of nowhere and streaked out of sight. He regained his composure and looked at the visualizer screen. To his surprise, the ship caricature depicted on the visualizer was the E647, the Yandan transport piloted by Officer Morg. The Commander shut off the recognition system alarm and put in an emergency communication to Yanda.

An annoyed Lead Trifect answered his private comm number. "Commander Fritase, why are you contacting me?"

"Sir, I'm sorry to bother you, but Officer Morg's ship just appeared out of nowhere and is on a course for Earth. Do you want me to pursue or intercept?" The Commander tried to contain his excitement. The appearance of the E647 was a genuine stroke of luck. Rather than sit in the dead of space for days or weeks waiting for something to happen, the game was afoot after a few short hours. If his ancestors from the hereafter looked upon him favorably, he would wrap up this assignment within a day. Then it was back to Yanda and retirement.

"What do you mean it appeared out of nowhere?"

"Sir, I don't know how else to describe what happened. One moment there was nothing in the adjacent quadrant and then Morg's ship appeared. I have no reason to think the recognition system failed. I'm sure it worked perfectly. Somehow, Morg's ship was hidden and then materialized."

The Lead Trifect pondered this new information and considered all the possible explanations.

"Commander, you know more about this than I do, but could the transport have been retrofitted with cloaking?"

"I doubt it. Adding cloaking to an existing ship is very expensive and time-consuming plus it leaves a shadow trail. The ship that just appeared doesn't have a trail which means it has been sitting idle for quite some time."

"Have you seen anything else suspicious out there?"

"Not a thing, sir."

The Lead Trifect contemplated the situation for a couple moments. His biggest fear was that the instantaneous and mysterious appearance of the E647 was part of some type of elaborate hoax. The situation didn't feel right, but his curiosity about what was happening on the transport got the better of him.

"Commander, intercept Morg's transport and board it. I want to know if everything is okay on that ship. If Morg questions why they were stopped, tell him Prefect Conway wants to communicate with his son. This might be the perfect opportunity to get that jerk off my back." The Lead Trifect's comment about Prefect Conway was unusual. It was rare when he verbalized an opinion about a planetary leader, especially one who might hold the fate of Yanda in his hands. The Trifect thought for a few more seconds and then added, "Commander, be extremely cautious." The Lead Trifect broke the communication but couldn't shake the thought that something wasn't right.

Fifteen minutes later, Commander Fritase overtook the decoy transport. He requested it to stop and submit to boarding by a representative of the Yandan Empire. When the transport refused, he brought it to a standstill by locking on with a harness beam. He didn't consider the transport's refusal as unusual. He would have taken the same evasive maneuvers if ordered to stop by an unknown interceptor appearing out of nowhere. He put on body armor, loaded up on vap guns and shock grenades and strutted off to the bridging ramp.

HE WAS surprised that neither Officer Morg or the Earthling greeted him when he entered the E647. He had identified himself when hailing the decoy transport so there was no reason for them to hide as though they were being boarded by an enemy. He wanted to call out to his fellow invasion trooper but something in his gut said, "Be quiet".

He squinted to see down the cabin corridor toward the bridge. The luminescent lighting was turned down, so his normal weak eyesight was close to worthless. He mentally berated himself for not bringing sight goggles. They were the most important piece of military hardware for a Yandan invasion trooper. Without goggles, he was at a distinct disadvantage if walking into a trap or ambush.

The Commander made a snap decision. There was enough physical and sensory evidence to believe there was something wrong on the transport. Whoever was behind this ruse wanted him to enter their web. He needed to get back to his ship, retrieve the goggles and scan the transport for evidence of life forms. He turned to leave the cabin but froze when he felt the transport start to move. The straining shadow drive motors sent a weak vibration throughout the ship's hull and his body. The momentum was slow at first but then snapped forward to a faster speed. Somehow the transport broke free of the harness beam and started moving swiftly away from the Shooting Star 38.

He squatted to make himself less of a target and held on to a support pole for stability. The situation was precarious, at best. The best he could hope for was that this was an elaborate joke Morg was playing on him. That thought lasted for less than five seconds. In all the years as a superior-ranking officer, he could not remember one instance of Morg instigating or participating in shenanigans. Morg was the ideal, straightlaced, by-the-book invasion trooper.

His acute hearing was the only defensive weapon he could rely on to detect danger. He turned his head slightly so the best of his three parabolic dish-like ears pointed down the corridor toward the bridge. He turned on his transceiver and entered the Lead Trifect's private comm number. The communication wasn't answered on the first, second, third, or fourth pulse.

Fritase began to worry that the transceiver's signal was being blocked. It was possible the transport's hull or communication deflection system was preventing a comm hook-up. He was ready to disconnect when he heard, "Are you on the transport, Commander?"

"Yes, sir. But, there's something wrong."

Fritase pointed the transceiver down the corridor so the Lead Trifect could see the ominous situation.

"What did you say? You have to speak up, Commander."

Fritase brought the transceiver closer to his voice hole and whispered, "I can't, sir. I've walked into a trap. Someone disconnected the harness beam and is piloting the transport to an unknown destination."

"Have you seen Morg or the Earthling?"

"No, sir. They didn't meet me upon boarding, and I have yet to see any life forms."

The Lead Trifect's worst nightmare was coming true. Unless his Commander was misreading the situation, the transport was under the control of someone other than Morg. This raised two simple questions. Where was Morg and who was in control of the transport?

"What do you plan?"

"I'm not sure, Lead Trifect. I think I'll take up a defensive position and wait."

"Do what you think is best, Commander."

There was dead silence for several minutes. Both Yandans were thinking about the circumstances and searching for a plausible solution. Was it possible they overlooked the obvious?

"Commander, do you think this is a ploy to steal the 38?"

"What do you mean, Lead Trifect?"

"Someone lures you onto the transport, breaks the harness beam and then kidnaps you. As you move further and further away, an unknown accomplice steals our 38."

"It's possible, Lead Trifect, but seems far-fetched. How would these pirates know I arrived in a 38 and, for that matter, how would they know about the 38? The 38 is an experimental ship. The only way your theory works is if there is a leak at Command Headquarters."

Fritase was instantly embarrassed. If he could have intercepted the remark about a Command Headquarters' leak before it traveled to Yanda, he would have done so immediately.

"Sir, I apologize. I don't mean to suggest you have a leak at..."

"No apologies needed, son. You might be right. In fact, I've often wondered if there is a leak here."

As the Commander and Lead Trifect discussed and analyzed the situation, JoJo and Tookie sat on the bridge watching the stars pass by. They were guiding the transport in a giant loop toward Ziptowtheon. From their gyro chairs they could see and listen to everything said between the two Yandans. All they had to do was wait until the Commander got up enough courage to move toward the bridge. When he entered the kill zone, JoJo would toggle the blue switch on the control panel and watch the Yandan go down.

JoJo looked over at the nervous Tookie and said, "This is great. We've got the Yandan confused and pinned down. It's only a matter of time before he moves on the bridge. All we have to do is remain calm and wait."

Tookie looked at JoJo and forced a grin his way. He was beginning to realize how psychotic JoJo was. Did the little fur-ball have a death wish or love and crave the adrenaline rush from dangerous situations? Either way, he wasn't someone to develop into a friend. If he got out of this situation alive, he promised himself to stay as far away from this loon as possible.

"Oh, shit!" The halo-screen monitoring the cabin to bridge corridor was flashing a deep red warning. The Yandan trooper moved rapidly into the kill zone. He moved with stealth and unusual speed for a large being. JoJo almost fell out of his gyro chair diving for the blue toggle switch.

Tookie was scared but didn't know why until he spotted the Yandan on the halo-screen. Minutes before, the Yandan was telling his superior about establishing a defensive position in the corridor. Now, he was charging the control bridge. The SOB had used misinformation and trickery to catch them by surprise.

The picture quality on the halo-screen was poor but good enough to see the trooper's battle armament. Tookie could see an assault rife slung over his shoulder and a vap gun in each hand. He wore body armor from the top of his head to mid-thigh on each leg. There was something shiny in his mouth. Tookie leaned closer to the screen to see a Katanian close-combat, fighting sword clenched between his fangs. This trooper meant business. Things would get very ugly if he got to the bridge.

Tookie slid down in his chair attempting to hide. He couldn't contain himself and screamed, "Holy shit, JoJo. He's attacking. Do something."

"Shut up, Tookie. I did."

JoJo expected the knockout gas to discharge and engulf the Yandan trooper in a deadly cocoon. When it didn't, he knew he was betrayed. He and Tookie were sacrificial lambs. And, he had just enough time to guess why.

"Turn around, you two." When neither chair turned his way, the Commander regretted his decision to rush the bridge. Something was wrong, and it was unlikely the situation would end without violence.

Tookie started to swivel his gyro chair, but JoJo continued to stare out the viewing port window. He decided to enjoy the sights for as long as he could.

"I said turn around. Do it now, or I'll fire."

That was the last thing Commander Fritase said before the decoy transport disintegrated. Twenty-seven military-grade, thermal grenades placed throughout the fake E647 went off simultaneously. The blue toggle switch on the control panel was the trigger. The result was a massive implosion which reduced the ship and everyone aboard to atomic sub-particles.

16

On Yanda, the Lead Trifect's transceiver screen turned a red-violet and then went blank. He doubted it was a malfunction. He hoped he was wrong but guessed the Commander was dead.

"Yes, Lead Trifect."

"Trifects, I'm sure Commander Fritase is dead. Have our interplanetary techs look for new, unexplained explosions within a light year of his last known coordinates. I need an answer by the time I get to headquarters. I'm on my way."

He signed off and started the twenty-minute walk. He could have taken a glider but needed the time to think about what happened. He took his transceiver and replayed the last forty-five recorded seconds over and over. One thing that stood out was the Commander not firing any of his weapons. Conversely, there was no evidence that he took fire from enemy combatants. This reaffirmed the Lead Trifect's guess that the transport no longer existed. Something or someone on board the transport caused its destruction, or it took a direct hit from another ship. How it met its end would take a lot more time to investigate. Time which was at a premium and the Trifect couldn't afford to waste.

He could also see the two gyro chairs on the transport's bridge were occupied by beings other than Morg and the Earthling. Whoever occupied the gyros had to be short because their heads weren't above the chair backs. It was obvious that Fritase knew the bridge occupants were not Morg and the Earthling. He referred to them as "you two".

The Lead Trifect was still looking at the playback recording when he stepped into the palace. The daylight glare disappeared immediately from the transceiver screen. When his eyes adjusted, images appeared on the screen which he hadn't noticed before. There was something beyond the gyro chairs. He fiddled with the contrast and imaging software to get a better view. Slowly, ghost images came into focus. Reflecting off the transport's viewing port window were the front sides of the gyro chairs. And, in the chairs were two beings he never saw before.

One appeared to be a furry little thing which could not have been over three feet tall. The other was slightly taller with a frail body. Neither fit the image of a pirate or kidnapper. The little one looked like a manual laborer, whereas, the other one looked like a nerd scientist, chemist, or quantum physics professor. The furball looked at ease and content. The nerd oozed fear and anxiety.

The Lead Trifect didn't stop staring at these two beings until he entered the headquarters offices in the palace.

"Lead Trifect, we have the information you asked for."

Without taking his eyes off the transceiver screen, he said, "Yes. What have you got?"

"There was a single explosion about forty-five minutes ago. It occurred at coordinates 2323565-507-003 which is very close to Commander Fritase's last known coordinates."

"What else do we know about this explosion?"

"It registered thirty-four dicrons which is a very large blast. It's much larger than any explosion which happens during an Interceptor dogfight."

"What would cause such a large blast?"

"We don't know, Lead Trifect. Possibly our munitions or military people can give us an answer."

"Make sure you get that. Is there anything else we know about this explosion?"

"That's all the information we have."

There was no sense continuing the conversation until the two Trifect were brought up to speed on what the Lead Trifect knew. He put the transceiver on the conference table and played the last communication from Commander Fritase.

When the recording stopped, one of the Trifect looked at the Lead Trifect who was at the Cannis dispenser. "I think you're right, Lead Trifect. Commander Fritase is dead. Most likely killed in the explosion we picked up."

He knew it was a mistake as soon as he asked, "What do you think we should do now?"

A deafening silence fell over the room. The two Trifect looked at each other and then lowered their eyes to watch an imaginary insect under the conference table.

Once again, the two Trifect subordinates were doing a lousy job of investigating. The Lead Trifect couldn't understand how they reached their present positions without inquisitive minds. They didn't think outside the box and rarely asked *what-if* questions. This was precisely what they needed to do to uncover possible clues and explanations. His two direct reports didn't have an inquisitive bone in their scaly bodies. He wondered what would happen to Yanda if he retired or met the wrong end of a vap weapon?

His frustration was rising, and he couldn't afford to waste more time playing games with the two underlings.

"Where is our Shooting Star 38?"

He could tell by the expressions on their faces that they hadn't given one iota of thought to the experimental Interceptor. The Commander was on the transport when it blew up. He specifically said the harness beam from the 38 to the transport was broken. Put two and two together and it added up to, "where the hell is the 38?"

"Trifect, considering the 38 is the most important piece of military hardware in the Yandan space fleet, don't you think it would be wise to find it?"

The two Trifect knew the Lead Trifect was mad. The tone of his voice and the ridicule in his words were meant as an obvious tongue-lashing.

"We'll get on it, sir."

One of the Trifect reached for the communicator on the conference table to start the search for the 38.

"Hold on. There are some other things to do, so let's discuss them before you get to work."

The Lead Trifect didn't wait for a response. He launched into a step-by-step review of what had to be done.

"First, find the 38. Use every resource at our disposal to find it. Check with our allies. Review our monitoring outpost recordings to see if the 38 flew by. Put out a reward bulletin for the return of the 38 or information leading to its whereabouts. Find that damn ship. It's value to the Empire is beyond calculation."

The Lead Trifect watched his subordinates scribbling notes besides recording everything he said.

"Next, get at least a half-dozen sweepers to the coordinates where the explosion occurred. I want forensic evidence to substantiate if it was our transport which exploded. Also, look for genetic evidence. Were Morg and the Earthling on board the transport or not? And, this brings me to my last directive. Watch this."

The Lead Trifect fast-forwarded the Commander's communication. He stopped at the point where the reflections in the transport's viewing port window were barely noticeable.

He fiddled with the enhancement software to bring out a decent image of JoJo and Tookie sitting in the gyro chairs. "Look closely. Do you see these two creatures? I want to know who they are and where they came from."

"Any questions?"

He didn't expect either of the Trifect to ask or say anything. He had embarrassed and ridiculed them enough. They were ashamed and wouldn't dare open their voice holes.

"Good. I'm leaving. It's time to put in a communication to Mr. Conway."

17

"Excellent. Very, very good, comrades. You executed the plan exactly right. You are to be commended."

The Crelon responded for the revolutionaries. "Thank you, First Comrade Joe, but all the honor and compliments belong to you. Your plan was perfect. All we did was follow it."

"Well, we can all share in the success of operation Decoy. The Earthling let everyone bask in the glory before continuing. "Now, can I assume our two little friends were vaporized in the explosion?"

"Yes, sir. JoJo and Tookie were martyred."

"They will be remembered as true patriots in the overthrow of the Yandan Empire." Comrade Joe didn't believe that, but it sounded good. By the end of the rebellion, no one would remember JoJo and Tookie or care what they did for the rebellion.

"And, we know for a fact the surveillance Interceptor was Yandan?"

"Absolutely. JoJo sent us a live feed of the Yandan trooper boarding the decoy transport. Plus, we've towed the Yandan Interceptor back to Ziptowtheon. You should see this thing, First Comrade."

"Why is that?"

"None of us have ever seen a ship like this. The shadow drive system is quite a bit different than a normal Interceptor. And, the aerodynamics and hull materials are innovative compared to the newest Interceptors. Everything about this ship is a radical change from the most modern Interceptors. Our technicians are reverse engineering it. The initial feedback is this is an experimental ship which can travel much faster than anything known to exist. Our technicians are referring to this ultra-fast speed as hyper-jump"

"Well, that would explain how the Yandans got a surveillance set up so fast." The Earthling went into one of his deep-thought modes. The more he pondered the advantages of having the Yandan experimental Interceptor, the more excited he got. If they could duplicate this new shadow drive system, they would be unstoppable. With super-cloaking and this new Interceptor, they would overrun the Yandan Empire with ease. A broad smile spread across his face as he thought about the glorious victories to come.

"Gentlemen, it's all ours. What could be more fabulous? The Yandans are most likely going crazy. They have lost their new baby. Its vanished into thin air. I love it."

The kid chuckled louder and louder. This led the four members of his executive revolution staff to smile, giggle and congratulate each other. Their egos could not have been more inflated. If they weren't already the most powerful beings in the rebellion, they would have promoted themselves on the spot.

When the laughter petered out, the Earthling resumed the meeting. "Okay, okay, let's move on. Before I forget, make sure our best technicians are working on the experimental Yandan Interceptor. He didn't bother to explain the benefits of having a fleet of hyper-Interceptors. "Have you begun the next phase of our plan?"

The Earthling made a point of giving credit to the entire council for all his plans. He believed that beings who had ownership and authorship for what was to happen executed plans with devout loyalty. In fact, some became zealots to ensure their plans were carried out successfully.

"Yes. Ziptowtheon is moving to the new location we selected. The other cloaked mini-planets and satellite weapon platforms are also moving closer to Yanda and their ally planets."

"Very good. Keep the speed down so our cloaked units leave a minimal shadow trail. I'm sure the Yandans are snooping around the Ziptowtheon coordinates. They'll try to find evidence of the transport, their experimental ship, and the passengers on those ships. Passengers like me."

When the irony of the Earthling's last remark registered with everyone, they broke out in another laughing fit. Each of them could imagine the Yandans wandering around a large sector of space like lost children. The thought of them wasting considerable time and money looking for something which didn't exist was priceless.

Everything was working out exactly as the Earthling planned. Word would leak out that the Yandan transport exploded and with it, Morg and the Earthling were now permanent residents of the afterlife. The kid was shielded by his fake death. He could now operate at will. He didn't have to worry bounty about hunters, mercenaries, the Trifect and whoever else hated his guts and wanted him arrested or dead. All he had to do was keep a low profile and not do anything stupid.

The only being who could upset his perfect plan was Morg. The Yandan had to be watched closely. Hopefully, he wouldn't make any more communications for quite some time. He believed the Trifect was investigating the cloaked star of Ziptowtheon. His offspring would be notified of his death. And, the daughters of his former mercenary friends were looking for a transport which supposedly no longer existed. If Morg did something unexpected which couldn't be negated, he could always be killed. The kid hoped it wouldn't come to that. He was beginning to like the Yandan.

The wild card was his father, the high and mighty Prefect Conway. What would the old man do when he heard the transport vaporized? Would he investigate or leave it alone? As hard as the kid tried, he couldn't guess what the old man would do. He was too unpredictable.

The Earthling broke the communication with his revolutionary council just as Morg wandered onto the bridge.

18

There was knocking at his bedroom door. He could tell by the perfectly timed raps, all delivered with the same force, it was the Mentat. He marveled at the Mentat's rigid and precise behavior although it could be annoying at times. To Conway, he seemed more like a robot than a living, breathing being.

"Prefect, are you awake?"

"Honey Nuts, when are you going to get rid of that thing. He creeps me out."

Conway rolled into a sitting position and hung his legs over the edge of the bed. He looked for something to cover his nude body. The fog of sleep was slowly evaporating and as his mind cleared, he thought about Beth's cutesy nickname. He asked her numerous times why she called him Honey Nuts. No badgering, gifts or promises could get her to reveal the reason. He finally gave up trying to pry the answer from her. After all, she was young, firm and the best ride he ever had.

"One day my dear. Right now, he's too valuable to me."

Honey Nuts Conway leaned backward and playfully gnawed on

Beth's shoulder. He followed with a quick peck and then casually strolled to the door as he wrapped himself in a bathrobe.

He opened the door wide enough to make sure no one else was with the Mentat. "I'm up. What's going on?"

"The Lead Trifect has requested a personal communication with you in .034 Tripes. He claims it is very important for you and him to talk."

Conway rolled his eyes and shook his head in mild frustration. He wondered why the Mentat continued to use alien terms he didn't understand.

"What the hell is .3 whatever Tripes? English. What's that in English for god's sake?"

"It's approximately forty minutes."

"Okay. Tell the Yandans I'll be ready in sixty minutes. I'm sure you know how many Tripes that is."

Before the Mentat could question Conway's re-scheduling of the communication, the door shut in his face. Conway slammed the door in partial retaliation for the Mentat using alien technical words. He also got a kick out of agitating the Mentat to see if he could get an emotional response from him. A simple curse word, fit of anger or laugh would go a long way to proving there was something inside the Mentat other than even-keeled, programmed responses. Thus far, Conway had been unsuccessful. The Mentat's responses were like those of an automaton.

Conway slid back into the bed and rolled over on Beth's backside. In this position, he loved how his body molded to her. "I have a surprise for you. Are you interested?"

Beth let out a loving coo and said, "Show me, Honey Nuts."

For the next thirty minutes, she only thought of how rewarding it was being the bed partner of the most important man on Earth. The last several years as his concubine were thrilling. It was exactly what she needed after that bum Joe deserted her. It could only get better when the reigning Prefect of Earth defeated the Yandans and became the Prefect of the Universe. But, if Conway stumbled during his rise to power, she would have no problem distancing herself from the middle-aged creep.

One hour later the Lead Trifect placed the communication to Prefect Conway. The Mentat answered and started making excuses for Conway's absence. As they bantered back and forth and started negotiating for a rescheduled comm time, Prefect Conway was strolling to the communications room. He wasn't the least bit concerned about standing up the Lead Trifect. The Yandan needed to be taught a lesson about who he was dealing with on Earth. Conway held the high cards in this game. Earth possessed the natural resources Yanda needed for survival. Yanda held nothing which Earth was in dire need of. That included their huge supply of Cannis which could be bought easily on the open market.

"Lead Trifect, I will contact you as soon as I speak with Prefect Conway. I'm sure he has a good reason for being late."

Ten light years away, a disgusted Lead Trifect reached to push the off-comm button on his communications panel. He paused long enough to see the Mentat's attention drawn to a commotion occurring off-screen. Prefect Conway walked casually into view, sat down, and poured himself a drink.

After two gulps and an obnoxious burp, Conway peered into his halo-screen transceiver. He twisted, turned, and cocked his head several different ways pretending to have focus and reception problems. The Mentat stood at his side wondering what the hell he was doing.

Finally, he said, "Lead Trifect, how good to see you again. What do I owe this honor to? Do you have some good news for me? Am I going to talk with my son today? After all, it has been a couple weeks since I asked to speak with him."

The Lead Trifect held his anger in check. He thought about how much of a jerk Conway was. Not one word of an excuse or apology for being late. How could he and the people of Yanda trust this jerk? The same thought kept looping through his brain. "Conway, you are pushing your luck, pal".

"Prefect Conway, your son is dead."

"What did you say?"

"I said, your son is dead. His transport exploded."

The Lead Trifect sat motionless and didn't flinch a scale on his body. He knew this revelation would likely end the CASETA Agreement once and for all, but he didn't care. It had become an extreme long-shot that Conway intended to sign the Agreement. So, there was no reason to hold back and try to hide the kid's death. In fact, it was worth seeing Conway's reaction.

Every ounce of color drained from Conway's face. He tried to stand but there wasn't enough energy or desire left in his leg muscles. They gave out and he fell back into his chair. He slumped over like an old man and put his face into folded arms on the table. The only time he looked up was to confirm the Lead Trifect's shocking news with his Mentat.

The Lead Trifect was tempted to end the communication but wanted to see how a jerk handled personal tragedy. There was a part of him that enjoyed seeing the man suffer. He sat in his office for twenty minutes waiting to see what Conway did. The kid's father hardly moved. Other than rocking his head back and forth in his arms, the jerk said and did nothing. No one, including the Mentat, came over and tried to console him. When Conway finally got up and left the room the Lead Trifect made some interesting observations. Conway had not wept over his son's death. His eyes were crystal clear, not bloodshot. The man looked normal, as though he was getting ready to go for an afternoon stroll in the park.

The Lead Trifect kept his transceiver on in case something happened on Earth. He sat there watching the screen and wondering about Conway's reaction. The man was either cold as death or putting on an exceptional performance. He would have paid any amount of Cannis to know exactly what was going through the Prefect's head and heart, if he had one.

Once Conway left the prying eye of the halo transceiver he straightened up and started walking at a brisk pace back to his personal quarters. He had a lot of work to do. First, he needed to figure out if his stupid son was really dead. The Mentat confirmed that the Lead Trifect believed he was but that meant little to Conway. Although accidents happened, he knew his kid was too smart to be blown to bits on a transport that was safety certified before it left Yanda. That left only one possibility. The transport explosion wasn't an accident. The transport either took direct hits from an external force like an Interceptor or espionage was involved.

The farther he walked the more dubious he became about his son's death. In a strange way, things were starting to make a sliver of sense. The kid lied repeatedly about where and why the transport stopped for repairs. He lied about the rogue planet and its inhabitants. And now, shortly after he left the rogue planet, the transport blows up. There had to be some kind of connection between the rogue planet and the fate of the transport. But what was it?

He stopped dead in his tracks and turned around to face the Mentat. His psychic servant was exactly where he expected to find him. Five steps behind, over his left shoulder, and quiet as a mouse.

"Mentat, did you overhear my conversation with that Yandan creep?"

"Do you mean the Lead Trifect?"

"Of course, I do. Who else would I be referring to?"

"Yes, I overheard your conversation."

"Good. Then here's what I want you to do. Tomorrow, I want you to contact the Lead Trifect. Ask him what his thoughts are about the CASETA Agreement. He'll be surprised by your question because you are giving him a ray of hope for finalizing the Agreement. After he tells you, find out as much about the transport explosion as possible. Where did it happen? Get the coordinates. When did it happen? How does he know my son was on the transport? Etc., Etc., Etc. Do you understand?

"Yes. How should I explain your absence from the communication?"

"Tell him I'm in mourning. I'm so upset I've locked myself in my bedroom and refuse to come out. Make up any excuse you want."

"Mentat, do you know why I've asked you to contact the Lead Trifect?"

It took less than three seconds for the Mentat to answer. "Because I can distinguish truth from lies?"

"Good guess. You are correct, my man. I need to know facts. Not innuendo or guesses."

"Am I correct assuming you doubt your son is dead?"

"I don't know. But I do know something doesn't smell right."

First Prefect Conway turned and walked away. The Mentat stood in the hallway watching his boss and wondered what his comment about not smelling right meant. These humans had an extensive library of trite idioms which meant something entirely different than what was said. Why they were so indirect and obtuse was a mystery to the Mentat. Why couldn't they get directly to the point and say what was on their mind?

The Mentat was also very curious about why the Prefect wanted to find out if his son was dead. He didn't like the kid. He bitched about him all the time. They were more like bitter enemies than loving father and son. The kid completed his mission for the old man, so why did the Prefect care one iota about what happened to him? In fact, he should be happy the kid was gone. From what the Mentat deduced, the elimination of his son was a wonderful stroke of luck. He got rid of someone who constantly mucked things up. Plus, a thousand secrets went to his grave.

The Mentat headed for his quarters. He needed to meditate, practice thought reading and walk through every possible scenario which might happen during the upcoming communication with the Lead Trifect. But the most important thing he needed to do was contact Millard Miller, the Secretary-General of Earth's Global Union Assembly. Everything he learned during the communication and afterward had to be passed on to this man. The fate of Earth and possibly the universe depended on timely and accurate intelligence passed on to Miller.

19

A COUPLE HOURS AFTER SETTLING INTO THE CAPTAIN'S GYRO chair on the bridge, the Earthling felt the first pains in his lower abdomen. He didn't pay much attention and took for granted it was normal digestive gases. After all, he did some heavy-duty partying on Ziptowtheon the night before. God only knew what liquids and foods he put into his body during the festivities. The last thing he remembered before passing out was the free-for-all debauchery enjoyed by every party-goer. He was sure the parties he and his buddies held were every bit as wicked and fun as the ones Caligula sponsored in ancient Rome. Plus, staying intoxicated helped him forget Beth.

Over the next two hours, the pains increased and moved from his lower abdomen into his entire stomach and chest. Soon his back ached like hell. It felt as though he lifted heavy weights all day. So much sweat ran down his forehead he could hardly see. He found an old rag and wrapped it around his forehead to sop up the salty drippings.

He didn't know whether to stagger to the bathroom or stay on the bridge and hope the pain subsided. Either way, he knew this illness wasn't going to leave as quickly as it arrived. This wasn't food poisoning or a minor upset stomach. He was down for the count. He would have described his symptoms to a doctor as a combination of pneumonia and the flu.

He thought about calling his co-conspirators on Ziptowtheon to see if they were sick. It was worth the risk even if Morg might wake up and come out to the bridge during the communication. As it turned out, he didn't have to worry about that happening. The pain became so excruciating, doing anything other than moan and groan was impossible. He finally passed out after promising God to be a good person if He would only end the pain.

Something woke Morg from a dream filled with bizarre places and beings he never met. The only thing familiar about this dream was it involved another mission he was unable to complete satisfactorily. Ever since childhood, all his dreams had the same basic theme. He was involved in a mission or event which needed a hero. He volunteered or jumped at the challenge only to be thwarted by some minor inconvenience. He never saved the victim or himself. He was so close each time; within an inch or minute. Sadly, he never made the grade of hero. Frustration was the only thing he ever accomplished in each of his dreams.

There was a slight difference this time after awakening from his dream. He felt too crappy to be frustrated by the outcome. He had a tough time lifting himself to a sitting position in the gyro cot. He had a splitting headache and aches and pains radiated throughout his endoskeleton.

Yandans didn't have sweat glands. Toxins discharged from their bodies through the same filter gills that removed noxious gases from the air they breathed. Morg forced himself to stand and walk over to a wash basin. It only took one look into the mirror to know he was damn sick. His normal facial colors comprised of different shades of grey and green had washed out to a pale beige. Tiny streamlets of a mustard yellow, pussy fluid ran out of each filter. He felt bad and looked bad. But, worst of all, he smelled bad.

The first clue to a Yandan's health was his odor. If he was in decent shape, without any infections or broken limbs, he was odorless. Any disease or imperfection caused a Yandan's defense system to react internally and externally. While microorganisms within the body fought the infection, a noxious odor excreted from glands behind each knee and elbow. It was so disgusting it sent everyone running. If the patient died, the odor increased ten-fold and became unbearable. Only a Yanda could tolerate handling a Yandan corpse. Any other being had to wear a heavy-duty hazmat suit with fragrance infused breathing filters.

Morg braced himself on the wash basin and stared at the image in the mirror. If he didn't know otherwise, he would have wondered who the being was staring back. His mind wandered, and he thought back to something he learned in the military academy as a Yandi. The reason Yandans gave off a hideous odor when hurt could be traced back to the beginning of their race. The legend was that hurt Yandans from ancient times stayed alive and recuperated faster when they ran off the enemy with a repugnant odor. What foe would come close enough to make the final kill if he had to smell that odor? An odor so vile it seeped into clothes and hung in nostrils for days.

As far as he knew there wasn't an enemy to run off the transport. Yet that didn't stop his body from producing the same odor his ancestors used thousands of years before to run off invaders and assailants.

He filled the wash basin with a mildly acidic liquid formulated especially for Yandans. The filtrated water the Earthling used was too harsh on Yandan gills and scales. With the bowl filled, he put his entire face in the liquid. He could stay under the liquid for as long as he wanted. There were two breathing gills on either side of his neck which took over when his nose was blocked. He was hoping that submersion for an hour or so would clear his head and make him feel better. After ten minutes he gave up. The achy pain had migrated from the front of his body to the rear. Whatever invaded his body was settling in and making Morg miserable.

Morg was afraid to lay down again on the gyro cot. He feared that he would never get back up. He forced himself into the uniform he took off for sleeping and trudged into the hallway leading to the bridge. Halfway to the bridge, he doubled over. It was like someone hit him across the back with a carbon-metallic, enforcement baton. He gasped for air and thought for a moment he was going to hack up his last meal. Nothing came out of his mouth, but a wad of slithery phlegm shot from his nose. At first, he thought an insect or small animal had somehow crawled up his nose passage while sleeping and now decided to escape. He took a closer look at the discharge. It wasn't a living creature, but it was the strangest thing Morg had ever seen come out of his or anyone's body.

He moved at a slow pace through the hallway. He could come back later and clean up whatever organism ejected from his nose. Before he could see the bridge, he heard the Earthling. The sound coming from the Earthling was like hearing the mortally wounded on a battlefield shortly before dying. The groaning mixed with crying out in desperation for help. Morg wanted to run to the bridge but he couldn't muster the energy. He would be lucky to get there by walking.

The Earthling was lying on the bridge floor behind the control panel. He was in a fetal position. Even from thirty-five feet, Morg could tell the kid was shivering as though he was in a Treptow arctic blizzard. The kid was going in and out of consciousness. When he wasn't passed out, he was crying for help. A couple times he called for Morg. If it wasn't Morg it was his god. He even pleaded for help from his father and mother a couple times.

There was no reason to question the kid or try to look for what ailed him. Morg didn't have the energy and the kid wasn't coherent. He needed to do something for the punk even though there was a part of him that wanted to leave the little jerk on the floor to writhe away in pain. He decided not to be vindictive. He reached down and grabbed the kid by the midsection and started to the sleeping quarters. The kid was usually light as a feather. This time he felt as hefty as a pregnant Slippteon bull moose. Whatever invaded Morg's body had zapped his strength. He struggled to get the kid to the sleep bay without passing out.

He laid the kid into a gyro cot and covered him with an all-temp blanket. The kid was going back and forth between burning up with fever and freezing. The all-temp blanket was a medical wonder. It would keep the kid's body temperature at a constant ninety-two degrees. It wouldn't cure him, but at least, he would be more comfortable.

He considered giving the kid an all-purpose injection made to fight non-life-threatening ailments. It worked wonders combating the common cold, flu, sore throats, and a host of viral and bacterial infections. Unfortunately, it couldn't ward-off serious infections. When given to a being with a serious affliction the results were usually disastrous. Whatever was in the serum made these illnesses worse and, in some cases, resulted in death. There was a large warning label on the syringe which read, "FOR USE IN FIGHTING MINOR ILLNESS. DO NOT USE ON PATIENTS HAVING SERIOUS INFECTIONS AND DISEASES. CONSULT QUALIFIED PHYSICIANS FOR THESE AILMENTS." The warning label was enough to convince Morg the kid was better off without the injection. Before leaving sleep bay, Morg gave the kid a general anesthesia which would make him sleep for at least four hours.

It was tempting to lay down in the adjacent gyro cot and go to sleep, but someone had to be on the bridge. The transport could be set to auto-pilot, but the ship's computers couldn't make logical decisions when confronted with unusual circumstances like a fragment-storm or contact with another ship. Maybe he could get comfortable enough in the captain's gyro chair to take a nap. All he would do is set the auto-pilot to alarm mode. If the transport encountered any unusual obstructions or contacts, an ear-piercing alarm would wake him.

Morg made it back to the bridge and fell into the captain's chair. He was getting sicker but tried to convince himself it was his imagination. The safety of the voyage depended upon his attentive leadership. He couldn't afford to be sick. Two minutes later he was sound asleep. For the first time in many years, he didn't dream. His body was so busy fighting off the illness it couldn't spare any energy or brain cells to create dreams.

Four hours later, the auto-pilot alarm brought Morg out of a deep sleep. How long it blared was anyone's guess. Morg shook his head back and forth trying to clear the cobwebs from his brain. He thought about another acidic head-dunking, but it would take too long to get to the wash basin. Besides, he didn't have the energy to make it there and back.

When his eyes cleared, he shut off the alarm and looked at the sub-space-sonar on the control panel. Sitting about ten quadrants away was a ship. Its shadow drive system was disengaged but its life-support systems were still working. The slight movement the ship made was known as space-drift. It resulted from flying into or landing in a sub-vacuum pocket. These were large areas throughout space which had less than zero atmosphere. They were like black holes but on a much smaller scale.

The ship was in the direct path of the transport's route. If it was off-set either way by a couple quadrants the transport could have flown past it without an alarm going off. But this was more bad luck. Besides being sick, Morg now had to screw around with a marooned vessel in deep space. He thought of bypassing the ship but decided to investigate. There was no reason not to investigate. The transport had already slowed down to a crawl to avoid a crash. If he was creeping up on the marooned vessel he might as well see if he could help whoever was in it.

Morg guided the transport within a quadrant and hailed the stranded vessel. He kept a close eye on their missile defense system in case this was a staged trap. There was no response from the vessel. He continued to hail the ship but got nothing in return. Finally, he scanned the interior of the vessel and picked up five life forms. Four were dead. Their bodies still gave off energy even though they died hours before. The fifth being had a life force signal but it was very weak. Morg pulled within boarding distance of the marooned vessel and attached a harness beam. He grabbed his assault rife in case this was an elaborate ruse.

He cautiously scoured the marooned vessel for survivors. As his transport scanners indicated there was only one. Morg recognized the being as a Trikian. They were short, squatty beings, completely void of body hair. Their heads were huge compared to their bodies. Morg always wondered how their slim, twig-like necks could support such large craniums. They were known throughout the universe as weaklings who hired other beings to do all their physical labor.

Trikians had two traits which separated them from every other race in the universe. First, they were true intellectuals. The speed at which they processed data and came up with correct answers and viable solutions was remarkable. Their brains worked at supercomputer speeds. In fact, they were often pitted against supercomputers in contests to see which was faster. The Trikian usually won.

The other fascinating thing about Trikians was their ability to find precious metals and gems. It didn't make a lot a sense that such weak creatures could go anywhere in the universe and find something of value hidden below tons of rock and dirt. Yet, that was the skill all Trikians were good at. And, it made them very rich.

Their mining operations were wildly profitable. They would land on a planet, find rich veins, and then lease or buy the rights to that piece of land. How they found the rich deposits was a mystery. Some thought they could smell the valuable minerals. Others thought they could see valuable gems below the planet's crust. No one knew for sure and the Trikians wouldn't give up the answer. There were many legends about Trikians who were tortured to death without giving up the secret to their mining success.

The lone Trikian survivor was passed out on the bridge. His breathing was shallow, and he exhibited many of the same symptoms the kid and Morg had. Before leaving their ship, Morg double-checked the other four Trikians to make sure they were dead. He also did a download of their past month's flight log. He would play it when he got back to the transport. He wanted to know where this ship had been. The log might provide some clues about the four dead Trikians and why their ship was drifting in deep space. It didn't make any sense. If anything, the ship should be locked onto a destination and moving toward it on auto-pilot.

Morg picked the surviving Trikian off the floor and slung him over his shoulder. Five minutes later he was back on the Yandan transport. He took the Trikian to an empty sleep bay and administered the same help he gave the Earthling. Again, he opted not to give the Trikian the general infection-killing serum. His symptoms were so like the Earthling's the fear of killing him with the serum made his decision easy.

Morg stumbled back to the bridge and loaded the Trikian disc into the control panel. The recorded playback was undamaged but portions of it were intentionally erased. Most of the recording was nothing more than the five Trikians going about their normal business on their ship. Morg put the recording into hyper-search and looked for keywords, phrases, and activities. To his surprise, the hyper-search produced some interesting results.

Of major interest was that the recording contained over four hundred minor segments where the Trikians talked about precious jewels, gems, and minerals. Even for beings who spent their entire lives looking for treasures, this seemed like an unusually high number. What was more interesting was that every one of these segments had been scrubbed. They were still on the recording, but only authorized beings could watch and listen to them. There was no sense trying to access these segments. It would take a lifetime to figure out the access code to these scrubbed segments.

The other thing which caught Morg's attention was that the Trikian ship had been to Feltte Six two weeks before. Morg wondered what a Trikian ship was doing on a planet that catered to criminals. As far as he knew, Trikians were very straight-laced. They didn't drink liquor, smoke, or do drugs. In fact, he couldn't ever remember hearing about a Trikian who took part in any type of vice.

They were too busy scouring the universe looking for treasure and getting rich.

After three hours of watching and listening to the recording, Morg gave up. He couldn't access the scrubbed segments and the stop-over at Feltte Six was interesting, but he didn't know what to make of it. Watching five beings get sick and dying one after another wasn't Morg's idea of good entertainment. It was especially difficult to watch because it looked exactly like what the kid and he were suffering from. He wondered if he had just watched a trailer of their soon-to-be deaths?

Morg sat back in the gyro chair and tried to get comfortable. Now that he didn't have anything to occupy his attention the pain radiating throughout his body was more intense. He needed to shift his mind to another subject. It was an old trick he used in combat. When he got hurt, he immediately started to think about anything other than the wound. His mate was one of his favorite subjects. Thinking about her made him impervious to the pain. At times it worked so well he forgot the wound and rejoined the battle.

It didn't take long for him to find a subject to take his mind off the illness. He wondered who erased segments of the recording and what was erased. He came up with all kinds of possible explanations. He tore each theory apart and assigned it a numerical probability score. The higher the score the more likely the theory made sense and explained what was erased. The lower the score the less likely the theory explained the erasures. These mental gymnastics were like a game. All he had to do to win the prize was to figure out what was erased.

After hours of playing the game, he was left with one explanation which stood apart from all others. The Trikian who did the erasures was still alive and in the transport's rest bay trying to stay alive. Knowing his mates had died, and he might be close to the same fate, he decided to erase all references to their latest treasure find. It was a reasonable thing to do for a being whose entire life revolved around finding treasure. By deleting all references to their treasure find, he guaranteed it would remain a secret until another Trikian stumbled upon it. There was no reason to give the location of this treasure bonanza to a non-Trikian. Especially a Yandan who stumbled upon their dead ship and bodies in deep space.

The pain, nausea, and fever came rushing back after he quit playing the *who-and-what* game. It was evident that everyone on the transport needed medical attention. No one was getting better. Morg had to get them to a medical station soon or another ship would be drifting in deep space with corpses on it.

20

"I hate to speak ill of the dead, but Conway's kid blowing up is great news. The only thing which would have been better is if Conway was on that transport. What was the kid's name again?"

"His name was Joseph Conway, Secretary-General Miller"

"Ah, yes. I remember that twerp. He made a career of getting under everyone's skin. He constantly caused trouble among the Assembly members. I was so happy when he disappeared. When was that? About eight to nine years ago? Ya know, I never understood where the kid went. One day he was here and the next, he was gone. I was so happy he was gone I didn't give a damn where he went."

Milliard Miller sat across the table from Conway's Mentat. Both were sipping from cups containing the rare Fuchi herb drink. The Fuchi tree only grew in a remote mountain area of Tibet. Its coveted leaves only sprouted every three years. They were dried and ground into an herbal powder which many people believed to be a fountain of youth. Besides slowing down the aging process, the drink had an unusual effect on human thinking. Earthlings swore their brains worked faster and better when they drank Fuchi. It was the favorite drink of those who relied on creativity and intelligence to make a living. Most artists, musicians, scientists, and authors found a way to afford the rare powder.

The Mentat had a rare half-day off. Conway thought he did such a wonderful job interviewing the Lead Trifect about Joseph's disappearance, he gave him a mini vacation. It was the perfect time to update Secretary-General Miller.

Miller was a man of fifty-something who exercised at least three hours a day. He looked ten years younger than his age. He still had a full head of hair which was the same color it was as a teenager. He was slim and trim and had the body of a professional male model. His goal was to live for a hundred and twenty years. He came from a good gene pool. Both his parents lasted until their mid-nineties. All he had to do was last twenty-five years longer than they did. He figured it would be a breeze.

His entire career was spent in government service. He devoted his life to doing the *people's business*. At least that's what he liked to say on the campaign trail when he was stumping for re-election. He was uncommitted to a partner because he enjoyed sex with a variety of beings. He was very selective in the mates he chose. His career came first. One bad sex partner could tarnish, if not end, a distinguished thirty years of government service.

The Mentat believed Miller was more trustworthy than Conway. He tried not to allow emotions to cloud his opinion of humanoids. But when it came to comparing these two men, there wasn't a choice. Conway was a scumbag. Miller was a decent humanoid who had a better grasp of reality. He was egotistic at times but also displayed humility when necessary. He was straightforward and rarely used underhanded tactics to discredit his opponents. The most important part of his personality was that he hated Conway. He had nothing in common with the man and knew that for the sake of Earth and the universe, Conway must be stopped.

"Ya know, I can still remember the day when Conway told the Assembly his kid was alive on the same planet we were negotiating with. What a coincidence. In retrospect, it was too much of a coincidence. I almost crapped my pants when Conway said the CASETA Agreement was on hold until his kid was released from Yanda and sent back to Earth."

Miller paused and shook his head back and forth remembering that horrid day when one dumb-ass kid became the major factor in negotiating an important contract between two powerful planets. If the Assembly had been using their collective brain, they would have told Conway to go screw himself. The kid should never have been a pawn in such an important negotiation. But now, the tables had turned against Conway. His kid was no more. He was blown to smithereens somewhere in deep space. There was a god after all.

"Are you sure Conway's kid is dead?"

"Before I talked with the Lead Trifect this morning, I was ninety percent sure he was dead. Now, I've lowered that estimate to around fifty percent. The Lead Trifect had a man on the transport when it blew up. The recording he made never shows Joseph Conway on the ship. The Yandan charged with bringing the young Conway back to Earth isn't in the recording either."

"How long was the Lead Trifect's man on the ship before it blew?"

"Only a few minutes, Secretary-General."

Miller squinched his eyes thinking about what the Mentat described. "That's strange, but it doesn't prove the kid wasn't on the transport."

"No, it doesn't. That's one of the reasons why my probability rating is still at fifty percent. Also, the transport had the same identification number and flight signature. ID numbers can be faked but I've never heard of a fake flight signature."

"That's very interesting. I guess this situation can be summed up in a couple short sentences. A Yandan transport blew up in deep space and Joseph Conway may or may not have been on it. If he wasn't, then where the hell is he? For that matter, do we care where he is?"

Miller rubbed his forehead hard hoping to resolve these questions. He hated situations which could be maybe-this-or-that. He liked black or white. He hated possible theories in the gray zone.

"I just thought of something. Who was flying the transport?"

"The Lead Trifect claims the recording doesn't show who is in the pilot gyro chairs. When he answered that question, I picked up stressf in his voice. I'm sure he was lying but he wouldn't say who or what he saw, if anything.

He didn't want to ask the Mentat the next question but knew he must. "Have you told Conway everything you told me?"

"Yes and no. I don't think he understood the implications of what I was saying. I think he assumes the kid was on the transport. I tried to stay as vague as possible, but I had to be specific about most things."

"Okay. I guess there's nothing we can do about it. Even if the kid is dead, I don't think that's going to change Conway one bit. He's possessed and determined not to sign the CASETA Agreement. I'm not sure what he's up to but it can't be anything good."

The Mentat agreed with Miller's assessment. Whether Joseph was alive, or dead, wasn't going to change Prefect Conway's plans. Signing CASETA with Yanda was kaput. Something else was in the works. Something which Prefect Conway thought was more beneficial. It may not benefit Earth more, but it would enrich Prefect Conway's status and pocket.

"Is there anything else I should know about?"

Before the Mentat could respond there was a knock at the door. Miller started to get out of his chair when the door opened a bit and Beth poked her head into the room.

"Beth, my dear. Please come in. Would you like a cup of Fuchi?"

"Why yes, that would be wonderful."

Millard Miller held Beth's chair for her as she sat and then went to the service bar to pour her the cup of Fuchi.

"Darling, you look stunning today. Living with the pig agrees with you."

Beth's half-smirk reminded the Mentat of the family cat who tried to hide eating the pet parakeet even though there were feathers hanging from his mouth.

"Yeah, it's a real treat. He must be the most obnoxious person in the universe. God, I'll be glad when...."

Beth stopped in mid-sentence and looked back and forth between Miller and the Mentat. She had seen the Mentat but didn't give it a second thought. She was so accustomed to seeing him around Conway's residence that running into him at Miller's seemed natural. But now she wondered what she could say and what he was doing in Miller's private office.

"That's okay, my dear. You can speak freely in front of the Mentat. In fact, he was filling me in about the death of Conway's kid before you dropped in. I believe it's fair to say that this gentleman is on our team. Would you say that's a fair statement, Mentat?"

The Mentat looked at Miller and debated what to say. He just learned that Conway's lover, Beth, was in alliance with Millard Miller. He was surprised, very surprised. He could not ever recall seeing the two of them say two words to each other. Yet, here they were openly discussing a man they hated. Should he come out in favor of their betrayal or play it conservatively? After all, if this woman could sleep with Conway and then stab him in the back, how much could she be trusted?

As though Miller read his mind, he leaned over and patted the Mentat's leg. "Hey, that's okay. You don't have to answer that question. I know this must be a huge surprise for you. There are some other things you'll learn once you get on the anti-Conway bandwagon, but that can wait. Take some time and think about this. We can use you, but I'm not going to force you, or anyone, to do something they don't agree with."

The Mentat could tell that Miller was completely truthful. However, that didn't help him make the decision he now faced. Should he join the anti-Conway group and do their bidding, or honor the contract his home planet signed with Prefect Conway?

"Yes, thank you, Secretary-General. It would definitely be beneficial if I took some time to consider your words."

"You do that, sir." Miller and the Mentat rose from the table and started to the door. The Mentat loved the fact that Miller referred to him with titles of respect. There was something about the titles, sir and gentleman, which made the Mentat feel special. If nothing else, they made him feel like a humanoid. He thought about a day in the future when he might have human friends.

"Was there anything else you wanted to discuss?"

The Mentat debated with himself. There was one last tidbit of information he planned to pass on to Miller but wasn't sure if the timing was right. He decided to take a chance and said, "I've figured out why the Prefect doesn't want to sign the CASETA Agreement with Yanda."

Miller put his arm around the Mentat as they walked. A weak smile crossed his face. "Let me guess. He's already made arrangements with the planet Florid to sell our sulfur and carbon toxic gases and compounds to them. Am I correct?"

The Mentat stopped suddenly and faced Miller. "You're right, sir."

"I know. Our girl, Beth, figured it out a couple weeks ago. But, thanks for the confirmation. It's always nice to have information validated by a second source."

The Mentat looked over at Beth who was still sitting at the table. She put down her Fuchi cup, gave him another Cheshire Cat smile and waved good-bye.

Miller reached to open the door. "Crap. I've forgotten the kid's name. What's his name again?"

"Joseph Conway."

"Thanks. I better write that down, so I don't forget. I'm sure old man Conway will want me to give the eulogy at the kid's funeral. And, of course, there are flowers to send and condolences and all that other bullshit. That's the downside of being the Prefect's closest friend." Miller and Beth started laughing. Taking sarcastic shots at the Prefect was one of the few ways they had to stay sane.

Miller patted the Mentat on the back as he ushered him out the door. "I'll talk with you later, sir." Miller watched the Mentat walk away. It was very noticeable how the Mentat reacted when he was called "sir". He stood a little straighter and taller. Simply giving the Mentat a bit of respect was winning him over. Miller was very confident the Mentat would join his anti-Conway group.

"Well, dear. What do you think?"

"That Mentat better keep his mouth shut or both our asses are cooked."

"Don't worry, my dear. He'll come over to our side soon enough. What do you think about the kid getting shredded to bits in space?"

"Considering what he did to me, I hope he died a long, painful death. Good riddance."

"Well, I doubt there was much pain if his ship blew up."

Beth stopped sipping and put her cup down. "What do you mean *if* he was blown up?"

"There's a small chance he wasn't on the ship. The Mentat told me about his communication with the Lead Trifect this morning. Apparently, there was a Yandan invasion trooper on the ship when it vaporized. From the time the trooper entered the transport to the time it blows, there's no Joseph Conway or escort Yandan on his transmission."

"Well, who was flying the transport?"

"That's exactly what I asked the Mentat. All he knows is that the Lead Trifect answered that question dishonestly. He might know who was piloting the transport but isn't telling."

"Shit, shit, shit." Beth took her Fuchi cup and threw it across the room. It broke into a hundred small pieces and shards. Miller didn't say a word about the cup or her eruption. He understood and sympathized with her frustration.

It took Beth a couple minutes to calm down enough to talk. "I wondered why the pig was in such a good mood this morning. I guess

I know now. He suspects the same thing you, the Mentat and Lead Trifect do. That prick-of-a-son somehow escaped death again. Well, have you got any ideas, Millard?"

"Yes, I've had a contingency plan ready for some time. It might be time to launch it. If the kid is still alive, his ship couldn't be any more than four to five light years away from Earth now. But, let's wait a little while longer. I want to see what else happens. Make sure you keep close tabs on the pig. Watch everything he does and listen carefully to what he says."

"Does your contingency plan include me?"

"Absolutely. What you've already endured is beyond description. You deserve some pay-back."

21

"That was an interesting conversation."

"That, my brothers, is known as a fishing expedition. It's quite popular among Earthlings when negotiating. This is the way it works. When one Earthling wants to know what another Earthling knows, he'll ask a series of innocuous questions. All the questions are on the fringe of the real issue. If done correctly, the questioned Earthling will be lulled into giving up valuable information. That information is then used to strike a better bargain. It can be quite an effective negotiating tactic."

"Did it work with you, Lead Trifect?"

"Yes and no. Both of us were fishing for information. I'm sure Conway told the Mentat what questions to ask me and how to ask them. That, combined with the Mentat's ability to detect dishonesty, got Conway a fairly accurate picture of what we know. I went along with this charade because I wanted to know what Conway knew about his kid and Officer Morg. Based on the questions the Mentat asked, I'd say Conway isn't sure if the kid is alive or dead. Most likely, he's leaning toward alive. He's also trying to figure out what to do next. Should he go looking for the kid or sit and wait. I'm sure he's as confused as we are about what happened on the transport."

"So, what do you think happened to Morg and the Earthling?"

The Lead Trifect shook his head back and forth. "Brothers, I don't know. My guess is that the kid and Morg may have survived, but I don't know how. There's a good chance we'll find out for certain within a couple days."

"What about the CASETA Agreement? Do you think they are reconsidering it?"

"Brothers, it was a ruse to get information from me. Conway has no intention of signing the Agreement. He has other plans. I wish I knew what. It would make my decisions a lot easier if I knew what he was planning."

Without looking at his underlings, he asked, "Do we have any way of getting that information? Do we have any spies within Earth's hierarchy? Can we buy the information from someone there? How about other members of their Assembly? Will any of them sell out Conway?"

He didn't bother to look across the table at his underlings. He could tell from the silence this was another opportunity missed by his brother Trifect.

There was no use dwelling on the Mentat communication. It netted the Lead Trifect exactly what he thought it would; a big fat zero. And, using espionage this late in the game to find out what Conway was up to was another waste of time.

He spun his chair and turned his back on the two Trifect. "Brothers, have you found the 38 yet?"

There was dead silence. There was no sense looking at them. He could feel their answer.

"Have our sweepers or any other ships found wreckage from the transport in the quadrant where it blew up?"

Again, no response. He turned back toward them. They were so easy to read. Their expressions screamed a giant *no* for each question.

It had been one of his worst mornings since taking over as Lead Trifect. It didn't seem like anything was moving toward a resolution. He felt like a juggler with a dozen balls in the air and no idea what to do with them. He didn't know for sure if the Earthling and Morg were alive. Should he plan an invasion of Earth to get the gases and compounds Yanda needed? Or, should Yanda write off Earth and let that fool Conway lead his planet to self-destruction? Their best military weapon had disappeared. Someone had it, but who? Things were not going well, and he wondered if it was time to pull the plug and retire. Even that thought was depressing. Who the hell would he turn the reins of power over to? The other two Trifect weren't competent enough to be office clerks.

He could walk away from his position and retire anywhere he wanted. His estate was massive, but there was one thing stopping him. In the lower depths of his being, he felt that something was very, very wrong. It had been growing steadily over the past year or two. It was far greater than missing transports and experimental ships. It dwarfed finding the correct toxic gases to load into the Yandan atmosphere.

Something big and evil was coming toward Yanda. What it was and when it would arrive were the unknowns. His gut told him it was real and out there somewhere, waiting to pounce. That's why it was imperative the Yanda Federation not mess up. And, that was the main reason why he couldn't walk away from his position now. Everyone on his home planet and within the alliance depended on him for safety and security. He tried to remain humble, but there was no one else in the alliance who could lead by making sound decisions. As much as he wanted to pack his duffle bag and leave, he couldn't.

He pushed these thoughts of doom and gloom out of his mind and went back to asking the other two Trifect questions.

"Brothers, I'm going to take the afternoon off. Is there anything else before I leave?"

"Ah, yes, Lead Trifect. Most departments in the government are getting communications from Morg's heirs. They want to know when he will be officially declared non-functioning. They want his estate, pension, and benefits."

"How did they find out about the transport blowing up? Did you two tell anyone?"

"No, Lead Trifect. We told no one, but I know it spread like a wildfire."

"So, on top of everything else, we have a leak here within the palace executive chambers. That's great."

Once again, the two Trifect sat at the conference table looking like two innocent school-age Yandies. They hadn't thought how strange it was that everyone on Yanda knew about the transport explosion. They didn't seem to care that information was leaking out of the palace. Or, they hadn't put two and two together to realize there was a leaker.

The Lead Trifect wanted to get up and leave the room. He feared if he stayed, he might overreact and throw half of the palace employees into solitary confinement. It was time to take care of the leaker in the palace.

Instead, he got up and walked around the room. His underlings knew better than talk while he did this. There was something gnawing at the deepest levels of his consciousness. It had been there for days, but he couldn't bring it into the open. On his third trip around the conference table, it hit him. It was so obvious. Why hadn't he realized it before? He must be getting dim-witted in his old age. A broad smirk crossed his face and he turned toward his brother Trifect.

"What is it, Lead Trifect?"

"I figured out why Commander Fritase rushed the transport bridge."

"What are you talking about?"

"Do you remember when I played his recording for you? You didn't see the entire recording, but when he first boarded the transport, he knew something was wrong. He decided to take a defensive position and hunker down in the hallway. He was going to wait and see what happened. Almost as soon as he said that he rushed the bridge. Why would he do that?"

The Lead Trifect didn't wait for them to guess. He went ahead and answered his own question. "Somehow he knew the transport was going to blow. Maybe he heard the detonation devices activate. Or, he saw or heard something which tipped him off. It was his last-ditch effort to avoid a catastrophe. If he could get to the bridge, he might have a chance to stop the detonation."

The two Trifect understood what he was saying but didn't understand the implications.

He felt a hundred times better now. Taking the afternoon off would be somewhat enjoyable rather than dour and anxiety filled.

"Brothers, Morg and the Earthling are alive. They weren't on that transport and Commander Fritase knew it. I don't know where they were, but they weren't there."

The other two Trifect had quizzical looks on their faces. They leaned over the conference table waiting to hear more.

"Don't change a thing. Keep sweeping the area for debris from the ship that blew. And, keep looking for the 38. It went somewhere. Someone has it. We need that Interceptor back. But, above all else, we must contact Morg. I know you don't know where he is, but you must figure out a way to get ahold of him. He's our only chance to exert pressure on Conway. If Conway thinks we aren't going to return his son, he might adjust his attitude and consider signing the CASETA Agreement. His son might be the bargaining chip we need."

He looked at his two underlings. He could see they were finally following his explanation. To be certain, he asked, "Do you understand what has to be done?"

"Yes, Lead Trifect. We understand."

"Brothers don't let me down. And, don't let Yanda down. Find a way to contact Morg. And, one last thing. You are not to mention to anyone that Morg and the Earthling are alive. If this leaks out, I'm going to send both your asses to the worst, most remote military station we have. Understand?"

"Yes, Lead Trifect." It was one of the few times he could remember the two underlings standing and saluting.

22

It was one and a half light years to the nearest medical depot. It put the transport closer to Earth, but they were still over three light years away from their ultimate destination.

Morg was doing the best he could to pilot the ship and take care of his two sick passengers. If he was well, nursing the Earthling and Trikian would be tolerable. But he was getting sicker and the energy he had available to devote to others was dwindling. The mere thought of walking from the bridge to the sleeping quarters to service patients was exhausting.

The Trikian was the sickest. It was most likely because he caught the disease or infection a week or more before Morg and the kid. When he wasn't comatose, he was delirious talking to invisible visitors, comrades, and family members. He went back and forth between a high fever and extreme cold. Morg was either piling thermal blankets on him or lowering him into a space chamber containing ultra-frigid molecules taken from outside the transport. The molecules were gradually warmed to fifteen degrees below the being's normal body temperature. At this cool temperature, a sick patient's temperature could be controlled. It was a simple and effective way to stabilize a being with a high fever.

Morg and the Earthling were exhibiting the same symptoms but to a lesser degree. It was only a matter of time before they became as sick as the Trikian. With luck, they would reach the medical depot before that happened.

On the morning of the third day after rescuing the Trikian, Morg was awakened by screams coming from the sleeping quarters. He couldn't make out what was being shouted but it sounded as if someone was fighting for his life. Morg shuffled as fast as he could to the sleeping quarters. He found the Trikian unconscious and flopping around on his gyro cot. He was screaming at someone about a rich deposit of Molum crystals. These were the most sought-after crystals in the universe. One crystal could power an entire city for a year or more. The cost of this mineral was outrageously high, but the pay-back was higher.

"What do you mean we can't lease this land? You're not using it and we've offered you an above-market lease price. Well, will you sell us the land?"

The Trikian trashed about as he whispered to a phantom comrade. "Don't say anything to Helmer about the crystal deposit. We must get this contract before someone else discovers what we found. It could be the largest deposit of Molum crystals ever discovered. The vein runs at least a hundredth of the circumference of the planet. I can't believe it's in a valley between two ancient lava flows."

The Trikian stopped wiggling in his stupor. A contented and thoughtful expression crossed his face. If Morg didn't know better he'd guess the Trikian was devising a scheme to get his hands on the crystals.

"I'm not sure what to do if Helmer doesn't lease or sell us the land. Maybe we should call in Bentwa. You know, Bentwa the fixer. He can be very persuasive. Remember the dope he talked with on Cresma? One look at Bentwa and he signed over the land to us immediately. By the way, do you still have his private comm number?

The Trikian stopped mumbling and started laughing. The only other time Morg saw beings laugh while unconscious was on the battlefield. Some mortally wounded troopers laughed hysterically right to their last breath. Morg assumed it was the body's way of dealing with extreme pain. Now, he wasn't so sure. It might be that the dying watched a review of their life and found a specific memory that was laughable. For a Yandan it wouldn't be something considered funny because they didn't understand the finer points of comedy. It was more likely to be something ironic or sarcastic. Could it be the Trikians had the same perspective on what deserved a laugh?

Morg wanted to lay down in the gyro cot next to the Trikian and sleep but this might be his last chance to learn what the Trikian was jabbering about. He forced his eyes to stay open and leaned closer to the patient. He had listened closely to the Trikian's speech patterns for the last couple of days. He thought he could imitate his dialect and pretend to be a fellow Trikian.

"Yes, I still have Bentwa's comm number. What would you like me to tell him?"

The Trikian didn't answer immediately. Morg started to worry that even in his stupor he knew another Trikian wasn't at his bedside. But it was too late to worry about what was going through the dying Trikian's mind. Morg had taken a chance and imitated the Trikian's language and dialect the best he could. If the dying being knew he was an imposter, so be it.

Morg got up and hobbled toward the adjacent gyro cot. If the Trikian was going to die without divulging any more information, then Morg was going to rest. He had seen enough death for one lifetime. Watching the Trikian die wouldn't be any different than witnessing a hundred battlefield deaths.

"Call Bentwa and see if he is available for a top-secret assignment. Offer him top pay to make himself available." Morg whirled around and looked at the Trikian. There was no question he was still unconscious. Droplets of yellow secretion were forming on his forehead and began to combine with other droplets to run down the side of his face. Morg sat down on the side of his cot again. His breathing had grown more labored in the last couple of minutes. Beneath his near-transparent, fluttering eyelids, Morg could see the Trikian's eyes gyrating every which way.

Morg waited to hear more. He didn't know if the Trikian was done speaking or taking time to piece together other thoughts. In a mind so fragile and under duress the Trikian couldn't be a hundred percent lucid. Morg resigned himself to another waiting game. A game he didn't feel well enough to play.

Shivers started to run up and down Morg's back. His head throbbed, and images were going in and out of focus. He needed to lie down soon. It was either that or fall to the floor unconscious. He caught himself before passing out and managed to lay down next to the Trikian. As sleep started to butt out consciousness, he heard the Trikian somewhere in the distance. "Tell Bentwa we will meet him at the Mytop 2212 glider tube in ...."

23

Morg was awakened by the transport's Roboland system. Several hours of sleep had restored a bit of energy to his body and clarity to his mind. Echoing throughout the ship, Morg heard the Roboland system giving instructions for docking at the medical depot. He needed to get to the bridge and make sure the transport landed without a hitch. He swung his legs over the side of the cot and prepared to stand. Before making what was now a huge effort, he remembered the Trikian. He looked over his shoulder to check on the sickest being aboard the transport.

Morg had seen enough corpses to know the Trikian was dead. There was nothing he could do for the alien other than cover his face with a thermal blanket.

He struggled to his feet and trudged toward the bridge. What normally took two to three minutes now seemed like hours. He weaved back and forth through the hallway, stopping every so often to grab a stationary fixture and catch his breath.

He made it to the captain's gyro chair in the nick of time. He fell into it and forced himself to do a quick review of the transport's auto-landing approach to the docking bay. Everything seemed to be in order even though he could only muster enough energy for a cursory inspection of the control panel. Thankfully the Roboland was an automated procedure. In his present condition, he would never be able to land the transport without Roboland.

"Engage gyro chair restriction belts. Prepare for harness beam lockdown in ten seconds. Ten, nine, eight, seven...."

A jarring thud pulsated throughout the hull as the harness beam attached itself to the transport. It would be another five minutes before the transport was pulled into the docking bay and set in its stall. Morg was exhausted even though he had done very little. As he sat in the captain's chair watching the medical depot draw closer, he started thinking about the Trikian's last words. So much of what the Trikian said was whispered, screamed, or slurred. There was a good chance the ship's surveillance system hadn't captured all his words correctly.

He needed to record the Trikian's last keywords before the illness wiped them from his memory. "Record on." Morg leaned forward and held his head with his two, oversized pincher hands. He squeezed slightly hoping this would lift the fog in his head and bring back everything the Trikian said.

"Molum crystals..., Helmer..., huge deposit..., in a valley..., between ancient lava flows..., Bentwa." That was all he could remember even though there was something nagging at him. There was at least one other keyword, but his illness was blocking it out. Maybe when he felt better a review of the ship's audio log would reveal what he was trying to remember.

"Record...." Morg stopped before shutting off the system. Mytop 2212. It was Mytop 2212. That's what he was trying to remember. The name of a Feltte Six vice and pleasure park catapulted into his head. "Glider tube..., Mytop 2212. Record off."

Even in his weak state, he was able to put two and two together and deduce that the Molum crystals might be on Feltte Six. Everything the Trikian said on his deathbed, plus the recording he pirated from the Trikian ship, pointed to Feltte Six. It seemed like an odd place to find Molum crystals considering how populated Feltte Six was and its extensive history.

Morg wondered how the crystals could remain undiscovered for thousands of years. Had erosion finally exposed the crystals? Or, did geothermal forces within the planet finally push the crystals to the surface? Both explanations seemed unlikely, but somehow the Trikians found them. After all, they were professional treasure hunters. They knew their business better than anyone else and had the riches to prove it.

THE DOCKING BAY on the medical depot planet was filled. Morg's transport got the last available stall even though there were several ships waiting outside the planet's flight boundary. The fact that the transport was Yandan gave it a priority and expedited clearance. The beings who ran the medical depot knew who paid their bills and salaries. The last thing they would do is delay docking privileges to a Yandan or Alliance ship.

When the transport came to rest Morg looked out the viewing port. It was mass confusion everywhere he looked. Medical orderlies and doctors wore hazard abatement suits over their entire bodies. Each suit was a forest green color and identified with a Yandan Medical Corp insignia. Air and waste filtering systems within each suit permitted the wearer to work without fear of contamination. Each suit also had a nourishment port which allowed the wearer to drink liquid meals.

Morg lost count of all the floatation stretchers he saw moving the sick and dead. With all this commotion, he wondered how long it would be before he and the Earthling were examined. That was the last thing he remembered until someone started to poke and prod his outer shell near his right arm.

"Officer, officer. Please wake up. I need to get you processed and in to see a doctor. Are you awake, sir?"

Morg opened his eyes to see two optic-scan lenses from a hazard abatement suit looking down at him. He had no clue what type of planetary being was inside the orderly suit. In his present condition, he didn't give a damn. All he cared about was getting medical attention for himself and the Earthling.

"Yeah, yeah. I'm awake. How long was I out?"

"I don't know sir. I'm too busy to notice things like that. Sir are you the only being on this ship?"

Morg shook his head from side to side trying to dislodge the last cobwebs in his mind. "No. There is an Earthling and Trikian in the sleeping quarters. The Trikian is dead. I'm not sure about the Earthling."

The orderly made a notation of what Morg said and headed for the sleeping quarters. "I'll be right back. Try to relax."

Morg wanted to laugh but he knew it would hurt too much. Try to relax? Was the orderly joking? Every tendon and skeletal membrane in his body screamed in pain. He had been wounded many times in battle, but nothing compared to this. Pain resulting from wounds was usually localized, but this illness radiated a pulsating pain throughout his entire inner and outer body.

Morg went back to watching the activity on the docking platform. The bustle hadn't let up since he passed out. Every floatation stretcher he could see held a body. It wasn't hard telling the dead from those still clinging to life. The death stretchers contained more than one body and were pushed by a robotic android. They moved at a speed much slower than the stretchers with a living being. The robots walked each death stretcher into the Refuse Room where the bodies were dumped into an acid tank. Within two minutes each corpse dissolved to nothing.

In the sleeping quarters, the orderly examined the kid who was in the initial stages of full-blown delirium. He thrashed about and talked with invisible visitors. If the orderly had bothered to listen, he would have heard an outline of the invasion of Yanda. He did take notice when the kid screamed at someone named Prefect Conway.

The orderly turned around and did a quick scan of the sleeping room to make sure this Prefect being was only a figment of the patient's imagination.

The orderly locked down the kid on the gyro cot, so he wouldn't have to fight with him during the examination. Fluid and skin samples were required of each new patient regardless of their condition, rank, or planetary affiliation. The samples went to the depot's testing facility for chemical and medical analysis. Within thirty minutes the doctor knew what disease or illness the patient suffered from. He relied on a data bank containing the records of every illness or disease reported in the last hundred years. If any other being in the universe had contracted the same disease, it matched automatically with the newest patient. The doctors wouldn't have to see the analysis report to know what was wrong with the Earthling. His symptoms were identical to thousands of other patients who arrived at the medical depot in the past couple weeks.

The orderly hated submitting each new patient's samples for analysis. It was an administrative nightmare which took over an hour per patient. He argued daily with his superiors about wasting the time to do individual analysis. It made no sense during an epidemic. Every sick being arriving at the medical depot had the same symptoms. The only thing that changed was the patient's name, age, and planetary classification.

He lost the argument each day. What he didn't know was that the Yandan High Command used the individual analysis reports from each depot to look for beings of interest. These included criminals, revolutionaries, the kidnapped and others wanted for assorted reasons. By the time Morg and the Earthling saw a doctor and were assigned to a treatment ward, the Trifect on Yanda would know they were still alive and their location. Then it was a question of whether this news could be kept secret and used to the Trifect's advantage.

"I'm sorry, Officer. I was trying not to wake you."

Morg had nodded off again and awoke as the orderly finished his last sample extraction.

"Yeah, no problem. What were you doing?"

"Taking fluid and exterior membrane samples. It's required for every new patient."

Morg wanted to protest but he knew it was too late. He was too tired to fight with the orderly. Plus, the depot may refuse to admit him and the kid if they didn't have the required samples.

"Officer, I'm done with my initial examination. As soon as there are available floatation stretchers, we'll get you two moved into the clinic."

"How long will that be?"

"Probably two to three hours, sir."

Morg made a snap decision. He couldn't wait hours for a ride to the clinic. "Wait right here, doc."

Morg reached deep within himself and found enough energy to leave the bridge and stumble to the sleeping quarters. He yanked the kid from the gyro cot and heaved him up onto his shoulder. Thankfully, the kid was unconscious. If he had been awake, he would scream in pain due to the rough texture and sharp edges of Morg's skeletal exterior.

The orderly was shocked by what he saw coming toward the bridge. He heard stories about the courage and stamina of Yandan Invasion Troopers, but here was a real-life example of it. Heading his way was the Officer carrying the Earthling. The Yandan was staggering but didn't let on that the load was too much for his sickly body.

"Let's go. Lead the way."

"Huh?"

"To the clinic. Now! My co-pilot and I aren't waiting for a damn stretcher."

The hardened stare from the Yandan was enough to get the orderly moving. There was no way he was going to challenge a pissed off trooper.

Morg and the orderly pushed their way through the crowded docking platform. There was so much activity their progress came to an abrupt halt several times. It was mass confusion caused by a lack of leadership. Yelling, screaming, and crying were coming from every direction. The smell of death hung in the air. Morg pushed aside a couple delirious patients who thought they should get off their stretchers and fight. Orderlies screamed to be heard over the commotion. Their assistants stumble-bummed their way through the crowds trying to follow orders.

"Sister, did you see that?"

Two Athlon mercenaries lay next to each other on a multi-body stretcher. They were sicker than some beings on the docking platform yet better than others. The illness clouded their memories of how long it had been since leaving Feltte Six. Their best guess was somewhere between one and two weeks.

There was a third body on the stretcher with them. It was their sister mercenary who died as their ship was towed into the docking bay. Their refusal to ride on single floatation stretchers was delaying their access to the clinic. The dead were not allowed to enter the clinic. Their stretcher wasn't going anywhere until the sister mercenary was loaded on a death stretcher and sent to the Refuse Room.

"See what, sister?"

"I think that was Officer Morg, the Yandan we're looking for. Look! Do you see that Yandan carrying a human over his shoulder?"

The mercenary who spotted Morg pointed his direction. She helped her fellow mercenary struggle to a propped-up position. "Hurry, he's being swallowed by the crowd."

"I can barely see a Yandan carrying something over his shoulder. I can't see his face. Are you sure it was Morg?"

"It sure as hell looked like him. It makes sense he would show up here. He was on Feltte Six too."

"We need to follow him, sister."

The two remaining daughters of Crex, Stex, and Blex started screaming. "Orderly. Orderly. Get a damn orderly over here and get this corpse off our stretcher."

Their stamina was draining fast but the one on the outside of the stretcher had enough energy left to grab a passing orderly. "Get this body off our stretcher and push us into the clinic, now." Having an Athlon mercenary growl orders was enough to scare the orderly into action. It didn't matter that they were female. They were big, ugly, and mean enough to beat him to a pulp. Sixty seconds later they were wheeled in the same direction as Morg.

24

"Why did you execute the leaker?"

"It seemed like the right thing to do, Lead Trifect. We couldn't afford to lose anymore...."

The Lead Trifect held up his hand bringing to a stop the idiotic explanation from his underling.

"Did it ever occur to you to consult me when you found the leaker in the palace communications office?"

"We didn't think you wanted to be bothered with such a trivial matter. You've been under a lot of stress, so we didn't want to add any more.

"That was very considerate of you but not smart."

"We don't understand, sir. Why wouldn't you want the rat exterminated?"

The Lead Trifect wanted to start screaming but realized it wouldn't do any good. He was dealing with two Yandans who weren't very clever. They were unable to think outside the box and see how a lousy situation could be used to their advantage.

He couldn't help keeping the sarcasm out of his response. "Was he divulging secret information for personal reasons or selling the information? Was he a lone rogue or working with others? What contacts did he have in the palace and elsewhere? Were there other things he leaked that we don't know about?"

The Lead Trifect was having difficulty keeping calm. He considered firing the two underlings. For a split second, he thought a firing squad might be a better remedy.

He gritted his fangs and spit out his final remark. "You've blown a perfect opportunity to use this leaker to our advantage." He looked across the table and could see that his underlings didn't understand what he was talking about. "Gentlemen, it's called misdirection. Once we knew who the leaker was, we could have used him to put out fake information. He was a valuable resource. You use traitors like this to your advantage before executing them."

The Lead Trifect closed his eyes and shook his head in disgust.

"From this point forward, you don't do anything unless I know about it. Do you understand?"

The underlings lowered their heads and nodded in agreement.

"Okay, let's see if we can unscramble this mess. Tell me exactly what happened."

"Medical depot Alpha 30 sent in a medical analysis on two sick beings who arrived there ten hours ago. The analysis reports matched with Officer Morg and Earthling Joseph Conway. They have the same illness which has become an epidemic. The report came in to our traitor. He then sent out this information to a couple private comm numbers. We're trying to establish who owns these numbers."

"Did you interrogate him to find out who the private comm numbers belonged to?"

A slight smile of satisfaction crossed their faces. "Yes, we did. In fact, we tortured him, but he wouldn't give up that information. That's when we decided to execute him."

"Do you see now how your overreaction killed our chance of finding out who he was feeding information to? If you had laid off him, we could have fed him fake secret information. Then our tech department could have unveiled the private numbers and his accomplices."

The Lead Trifect let the scolding sink in before he continued. "The chance of you finding out now who belongs to the private numbers is remote, at best. I'm going to assume he sent the information to Prefect Conway. Who belongs to the second private number is anyone's guess?"

"What should we do Lead Trifect?"

The Lead Trifect began walking around the room. It was the easiest way for him to solve difficult problems. He mumbled under his breath, talking, and debating with himself. It didn't take long for him to realize his options were limited.

"If Prefect Conway knows his son is alive then it won't take long before the news spreads across the universe. Do you remember how fast the transport explosion news traveled? The same thing is going to happen with this. So, what can we do? We can't get the Shooting Star 38 to Alpha 30 to pick up Morg and the Earthling because we lost it. Do we have any agents on Alpha 30 we trust?"

"We will have to check, sir."

"Do that. I want an answer within the hour. I want to know who they are, their backgrounds and how long they have been in our service. If we don't have a trusted agent on Alpha 30 then locate the nearest one who can get there within a day. Do you understand?"

The underlings saluted and scampered off to check confidential agent profiles for Alpha 30 and nearby quadrants. After screwing up so many times they were beginning to question their competency. It seemed like every decision they made was exactly the opposite of what the Lead Trifect wanted.

The Lead Trifect sat at the meeting table and searched for positives in this predicament. He finally stumbled on one. He now knew where Morg and the Earthling were. With a bit of luck, he could contact Officer Morg, explain the situation and set a sound plan of action.

Maybe things weren't as bad as he thought at first. The Earthling and Officer Morg were too sick to go anywhere, unless...unless they were taken forcibly. The Lead Trifect jumped up out of his chair. How could he have been so blind? If he knew where they were then others knew their location. The palace leaker had seen to that.

In their sickly condition, Officer Morg and the Earthling were prime candidates for kidnapping or worse.

Under his breath, he said, "Brothers, please don't screw this one up." He sat back down and waited for the return of the other two Trifect.

25

Eight hours later, Morg and the kid finished the doctor examination and a battery of tests. The medical staff wanted to assign them to different recovery wards. They used every excuse and reason they could think of to separate the two of them. Morg wouldn't have any part of it. He wasn't going to let the kid out of his sight. It was hard enough keeping track of him when he was in good health. God only knew what mischief the kid could get into being delirious.

"Do you realize Officer Morg that Joseph Conway is sicker than you?"

"Yes, I understand, doc. And, I'm sure you are going to tell me that if I go in his ward with other patients like him it will delay my recovery."

"That's precisely what I was going to tell you because it's the truth."

"I understand and hold you blameless if that happens. I can't afford to let him out of my sight, doc."

The doctor gave up trying to convince the Yandan officer. He had too many other patients to see and worry about to continue arguing.

"Okay, son. I give up. It's your health so good luck to you. I've given you a double dose of serum. It's not a cure but you should start feeling better in a day or two. From that point on, it's up to your body. Only time will tell. You'll either recover or die. We don't know why some patients recover and others don't. This is an odd illness with a mind of its own. So, good luck. Hopefully, I'll see you around the hospital a week from now."

The doctor gave Morg a friendly pat on the back and walked off. He had dozens of new patients to see before his eighteen-hour shift ended. So far, he was lucky and not caught the illness. The continuous molecule scrubbers in the hospital were invaluable in preventing the disease from spreading. The doctor didn't know who invented molecule scrubbers but wanted to meet him. He wanted to personally thank this being for saving his ass many times over.

Morg looked at the Earthling who was in the bed next to his. The kid was out cold. Between injections, inoculations, painkillers, and other drugs, the kid might sleep for a solid week or more. At least, that's what Morg hoped. It was a lot easier keeping an eye on a semi-comatose Earthling as opposed to one who was wide awake.

Morg lay back and thought about closing his eyes. He needed more sleep, but something stopped him from nodding off. It was a gut feeling that someone was watching him. It had started hours before when they were assigned to the recovery room. It was the same feeling he experienced on the battlefield. A couple times he felt snipers watching him from several miles away. He couldn't see them but knew they were out there somewhere. It was the same feeling he had now. Someone was watching, and their intention was to inflict pain, just like battlefield snipers.

The only advantage he had was that the recovery rooms held thousands of patients. It was unlikely his enemy would attack in a sea of witnesses. The downside was that so many beings wandering around made it difficult to pick out the enemy. Even if he caught someone staring, it wasn't proof they intended to harm him. His only hope was that the enemy wasn't a lunatic. A suicide killer using this mob of beings as cover would be damn near impossible to stop. He couldn't stop his eyes from closing. He fell asleep wondering if there was a private room the kid and he could move to.

"Officer Morg. Officer wake up. Do you hear me, officer?"

Morg's eyes popped open as fast as a thermal missile leaving its silo. He reached out to grab the being bending over his recovery cot. He was frightened and ashamed that any unknown stranger could get this close. His internal danger alert should have resonated throughout his body and woke him up. He had every intention of breaking the intruder's arm and disarming him. Instead, he stopped before applying any pressure to the arm.

Looking down at him was a female Landan. At first, he thought it was Luna from Feltte Six. She had the same natural beauty. Her hair, eyes, and complexion were the same soft beige color. The only difference was that this female was older with age and stretch marks on her face and neck. She could have easily passed for Luna's birth giver.

She gave Morg a broad smile as she pretended to be a medical aide. She took each of the three medical analysis devices from her smock and ran them over Morg's head, abdomen, and lower body. When she finished looking at the read-outs on each device, she pushed a couple of buttons. A concerned look crossed her face as she started talking to Morg.

"I sure wish I knew what all this crap meant." She put the devices aside and continued. "Officer, don't say anything, just listen. I'm a Yandan agent. It's not important you know my name. I've been sent here to get a message to you from the Lead Trifect. If you understand what I've said, roll your head to the left and then to the right."

A smile crossed the agent's face as Morg did as she instructed. She began a hand examination of his head and chest area attempting to replicate how a real doctor would examine a patient.

"I'm going to give you a placebo pill. As I lift your head to take a drink, I'm going to slip a recording button into your ear. On the button is a message from the Lead Trifect. To activate the button simply touch it with a hand appendage. It will continue to play the same message until you want to stop it. To stop it, touch it again with an appendage. When you get up and walk around, crush the button between your appendages and dispose of it. If you understand, roll your right eye to the left."

"Good. Excellent. Okay, officer, here's the placebo."

Morg leaned forward and tried to lift his head like any good patient. He could barely feel the button entering his ear passage. There was no question the Landan had done this type of insertion before.

"Good luck to you, officer." The pretty aide winked and started an inspection tour of the ward as she made her way to the exit. She was lucky none of the patients asked for assistance and other aides didn't give her a second look.

Out of the corner of one eye, Morg watched the Landan walk away and eventually leave the ward. He didn't want to activate the button until she was gone. He kept his mind occupied by wondering once again what a wink meant.

"Officer Morg, this is the Lead Trifect. To confirm my identity, your commanding officer during the invasion of Goltog was Fritase and your mate is non-functioning. You have sent us one message in the ancient Yandan language used in battle. You have three offspring and they are driving us nuts trying to inherit your estate and benefits."

Morg was skeptical about the Trifect's identity until he described what his offspring were up to. After hearing that, he was absolutely certain the Lead Trifect was on the button recorder.

"Officer, I have a number of things to tell you. First, you are in extreme danger. I have reason to believe you and your cargo are kidnapping targets. It is likely that Prefect Conway from Earth will attempt to kidnap his son. There may be others looking to kidnap or kill you and your cargo. Unfortunately, I don't know their identities. Secondly, word has gotten out that you and your cargo were not killed in the transport explosion. When you checked in at Alpha 30 your identities were flagged and sent to the Palace. Unfortunately, we had an espionage agent in the Comm Center who intercepted that information and gave it to our enemies. Also, I'm sorry to report that Commander Fritase was killed in the transport explosion. I know the two of you had a deep respect for each other."

Morg wasn't sure he heard the Lead Trifect correctly. Transport explosion? Commander Fritase killed on the transport? What was the Lead Trifect talking about?

"We're not sure how you got on the ship that took you to Alpha 30. Thankfully, you avoided the explosion and found a way to the medical depot. The agent who inserted your recorder button has given us the information on your new ship, so we can track it. We ran the ship's identifier number and came up with nothing. According to our records, TED88987 doesn't exist. If you can, please provide the ship's flight signature."

Morg was becoming more confused as the recording played. The only thing which made sense was that he and the kid were in danger.

"We are confused by the coordinates you sent us in your coded message. There isn't anything at these coordinates. How could you stop at this location for repairs? Did you make a mistake? Please explain."

Morg understood that stellar charts wouldn't show a cloaked planet like Ziptowtheon. He needed to explain this discrepancy, but it seemed of secondary importance to everything else the Lead Trifect spoke about.

"Lastly, Officer Morg. I want you and your cargo off the medical depot planet as soon as possible. The longer you stay the more of a target you become. I understand the two of you are deathly ill, but you need to leave quickly. The Landan agent has hidden medical supplies and instructions in the cargo bay of your new ship. Await further instructions before proceeding to Earth. To communicate directly with me, use private comm number MIKE8788761. Good luck Officer and get well. I look forward to decorating you after the completion of this mission."

Morg listened to the Lead Trifect's message a half-dozen more times. Re-playing it didn't resolve any of his confusion. The transport no longer existed? The cargo bay of your new ship? What the hell did the Lead Trifect mean? It didn't take a genius to know the answer to these confusing details lay in the adjacent cot sound asleep.

There was no question his gut feeling about being watched was right. It also made him wonder how many assassins, kidnappers, and miscellaneous bad guys were gunning for them.

26

Morg woke to the Lead Trifect's message still playing. He had listened to it sub-consciously hundreds of times in his sleep.

The sleep and drugs rejuvenated him. He felt a little better and for the first time in days wanted to eat and go to the bathroom. This illness created strange symptoms and side effects. He couldn't remember the last time he relieved himself. And, food was the furthest thing from his mind. Morg loved to eat but this illness erased his desire for nourishment. For beings who were overweight, the illness was a great diet.

Morg glanced over at the Earthling. The kid was still out cold, softly snoring, and smiling at whoever was in his dream.

Morg rose carefully from his cot hoping he wouldn't lose his balance and topple over. Before he stood, he knew a simple task like walking was going to be a challenge. It was amazing how his legs and back weakened even though he spent less than a day resting in the cot. He finally stood but didn't attempt to walk. He had a bad case of vertigo and it needed to pass before he took the first step.

Ten minutes later he was out of the recovery ward and walking the aisles of the hospital. He felt reasonably well even though he moved like an old Yandan. Doctors, orderlies, and assistants ran every which way. The number of sick patients arriving at the medical depot almost doubled in less than two days. Morg hugged the hallway walls to avoid running into anyone. He was out for a stroll and a bit of exercise. He moved aside for the beings who were either in the process of dying or trying to save the dying.

Every so often Morg looked over his shoulder or used a reflective partition or window to look behind himself. He couldn't shake the feeling of being followed. Even with years of experience in espionage and counter-espionage, he couldn't identify the tail. Whoever was following him was very sneaky. This being was not a first-timer to the spy game. He was well-versed in the art of surveillance.

Up ahead Morg spotted a comm center. He ducked into one of the comm cubicles and shut the door. The door was a solid composite of noise abatement material and carbon metallic. It prevented anyone from seeing or hearing what he was doing, but it also prohibited Morg from seeing out. He didn't know if keeping his activities secret was a good trade-off for not spotting his follower.

On the second pulse, Jimmy Washington answered. The quick response caught Morg by surprise. He stumbled over his words until he could get his voice hole working correctly.

"Jim...., I mean, Jimmy. There you are. Morg here. I guess you know that. You can see me, can't you?"

Jimmy was having fun watching and listening to Morg trip over himself. He decided to take over the conversation so Officer Morg could collect his thoughts and calm down.

"Officer Morg, how are you? You don't look like you are in the best of health. Where are you?"

"I'm on Alpha 30 which is a medical depot. The Earthling and I are sick as Mulange dogs. I'm starting to feel a little better, but the kid's recovery is touch and go." Morg took a good look at Jimmy and could see his bruised and swollen face was nearly healed. What a change from the last time they communicated. "You look great, Jimmy. Have the enforcers left you alone?"

"Haven't seen them again, Morg. Of course, damn near everyone on Feltte Six is sick. The entire planet is quarantined. We haven't had a visitor ship in quite some time."

"How are Luna and Sam?"

"Not so good. They've been sick for days. I thought I was going to lose Sam the other night, but she pulled through."

"And you haven't caught the illness?"

"No, I've been very lucky. Just about the time I started recovering from my injuries, Luna and Sam came down with the illness. So, I've been taking care of them. What a twist of fate, huh?"

"It's incredible you haven't caught the bug yet. This medical depot is wall to wall sickness and death."

"Same here, Morg. The latest estimate I heard was about thirty percent of Feltte Six's population will die from the bug. They think it started here but don't know why. Another theory is it was brought here on a visitor ship. Some areas of the universe are referring to it as a plague."

Morg wanted to say something but could feel his energy waning. It was better to let Jimmy rattle on and save his energy for later in the conversation.

"I don't have the time to worry about how it started. The girls and I are barricaded in Luna's home. We have enough supplies to wait until this thing burns itself out. Well, that's enough about us. What are your plans, Morg?"

"Just get better, Jimmy. I'm not worrying about anything else other than that." There was no sense telling Jimmy about their troubles. It would take forever explaining the crazy things which happened to them after leaving Feltte Six. Some of it Morg couldn't explain because he didn't understand it. Besides, if Jimmy didn't know anything then it couldn't be beaten out of him.

"Jimmy, can I ask you a couple questions?"

"Sure, dude. Lay it on me."

Morg wasn't sure but thought Jimmy agreed to field his questions.

"The last time I spoke with Luna, she mentioned there were

three female Athlon mercenaries looking for me. Have you heard any more about these three?"

Jimmy squinched his eyes indicating he was thinking back to anything the girls may have said about the Athlon mercenaries. After a minute, his eyelids opened to reveal a gleam. "Yeah, Luna did say something. It was just a passing comment that she hadn't seen the Athlons in the blind pig since talking with you. That's about it."

"Okay. Just wondering." Jimmy knew there was a damn good reason why Morg asked about the mercenaries. Chances were that he was worried about them for a good reason. If Morg wanted to volunteer more about this subject, he'd say something. Otherwise, Jimmy wouldn't push Morg for more information.

"Another question for you. Have you ever heard of ancient lava flows on Feltte Six?"

This time, Jimmy had a quick answer. "Yeah, there's an old Feltte Six legend about lava fields. I don't know much about it, but it has something to do with the first beings who landed on Feltte Six. Supposedly, Feltte Six was a very inhospitable place at that time. Volcanoes were exploding often and spewing lava and poisonous gases. Most of the volcanic activity happened on the other side of the planet from where Sam and I live. Anyhow, the first inhabitants learned how to use the lava flows to stay alive. They became adept at using them to cook, stay warm and heat their homes. Here's the part that's very strange. Somehow, they used high-temperature lava to create oxygen and nitrogen in the planet's atmosphere. That, in turn, created water vapor which produced moisture. The moisture turned to rain which fell back to the planet. As the rain pounded the planet's surface the lava started to cool. It was a giant ecological circle which lasted thousands of years. Eventually, the volcanoes went dormant and the lava flows stopped. That's about all I know, Morg. I don't know if it's true or a fairy tale."

This time Jimmy couldn't help himself. "Morg, that's a really weird thing to ask me. What's up?"

At times it was hard for Morg to follow the words and terms

Jimmy used. He wasn't sure what a fairy tale was. He guessed it was the opposite of truth.

Morg wanted to be up-front and honest with Jimmy but explaining the reason for his question about lava fields was best left unsaid. Jimmy would have a tough time believing that Morg met a dying Trikian in deep space who might have found a Molum crystal mother-lode on Feltte Six. In fact, Morg was having difficulty believing such a far-fetched story. "Jimmy, I can't tell you now. But, after I do more research, I promise to explain."

"Okay, Morg. Just don't get your ass blown away. I want to hear this explanation." Even though Jimmy's comment was in jest, he knew Morg lived a dangerous life. It was his semi-sarcastic, thoughtful way of telling Morg he cared and wanted his friend to stay alive.

"Don't worry, I'll survive. Jimmy, I hate to ask you again, but can you send another message for me?"

"Sure. Sam did it the last time, but I remember how she did it. Is it going to the same private comm number?"

"No, different number this time. If you are ready, I'll give you the new number and message."

"The transceiver recorder is on. Go ahead, Officer."

Morg switched to the ancient Yandan dialect. He spoke slowly and carefully so the recorder picked up every nuance in his message. "Lead Trifect, Officer Morg. I received your message from the Landan agent. There must be some mistake. The Earthling and I took the E647 to Alpha 30. When the transport was refurbished on cloaked planet Ziptowtheon, it was given the new identifier number and changes to its exterior. The number is fake. The transport still has the same flight signature. Do not know what ship exploded. Do not understand how or why Commander Fritase died in explosion. I will interrogate cargo about these discrepancies when he recovers from the illness. Will leave Alpha 30 as soon as possible. Please confirm that primary destination Earth is on hold."

Morg stopped using the ancient Yandan dialect. "Jimmy, that's it. Send directly to private comm number MIKE8788761."

"Will do, Officer. Is there anything else you need?"

"I don't think so. That should be it. Say hello to the girls for me."

Morg was ready to end the communication when another thought raced through his mind. "Jimmy, wait. I have another question. Do you know anything about Luna's female life-giver?"

Morg's question about the lava flows was strange but this question was really off-the-wall. "Not a thing, Officer. Why would you ask that?"

"It's not that important, but I ran into a female Landan here who looks like an older Luna. The similarity is uncanny."

"Oh. Well, I'll ask Luna when she is feeling better. If it's her mother, I mean female life-giver, do you want to know?"

"No. It doesn't make any difference to me. Just thought Luna might like to know where her life-giver is. That's assuming they are related. Jimmy, take care. I'm signing off now."

Although Morg sat through the communication, the exchange with Jimmy drained most of his energy. He considered taking a nap in the comm cubicle which was very quiet. He decided not to because it would be too difficult sleeping upright. He needed to lay horizontal on something like a recovery cot. The downside of sleeping in the recovery ward was hearing the hacking, sneezing, moans, and groans of the other patients. His acute hearing made it much more difficult falling asleep. If it hadn't been for the side-effects of the bug and utter exhaustion, he may never have fallen asleep in the ward.

Morg left the comm cubicle and began the long, draining trek back to the recovery ward. He still had the feeling of being watched. He took every opportunity to check the halls and rooms for surveillance tails.

"Officer Morg, I have a vap pistol in the middle of your back. You are going to take us to your little friend."

Out of the corner of his eyes, Morg could see a burly being over each shoulder. The one on his left held the vap pistol in his back. Both were coughing and sneezing which meant they were sick and most likely registered patients.

"Which little friend is that.... what's your name?"

"Never mind who we are. Just take us to that punk you brought to Feltte Six."

Now he knew who he was dealing with. It was the two enforcers that wanted to interrogate the Earthling about something which happened on Feltte Six. God only knew what mischief the kid got into at the Detroit 67 park. It must have been bad if two Feltte Six enforcers went AWOL to track the kid across the universe to a medical outpost.

"I don't think you'll get anything out of the Earthling."

"Why is that, Yandan?"

"Because he was out cold when I left him an hour ago. He's sick, just like you two. In fact, he's sicker than either of you."

"We'll worry about that. Your job is to get us to him if you want to stay alive."

Morg thought about disarming the two Feltte Six enforcers but knew he didn't have enough energy. Any other time they would be on their backs gasping for air.

As they meandered through the hallways, Morg wondered what the enforcers planned to do. They certainly couldn't assault the Earthling with hundreds of patients and workers in the recovery ward. They could silently kill the Earthling, but their chances of escaping Alpha 30 were slim to none. That left only one reasonable idea; kidnap the kid. Morg hoped these two slugs would take him along. He wanted to hear what the kid did on Feltte Six. Plus, he needed to hang on to the kid for the sake of his home planet and whatever scheme the Lead Trifect was cooking up. If the enforcers made the mistake of trying to assassinate him, they would end up on the wrong end of six decades of invasion trooper martial arts.

"Who are those two beings?"

"I don't know. They obviously don't like Morg. That's a vap pistol in his back."

The two female Athlon mercenaries lay on separate floating gurneys pretending to be deathly ill and uninterested in anything other than their illness. When Morg and his two captors walked by, they were no more than twelve feet away. They might be able to take out Morg at this distance, but then they would have to shoot it out with his captors. Until they figured out what was going on, it was better to get off their gurneys and follow at a discreet distance.

"Sister look at the pants those two are wearing. Aren't they the same design as the pants worn with Feltte Six uniforms?"

"I think you are right, sister."

"I wonder what two Feltte Six enforcers want with Officer Morg?"

"Maybe it has something to do with the death of our fathers."

"Possibly, but I don't think Feltte Six would send enforcers after Morg just because some of their visitors were killed by another guest. That doesn't make sense."

"You're right, sister. There must be another reason. I just hope Morg isn't taken back to Feltte Six for trial and execution. I want that privilege."

27

"Welcome, sir. How are you? I was very glad to get your message about meeting today."

The Mentat entered Millard Miller's private office and sat in the chair of authority at the meeting table. Normally, he wouldn't take the chair at the head of the table but referred to as "sir" gave him the courage to flaunt his new-found, self-confidence.

"Mr. Miller, the pleasure is all mine."

"Have you considered what we talked about the last time? Have you made a decision?"

"Yes, Mr. Miller, I have made a decision. I want to join your crusade against Prefect Conway".

Miller and the Mentat didn't say another word. Each was wrestling with thoughts racing through their minds. The Mentat questioned whether his decision to join Miller was wise. He had no problem sticking a knife in Conway's back. The man was an obese, abusive low-life. Everything and everyone he touched wilted and died a slow and horrendous death. He was bad for Earth, the solar system and universe. No matter how good his promises sounded they ultimately ended in doom.

What disturbed the Mentat was breaking his promise and contract with his superiors. If they found out about his disloyalty, he would be banished from the Mentat ranks and never allowed to return to the home planet of Mentattis.

Being chosen and trained as a Mentat was a great honor. Only the best of the brightest were selected for a Mentat internship. The training was arduous and lasted twenty years. It wasn't easy learning how to read the minds of other beings. Mentat interns gave up all personal relationships and once they entered training, contact with friends and family ceased. The drop-out rate was close to fifty percent. Those who didn't make the grade were banished to an outlying planet to live out the rest of their days in Spartan-like conditions. Their brains were neuro-cleansed so none of the secrets from Mentat training were passed on to outsiders.

He tried to convince himself that what he was about to do was for the betterment of the Mentat Service. It was a very risky gamble considering the Service produced most of the income for their planet. Deep-down he knew his disloyalty would be considered treason. There was no explanation or excuse the Mentat Service Ruling Council would accept. If they gave in to his argument for turning on Conway, the credibility of the Mentat Service was worthless. No leader or being of prominence in the universe would hire another Mentat. The fall-out from his disloyalty would have devastating consequences for every being on Mentattis. The economy would crash, and disorder would ripple throughout the universe.

Millard Miller knew the Mentat's cooperation was a double-edged sword. With the Mentat close to Conway it would be easier to keep tabs on the louse. Even though he was unpredictable, the information provided by Beth and the Mentat would help to checkmate every move Conway considered.

The downside of taking the Mentat into their rebellion group was that nothing could be kept from him. The Mentat could read minds as easily as a Rheno beast could shed and grow a new horn. Millard knew he would have to be upfront with the Mentat on everything. It would be impossible to lie or tell half-truths. Hiding or sugar-coating information was out. Only straight-up, unadulterated facts were acceptable.

The point of turning back on their allegiance passed when the Mentat sat down at the meeting table. From that point on they were comrades in rebellion. Their goal was simple. Keep Prefect Conway from upsetting the balance of power in the universe. The difficulty was anticipating Conway's irrational behavior and fighting him on multiple fronts. Plus, his secret police were everywhere.

"May I ask you a question, Mr. Miller?"

"Of course. You are part of the brotherhood now. What's on your mind?"

"Is Beth loyal to our cause? Can we trust her?"

Miller expected some tough questions from the Mentat but didn't anticipate this one. It was a loaded question with several considerations. His answer wouldn't be simple. It would be as complex as the question.

"Before I answer, why do you ask?"

"I'm not an expert on human behavior, but it seems to me that anyone who sells their body and mind as easily as Beth might do the same with their loyalty. Do you understand my concern, Secretary-General Miller?"

"I understand completely. The only answer I can give you is that Beth hasn't done or said anything to make me doubt her loyalty. However, she is a woman subject to emotions you and I don't understand or experience. Can she be bought for a price? Frankly, I don't know. My advice is to be cautious around her. Treat her like a poisonous viper you have raised from birth."

The Mentat detected no deception in Miller's answer. In fact, the truth in his answer was flawless.

"What do you need me to do?"

"Now, nothing other than report on what Conway is doing and thinking. That would include anything about his son, the CASETA Agreement with Yanda and his new alliance with Florid."

The Mentat knew Miller's answer was incomplete. It wasn't dishonest, it was simply missing pertinent information. He waited to see if Miller would add the remaining facts.

"Is there anything else, Secretary-General?"

Miller knew he was backed into a corner. The Mentat was picking up on his partial answer. He now had a choice. Tell him the entire truth or delay the truth.

"Sir, I appreciate your ability to know when I'm withholding information. That's the case now. To be honest, I can't tell you everything now. When the time comes, I promise to provide you with the remaining information. I'm sorry, but that's the best I can do for now."

Miller's explanation was straightforward and honest even if it didn't plug all the holes. The Mentat had a choice. Either get up and quit the rebellion or accept Miller's explanation. He decided to trust Miller and wait. He would give Miller a reasonable amount of time to divulge whatever he was withholding. If this veiled item continued to linger beyond a reasonable amount of time, he could always withdraw from the rebellion. At least, he hoped that was an option.

"I will defer to your judgement, Secretary-General."

"Thank you. I promise to pass on the remaining information as soon as I can."

The Mentat began to get up from the table to leave even though he perceived something else on the Secretary-General's mind. Leaving a meeting abruptly was one tactic Mentats used to get more information. Most beings spoke whatever was on their minds rather than let a trusted Mentat leave a meeting in haste.

"Sir, there is one other thing I need to tell you."

The Mentat pretended to be surprised and sat back down in his chair.

"I have sent an assassin to Alpha 30 to deal with Prefect Conway's kid. He should arrive there within a couple hours."

The Mentat concealed his surprise even though he was somewhat shocked. He had no idea Conway's kid was alive. This was the first he heard that the kid survived the explosion and wasn't blown to bits in a deep space. Prefect Conway doubted his son's death from the first reports of the explosion. But that was sheer conjecture which obviously wasn't speculation any longer.

"Our source at the Yandan palace told us that Joseph Conway checked in at Alpha 30 which is a medical depot. The kid is quite ill. I was hoping to get lucky and the kid would not survive the epidemic, but I've been told he will recover. Now, I must take matters into my own hands."

Miller paused for a moment trying to get an idea of whether this was new or old news for the Mentat. It was no use. The Mentat had a poker face and didn't make any movements which might indicate what he did or did not know.

"Did you know Conway's kid was still alive?"

"I did not, Secretary-General. I did know Prefect Conway was withholding vital information but didn't know what it was. The problem with the Prefect is that he is always withholding information from me. Also, he won't field any questions so it's impossible to determine what he is withholding. The only time he gives up information is when he gets mad and blurts out what is on his mind. At times, he will be careless with his thoughts when he is around Beth."

"Well, you know now. Keep tuned in to Conway for more information about his son. As I said, you should hear soon what my assassin does to the kid."

28

BETH AND PREFECT CONWAY WERE HAVING A QUAINT MORNING chat over Fuchi and pastries. It was unusual for Conway to sit and talk with her after sex. Normally, he bolted from the bedroom and sprinted to his office to plot havoc and chaos throughout the universe. Planning the takedown of the Yandan empire was his true sexual release. Beth was only a fill-in.

"Beth, can you keep a secret?"

She rolled her eyes and said, "I can't believe you asked that, Honey Nuts."

He could see the irritation under her smile so he backtracked quickly. "Okay, okay, I was kidding. But you have to promise to keep this a secret."

He waited for her to agree but she continued to stare a hole into him. She wasn't going to agree to anything more this morning. Sex was enough.

"My son, Joseph, is alive. Isn't that great?"

The bite of pastry in Beth's mouth almost flew out. She took a quick sip of Fuchi to flush the pastry down before choking on it.

"How do you know that? I thought he was killed in an explosion."

"It doesn't matter how I know, I just do. He's on a medical depot planet getting treated for the epidemic. I knew the SOB was too smart to get blown up by a terrorist or rogue interceptor. And, there was no way his transport accidentally imploded with that much force. I'll tell you, Beth. He's a pain-in-the-ass but smart as hell. He's exactly like his old man."

Beth acted mildly interested. If she acted very interested and asked a bunch of questions, Conway would get suspicious. She took another bite of pastry and sip from the Fuchi cup. She held herself back from racing over to the Cannis dispenser and taking a couple hits. It would be easier stomaching this terrible news if she were high.

"Is he going to get well?"

"My sources tell me he will definitely recover, but I'm going to make sure he gets home safe and sound."

"What do you mean?"

"I sent someone after him. He needs to get to Earth quick. It will be good for his health and I need him."

Beth gave Honey Nuts a weak smile as he got up to leave the room.

"You have a wonderful day, Bethie." Conway leaned over and gave her a peck on the cheek.

Beth sat at the table dumbfounded as she watched him strut from the bedroom. She didn't know whether to cry, laugh or puke. He was so elated by the news he called her Bethie. She had warned him once before never to call her that. Now she would have to punish him somehow. Withholding sex for a couple weeks always worked well.

Finding out that Prefect Conway's brat kid was still alive ruined her day. She had a severe headache and thought about going back to bed. But duty called. She needed to pass this information on to Millard Miller. He would be her first stop of the day. Good old Miller would know what to do. He was a clever guy who could figure out how this news affected the group's plan to overthrow Prefect Conway.

29

"Do you have to hold that vap pistol so damn hard against my shell? I'm not going to run away. I can hardly walk."

The enforcer took the vap pistol off Morg's shell. From one to two inches from his back, the pistol could put Morg down before he took one step in the wrong direction.

"Remember Yandan, the pistol is still close enough to put a big hole in you. So, don't try anything stupid. Understand?"

"Yeah, I understand." Morg took a few more steps before asking another question.

"What did the Earthling do on Feltte Six to get you two so ticked off?"

The enforcer debated whether he should answer or not. He didn't owe the Yandan an explanation but talking might draw less attention and help them blend into the crowd.

"He was a bad boy. He didn't dispose of a few corpses. In fact, you are guilty of that violation too."

"What do you mean, I didn't kill anyone?"

"True, but you are responsible for the kills your buddy made."

"How can I be responsible? I didn't know he killed anyone."

"That's your problem, Yandan. You arrived on Feltte Six with him, so he was your responsibility. You were told the rules at the reception center."

The enforcer was right, but the rule didn't make sense. How could a being be responsible for something he didn't know about? So much for the ancient axiom, ignorance is bliss.

"So, what is the penalty for this ghastly crime?"

"Up to and including death. And, I can do without your sarcasm, Yandan."

Morg could only shake his head in disbelief. There was no use debating with the enforcer.

"That's one hell of a regulation you have. By the way, who did the Earthling kill?"

"Athlon mercenaries."

Morg froze. The enforcer was looking around when Morg stopped walking. He bounced off the larger Yandan and caught himself at the last second before taking a tumble. Morg didn't know how close he came to a vap hole in his back. The enforcer could have easily squeezed the trigger on the vap pistol by mistake.

Morg thought about calling the enforcer a liar, but deep down he knew the revelation was correct. It explained how Crex, Blex, and Stex fell off the grid one-by-one. It also explained how the Earthling avoided three trained assassins gunning for him. The kid had turned the tables on the mercenaries and made them his prey.

Morg couldn't understand how three professional killers could fall victim to a twerp like the Earthling. They were in better physical condition and had years of experience hunting together like a pack of Beltrini wolves. There was only one possible explanation. The kid was smarter. He used intelligence to outwit his pursuers.

"Move ahead, Yandan."

Morg started walking again. It was another fifty steps before he asked, "Is that all he did on Feltte Six?"

"No, your little friend thought it would be fun to burn down a brothel and kill one of my brother enforcers."

Finally, here was the crime which got the enforcers upset enough to travel across the universe to hunt down the kid. Morg didn't bother to say anything. The kid was dead if these enforcers got to him. And, they wouldn't think twice about taking out the Yandan escort too.

"What are your plans for the Earthling?"

"We're taking him back to Feltte Six for judgement. But, if he gives us a tough time, he might not make it there."

Both enforcers chuckled under their breath. Morg knew what that meant. These two had no intention of taking the kid any further than a remote field to kill him.

"I shouldn't tell you this, but the Earthling is under Yandan diplomatic protection. You harm him, and you'll have to answer to the Yandan Trifect."

"We're not going to worry about the Trifect. What they don't know can't hurt us."

Morg knew he had to figure out a way to get rid of these two. They were out for blood and nothing was going to stop them. He thought the best opportunity to take out the enforcers was in the recovery ward. The place was a chaotic circus. Beings scurried every which way, bumping into each other and stumbling over fixtures. With luck, something would happen to attract the enforcer's attention for a fraction of a second. That's all Morg needed to neutralize these two buffoons. If something didn't occur by happenstance, then he would take a chance and attack.

"I'd give anything to know what they are talking about."

"Do you think we dare get closer and try to listen?"

"No, better not. We'll keep a safe distance. Did you see how Morg stopped dead in his tracks? Something the Feltte enforcer said got to him."

The female Athlon mercenary on the floatation gurney grunted in agreement. At the next hallway corner, she would switch places with her sister. Pushing the gurney would give her a better surveillance view of Morg and his captors.

As they walked along, Morg had time to think back to all the bizarre things the Earthling did on Feltte Six. It now made sense why he dressed up as a redhead female to board the transport. The authorities were after him and only a disguise could get him on the ship. Then, he was in such a hurry to leave the planet. And, when the Feltte Six Interceptors appeared, he begged Morg to destroy them with Thermax projectiles. Yes, the kid was a felon on the lam and his past was catching up with him.

Morg thought he saw the entrance to the recovery ward fifty-yards ahead. As they drew closer, he could read the large sign above the entrance door; "RECOVERY WARD C". He knew there were less than ten minutes to make something happen. It had to be something favorable which would get him and the kid out of the jam they were in.

His hope for a momentary distraction happened as they entered the recovery ward. Halfway down the main aisle, on the right side of the ward, Morg saw a cluster of beings gathered around a recovery cot. The cot was exactly where Morg left the kid. He guessed the group size at a dozen beings. There were a couple doctors and two or three assistants. Other than the hospital personnel, Morg had no idea who the others were. With his acute hearing, Morg could tell these beings were arguing. He couldn't hear individual words, but the tone of their argument was combative. At one point, a non-medical being pushed a doctor away in disgust. Two other beings came to the doctor's aid and a small ruckus of pushing and shoving broke out.

The two enforcers talked to each other between sneezing and wiping gunk from their eyes. In the brief time they were at Morg's back, their health deteriorated. Morg didn't think they were aware of this change. Also, they had no idea they were being led into a physical altercation. Morg's odds were increasing. Maybe a good old-fashioned brawl was all he needed to shake off the crazed Feltte Six killers.

Within thirty yards of the kid's cot, Morg could hear every word bantered back and forth between the antagonists. The gist of their argument was whether the kid was well enough to leave the recovery ward. The doctors and assistants insisted he was too ill to leave. They were backed by a couple of hospital security guards. The remaining beings in the group were Earthlings who demanded to have the kid released. One Earthling claimed to represent the kid's father, Prefect Conway. The other Earthling didn't identify himself.

In the midst of the argument, Morg heard the kid make a couple comments. His voice was weak and hard to pick out, but it was him. At times, he wanted to leave the ward with an Earthling. Then he changed his mind and was too weak to leave. Morg couldn't see the kid but could tell he was still dazed.

Before the Feltte Six enforcers knew what happened, Morg walked them into the middle of the argument. The two female Athlon mercenaries who were close on their heels couldn't help themselves. When they lost sight of Morg, they marched into the small mob like flying insects to a bright light at night.

Morg separated from the enforcers and went to the kid's bedside. Even though the kid was awake and sitting up, it was obvious he was still quite ill. He was as white as a ghost and his bleary eyes showed little interest in his situation. He was in no condition to travel anywhere.

"Earthling, can you hear me? It's Morg. Can you understand me?"

The Earthling slowly turned his head around to look at Morg. A slight twinkle lit his eyes when he saw Morg. He opened his mouth to say something. Morg leaned close to hear his words over the shouting and screaming happening around the cot.

"Morg, who are these beings?"

"It doesn't matter. I'll explain later. Listen closely, kid. Are you listening?"

"Yeah, yeah, I hear you Morg."

Morg whispered in the kid's ear, "When the fighting starts, roll off the cot and lay flat on the ground. Do you understand?"

Morg didn't have a chance to hear the kid's answer. The argument around the cot escalated to a full-scale brawl. Threats, accusations, and foul-mouth descriptions flew around the circle. Each adversary claimed authority over the Earthling. They took turns demanding the others leave immediately. Everyone stood their ground. Yelling turned to screaming, pushing led to thrown punches. It was a free-for-all with each assailant turning on the others.

The Earthling was having difficulty getting off the cot. Morg gave him a push in the back and watched him fall to the floor. He then dove under the cot from the opposite side and grabbed the Earthling. As he pulled the Earthling under the cot the first vap pistol rounds exploded. One of the female Athlon mercenaries fell to the floor with a vap hole through her head. Luna's description of the female mercenaries was right. They were butt ugly and smelled terrible.

Another body fell to the floor on the kid's side of the cot. Morg had no idea who this Earthling was.

The battle escalated. Vap and laser rounds flew in every direction. Most of the patients in the recovery ward were too sick to care about the death and destruction taking place close by. The healthier ones hobbled or crawled to the nearest exit. Every so often, someone cried out in pain. It was easy for Morg to distinguish the mortally wounded from the injured who would recover.

Morg looked out from under the cot. On every side, he could only see for twenty to thirty-feet before his vision was blocked by overturned fixtures, cots, and bodies. None of the combatants were observable. Based on the ricochet echoes from the vap rounds, Morg estimated that each combatant was concealed at least fifty feet from his location.

Nothing good was going to come from this battle. The longer they stayed in the middle, the more chance they would be casualties. Morg grabbed the dead Athlon's vap pistol and crawled out from under the cot. He scurried like a crab across the floor dragging the Earthling. He was surprised they weren't peppered with pistol fire. It could only mean the combatants were too busy shooting at each other to notice the Yandan and near-lifeless Earthling.

Morg was within ten feet of the exit door when he was hit in the left shoulder by a pistol round. He rolled to his right side and put a round between the eyes of his attacker. The Athlon enforcer fell face-forward to the floor. A "what-the-hell-just-happened" expression was still on his face after bouncing off the floor.

Morg ignored the wound and pain and scurried toward the door. Getting to safety, outside the perimeter of battle, was more important than doing a field dressing on his shoulder. Five feet later he cleared the recovery ward exit doors and ducked behind a wall with the Earthling. Three or four rounds sliced through the door closest to him. As the door swung back and forth, Morg took a quick peek into the ward to see who fired the rounds. Whoever it was ducked behind an obstruction. He knew approximately where the assassin was in the ward but couldn't see him or her.

The hole in his shoulder was one inch in diameter. It wasn't a direct hit going completely through the shoulder. It entered slightly above the armpit, at an acute angle, and exited at the top of his shoulder. Morg moved his arm to assess the damage. He could only lift it to a ninety-degree angle. During his career as an Invasion Trooper, he'd suffered several more serious wounds, but this one ranked high as most debilitating.

Time was in short supply. He had to get himself and the Earthling off Alpha 30. Morg grabbed a linen off a floatation gurney and ripped it into a couple five- by eight-inch strips. He took one of the strips and jammed each end into the entry and exit points of his wound. This would slow down the loss of body fluids until the wounds could be surgically cauterized and closed. He tied the remaining strip around his wrist for later use.

Putting the floatation gurney linen into his exposed wounds was a huge risk. It was probably swarming with infectious bacteria and viruses. But, in the middle of a fire-fight, he couldn't be picky. His first priority was getting to the transporter and blasting off. If the Trifect's Landan agent was truthful, there were medical supplies in the transport's cargo bay. He could patch himself up the best he could and then wait for the kid to get better and finish the job.

Morg picked up the kid and tossed him onto the empty floatation gurney. It would be a lot easier pushing the kid through the hallways to the departure dock than carrying him. He laid the vap pistol next to the kid and trotted away. He wanted to run but his gnarled feet with spurs on each heel limited him to a fast trot.

Morg pushed the gurney as hard as his sickly body allowed. He could see that the hallway ended at a "T" approximately fifty yards ahead. He didn't have a clue which way led to the docking bay. He decided to take whichever hallway had the most floatation gurneys in it. With all the new arrivals landing on Alpha 30, the hallway flooded with gurneys should be the one coming from the docking bay.

He rounded the corner at the "T" just ahead of two laser rounds shattering the wall. Bits of the hallway rained down on everyone within thirty feet. He didn't need to look back at the damage caused by the laser rounds. One second slower and he would have been splattered over everyone in the hallway.

The new hallway was jammed with gurneys, doctors, assistants and the sick. Most of them heard the laser rounds but were confused about what was happening. They were frozen in place blocking Morg's path.

"Get out of the way. Take cover. Move. Take cover. Get out of the way, dammit."

None of the beings moved. They stared at Morg like he was a carnival freak. Unless he could get them to move, he and the kid were headed for an intense firefight with whoever was chasing them. In an act of desperation, Morg took his vap pistol and fired several rounds down the hall, slightly above head level. That's all it took. Every being in the hallway scattered. They disappeared into adjacent rooms or tried to make themselves invisible by hiding under gurneys and behind each other. Morg did a double-take and smiled at a being hiding behind the gurney linen he held up.

Morg took off again winding his way through the remaining clutter in the hallway. Every forty to fifty yards he fired a few more bursts from the pistol. He found it ironic how the sound of a vap pistol could get the sickest beings to find enough energy to flee in fear.

Morg almost missed the entrance door to the docking bay. At the last second, he saw the ships lined up through the door window. He did a U-turn with the gurney and burst onto the docking bay platform. Less than three ships ahead were two hospital security officers. Their job was to provide security and safety to incoming patients and hospital staff. A good amount of their time was spent preventing theft from the ships and patients.

Morg could tell from the expressions on their faces that they were looking for something or someone. He guessed they received word about pistol-wielding maniacs heading toward the docking bay. He needed to get by them as fast as possible and find the transport. He vaguely remembered that the transport was on the other end of the docking bay.

He tucked the vap pistol under the Earthling and pushed the gurney up to the security officers. Sobbing and acting like a frightened child, he pleaded with the officers. "Please help me and my friend. There are crazy beings shooting laser guns in the hallway. They are right behind me. They'll be here any minute. Please stop them. They are killing everyone in sight. They're out of their minds."

Morg's acting had the desired effect. "Move along Yandan. We'll take care of this." The officers unharnessed their weapons and proceeded to the entrance door.

Morg didn't wait to see what happened. He dashed off, pushing his way through the mob of beings on the dock. When he couldn't move the gurney any further, he hoisted the Earthling onto his shoulder and forced his way through the crowd. Within two minutes, weapon fire erupted at the end of the docking bay he came from. He wanted to believe the security officers either killed or stopped the aggressor, but his gut knew better. Officers working on medical depots rarely had military and combat experience. They were outmatched by the aggressor gunning for Morg and the kid.

He could see the transport tethered by a harness beam in its stall.

All he needed was another two to three minutes to get safely aboard. With the Earthling on his shoulder, Morg ran up to the transport and yelled out the voice recognition entrance code. "Officer Morg-Operation Earth".

As Morg waited for the ramp to open, he scanned the docking bay. The weapon fire had stopped at the far end of the bay. The pursuer had made short order of the security officers. Although he couldn't see the enemy hunter heading his way, he could feel him closing in.

"Earthling, can you hear me?"

A weak, "yeah" drifted down to Morg.

"Listen. If anything happens to me, there's epidemic medicine and supplies in the cargo bay. Got it?"

Morg didn't know if the kid responded or not. He was too busy scurrying up the boarding ramp. The clackety-clack noise he made on the metallic ramp could have easily drowned out the kid's response. By the top of the ramp, he was winded from carrying the kid and had little energy left.

He gave the closing voice command and started to lower the kid to the floor. He needed to get to the bridge and prepare for take-off. The kid could stay where Morg dropped him until they were outside of Alpha 30's space boundary.

Morg took one step toward the bridge and was hit in the back by a laser round. It sent him flying head over heels. He came down hard on his face. The last thing he remembered was hearing the ramp door close with a thud.

30

"Can't I spend one evening with my mate without interruption by some type of universe emergency? Why is it these *can't-wait* emergencies never happen during the normal working day?"

"We're sorry, Lead Trifect. You instructed us to inform you about every important new incident."

The Lead Trifect fell into the primary chair at the Trifect conference table. So far, it was a terrible night. He wanted to spend a quiet evening at home but ended up arguing with his mate. He couldn't even remember what the dispute was about. Getting called to the palace by his underlings was the lesser of two evils. However, he wouldn't admit this to them.

"Yeah, yeah, yeah. Okay, you're right. So, what's so important it couldn't wait until tomorrow?"

"There's been a deadly firefight at the Alpha 30 medical depot. It involved Officer Morg and the Earthling."

"Are they still alive?"

"We're not sure, Lead Trifect. The ship they arrived in blasted off around the same time as the firefight. The authorities on Alpha 30 are trying to identify the dead and account for anyone missing. It's going to take a while because they are stretched to the limit taking care of epidemic patients. The number of sick arriving at the depot hasn't let up yet."

The Lead Trifect began to analyze this latest information. He predicted a kidnapping attempt of the Earthling but never thought it would erupt into a firefight. He looked across the table at the other two Trifect. He could tell by the expressions on their faces they were withholding more bad information.

"Is that it?"

His underlings hemmed and hawed. "Well, there's a couple more things, Lead Trifect."

"Out with it. I haven't got all night."

"Our Landan agent on Alpha 30 was assassinated. She was found in a utility closet with a vap hole in her head."

The loss of one agent wasn't going to upset the balance of power in the universe, but in this case, it was significant. The agent's death told the Lead Trifect the assassin was most likely a professional. He was a sly and shrewd killer. He saw through the Landan's doctor disguise and probably saw her put the recording button in Morg's ear. It was also reasonable to assume the assassin followed the Landan agent and watched her load supplies onto Morg's ship. God forbid, he got the ramp entrance code out of her before putting a vap hole in her head.

"That's very bad news. Don't ask me to explain. It's too late. I'll explain some other time. What else have you got?"

One of his underlings was about to answer when the Lead Trifect interrupted. "What direction did the Morg and Earthling ship head when it left Alpha 30?"

"To Earth at normal shadow-drive speed."

The Lead Trifect put his head face down on the table. He wanted to sleep and tune out the rest of this conversation. The last thing he wanted to hear was that Morg's ship was heading to Earth. Morg was under direct orders to avoid an Earth flight pattern until instructed to do so. Morg would never ignore Trifect orders, so someone else must be in command of the ship. That left only three possibilities. He was either dead, comatose or under restraint by a captor. Of course, this assumed he was on the ship.

"I'm afraid to ask. Is there anything else?"

This time the underlings were very hesitant to answer. They spent a half-hour before the Lead Trifect got to the palace trying to figure out how to explain this next bit of information.

"Ah, ah, this doesn't have anything to do with Alpha 30, Lead Trifect. This concerns something else we haven't talked about for a few days. We didn't know anything about this, so please don't ...."

"If you don't spit it out now, I'm going to throttle both of you. Now, knock off the crap."

"The Shooting Star 38 has a destiny explosion device on it."

"What the hell does that mean?"

"It means the Shooting Star is linked to its assigned pilot by genetics. If the assigned pilot doesn't sit in the captain's gyro chair once every five days, the 38 self-destructs."

"Whose idea was that?"

"We've been told it was the idea of one of our physicists. He thought the ship needed an extra level of protection from espionage because of its new and sensitive technology. That's why he put a destiny explosive on it."

"Interesting. Let me see if I have this right. Commander Fritase was the assigned pilot for the Shooting Star. The Commander is dead, so he won't be sitting in the captain's gyro chair. So, in a couple of days, the Shooting Star will self-destruct, wherever the hell it is. Of course, we don't know, because we lost it. Is that an adequate description of the Shooting Star situation?"

"Well, there is one other thing. If we find the Shooting Star within the five-day limit, the destiny explosive can be overridden from Yanda."

The Lead Trifect broke into a smile which was rare for a Yandan. The smile led to a laugh which led to a deep belly laugh. The underlings didn't understand what was going on. Laughing was almost unheard of for a Yandan. All the underlings could think of was that the Lead Trifect was very mad and the laughing was a cover-up.

It took the Lead Trifect a couple minutes to stop laughing and wipe the secretions from his sensory gills.

"Gentlemen, that's the best news I've heard tonight. Again, don't ask me to explain. I'm going home to get some rest."

The Lead Trifect's mood improved considerably since arriving at the palace. The underlings had no idea why but felt good about a meeting ending with laughter. Most meetings ended with the underlings cursed and crawling off like whipped dogs.

The Lead Trifect got up from the table and headed for the door. At the last second, he turned around and said, "Get ahold of the Alpha 30 director. Tell him he's got three hours to provide a list of the dead and missing. Also, I want to know exactly who was on the ship that took off. I'm sure there are video recorders on their docking bay. I don't give a shit about the epidemic patients. Getting my information is more important. If he values his budget for next year, he'll do precisely what I ask and fast."

31

"Good god, Morg. What did you do to yourself?"

As the Earthling worked on Morg's wounds, he kept talking to himself. When he ran out of gibberish to say, he whistled tunes from his teenage years. It was the only way he could stay awake. He had at least another hour of surgical repair on the Yandan before bedding down for some much-needed sleep. If he didn't get the wounds cleaned, cauterized, and filled in with surgical putty before passing out, the Yandan would die.

He needed the Yandan to survive. In fact, he was desperate to make sure Morg pulled through. Without another experienced pilot, he was sure the maniacs who tried to kill them on Alpha 30 would overtake the transport and board it. Any other time auto-pilot was good enough while he and Morg recuperated. But, not this time. Auto-pilot couldn't evade and destroy pursuing interceptors.

"Ya know, Morg. You are one large-ass being. It took me over an hour to drag you to sickbay. If it wasn't for the hydraulic lift, I never would have gotten you onto this cot."

The kid snipped away Morg's outer vest and scales around the wound holes. The scales were damaged beyond saving. If he did an adequate job of patching, the scales would grow back.

"Okay, let's see what we've got. Ah, two entrance and two exit holes. All are in the trilateral quadrant of the left shoulder. Looks like only one of the lipten conduits was hit. That conduit needs to be fused back together, which I'll do right now."

The Earthling lowered a magnifier over the wound, so he could get a better view of the conduit damage. "Okay, I'll fuse here and a little bit over here. Looks like the seepage is slowing down. Ah yes, here's another big perforation. I'll fuse that, once, twice, and a third time. And, that should do it. No more loss of lipten. One problem taken care of."

The Earthling leaned back and admired his work. He had never done surgery like this. He had read about Yandan anatomy and the use of fusegranators. With that knowledge and a genius IQ, it was only a matter of fusing body parts back together. It wasn't much different from the construction set he played with as a child.

He went on talking as he worked on the Yandan. "It's a damn good thing you're passed out Morg. With this much probing and cleansing of your wounds, you'd be screaming for mercy if you were awake. Even with heavy doses of painkiller you would be howling. I don't care how much of a badass Invasion Trooper you are. This would hurt like hell. Don't wake up, buddy, if you know what's good for you."

The Earthling rotated his head and arched his back to prevent getting cramps. "Okay, let's take a look. Everything is cleaned out pretty good. I don't see any other conduit or organ damage. Crap, there's a torn tension ligament. Well, I knew this was going too smooth. I'll put this growth patch between the two ends of the ligament. Over time it will grow back together good as new. There we go. Now, I can start the sterilization and then close up everything."

The kid continued patching and repairing Morg's shell. Anyone watching would have thought he was a trained battlefield surgeon.

He used the manual and automated surgical tools and supplies with the precision of a trained medical professional.

"Ya know, Morg. It's a damn good thing I have a photographic memory. Can you believe I remembered how to repair your lipten conduit? Now, be honest, Morg. Who else, other than a trained surgeon, would know how to mend these wounds? What did you say? You're right! Nobody in the universe could do as well as your buddy, good old First Comrade Joseph Q. Conway."

The kid gave himself a few moments of quiet time waiting for Morg's response which would never come. "I bet you didn't know I had an official title. That's right, I'm a First Comrade. I'm a big deal, Morg. I have an army of ten thousand warriors waiting for my command to invade Yanda and her allies. And, that's not all. I plan to take out my old man as soon as Yanda is conquered. Now, here's a trick question for you, Morg. You ready? Okay, once Yanda is crushed and my old man is disposed of, guess what I'll be?"

"Tick-tock, tick-tock, tick-tock." The kid pretended to be an antique clock counting down the remaining time available for the comatose Morg to answer the question.

"I'm sorry, Morg. Time's up. The correct answer is; drumroll please." The kid slapped his knees in quick repetition, imitating a drum. "Yours truly will be King of the Universe. And, my queen will be the graceful and lovely Beth from planet Earth. Can you believe it, Morg? The putz you spent weeks with flying in this transport tub will rule the universe. Hell, I might have a position for you when I take over."

The kid started laughing but stopped when his lungs protested in pain. They felt like they were on fire and got worse when the coughing started. The coughing fit, chills and spasms were a reminder he was still at the mercy of the epidemic. The medicine he found in the cargo bay helped but it would be a long road back to total recovery.

It took close to five minutes before the kid caught his breath and finished Morg's surgery. "Damn, that hurt. That's another good reason you should stay unconscious, Morg. You won't have to deal with this lousy illness. By the way, I owe you an apology. I'm ashamed to tell you this, but I was the one who killed your mate. She came to the transport to see you and ended up overhearing my communication with a fellow co-conspirator. I tried to reason with her, but she wouldn't have any of it. I didn't have a choice. I couldn't let her tell you or anyone about my plans to overthrown Yanda. I knifed her when she turned to leave the transport and then carried her into the cargo bay. I made myself a sandwich and sat down to decide what to do with her. A couple of docking bay agents boarded the transport, so I stashed her body behind some containers. I thought I'd have time to dispose of her but never got around to it. The next thing I knew, we launched and were well outside Yanda's boundary. I figured you'd smell the corpse, but you never did. That's why I finally said something about it. Sorry, buddy. It wasn't intentional."

The kid worked in silence for a while. The story about Morg's mate depressed him enough to keep quiet and finish applying surgical putty to Morg's wounds.

Soon his mood lightened, and he started talking with Morg and himself again.

"Let's see, what haven't you and I discussed yet? Oh, I know. This is very weird, Morg. I don't remember launching our ship off Alpha 30. I know you sure as hell didn't do it, so I must have. Man, I must be really sick not to remember launching the transport. Yet, it must have been me."

"No, you fool, it was me!"

The kid spun around in his gyro chair to face a Verasiun with a vap pistol pointed directly at his chest.

"Who the hell are you?"

"Let's say I can be your best friend or worst enemy, Joseph Conway."

The Verasiun had the kid at a disadvantage. If he knew the kid's name, he must be working for someone who knew a lot about the Earthling. The kid sat up straight and sized up the intruder. He did a quick search of his photographic memory to pull up everything he knew about Verasiuns. The Verasiun race was an enigma. No one knew for certain where their home planet was located. They could be found living on virtually every planet in the universe. They were cliquish but mingled with everyone regardless of race, status, or income level. They were experts at collecting data about others, without divulging one useful fact about themselves. The useful information they collected was sold to the highest bidder through trusted brokers. A Verasiun never dealt directly with the purchaser. He stayed at arms-length from the purchaser's identity and money. In a social setting, they acted naive and boring. But, at the most unexpected times, they surprised everyone with clever plans and solutions.

If their behavior wasn't strange enough, their appearance was more so. Every Verasiun was rail thin yet deceptively strong. Unconfirmed reports circulated about Verasiuns who could move and lift objects ten times their body weight. Their glowing orange skin drew everyone's attention at first. After a couple of minutes, they were the most ignored beings in a crowd.

"So, Joseph, what's this about you leading a rebellion against Yanda and Prefect Conway? I didn't know you were such an ambitious young man."

The kid dug deep into his bag of lies and let out a theatrical laugh. "You didn't believe that, did you? If you knew me better, you'd know I make up shit all the time. Plus, I haven't been thinking too clear since getting sick."

"Is that so? You sounded very convincing to me. And, what's this about you becoming the King of the Universe? I must say, you have very high goals."

"Oh, come on! King of the Universe? There's no such title. That alone should prove I was fantasizing. I was pretending like a character actor."

"Then you won't mind if I tell my employer and a few other interested parties about your make-believe life and plans?"

The kid wanted to ask who his employer was, but the Verasiun was too clever to divulge that information. The fabricated denial wasn't working so the kid decided to use a different tactic.

"Verasiun, I'm getting bored by this. I need to get back to my patient. What do you want?"

"Very good question, Earthling. You remind me of someone else I know who doesn't have much patience."

That was the final clue. The kid was now convinced the Verasiun worked for the son-of-a-bitch known as his father.

The Verasiun took a couple steps backward and started pacing back and forth. He kept the Earthling in his peripheral vision and didn't lower his vap pistol. If the Earthling was anything like his old man, he was crafty and dangerous.

"Here's the thing, Joseph Conway. I believed everything you said to the Yandan. You killed his mate and you are the leader of a group of revolutionaries. I can either pass this information on to beings who would find it very interesting or we work out a deal. I'm sure you have something which will buy my silence."

The grin on the Verasiun's face infuriated the kid. He wanted to slap it into the next quadrant. But there was no use daydreaming about something he didn't have enough energy to do. He would have to play this situation out and wait for an opportunity to outwit or overpower the Verasiun.

He didn't have to wait long. From every corner of the ship, red warning lights and high-pitched, screeching alarms erupted.

32

"Lead Trifect, I have Dr. Molusko on the halo-screen from Alpha 30."

"You're late, doctor. I gave you three hours to get the information I asked for. It's been three hours and ten minutes."

The elderly director of Alpha 30 didn't say a word. He wasn't happy taking valuable time from his day to compile a list of fools involved in a firefight. Especially fools who jeopardized the welfare of everyone in his hospital. He was less happy being dressed down by the Lead Trifect. He ran a hand through the frizzy, silver mane on his head and then wiped his face with a cleansing towelette. The long days fighting the epidemic had taken him to the breaking point. He was in no mood to put up with more guff from anyone, including the Lead Trifect.

"Do you want this information or not?"

"I'm waiting, doctor."

Halovision inserts instantly appeared on the screen. "Here are visions of all the beings involved in the firefight at the hospital. Starting in the upper left-hand corner are two female Athlons. Both are dead. They checked in to the hospital under the names of Clexinia Trimex and Stextlen Xpls. We could not determine if these were their real identities. They arrived with a third female Athlon who died on the docking bay. We don't know what her name was. All were wearing body armor. Stextlen and Clexinia secretly brought vap pistols and rifes into the hospital. I think it's safe to say they were here for more than epidemic treatment.

Dr. Molusko paused to see if the Lead Trifect had any questions.

"Go ahead, doctor."

"Next to the Athlon women, you will see two males. One is dead, and the other is hospitalized with multiple wounds. He has a fifty percent chance of pulling through. If he survives, he'll be minus a couple limbs. Both of these beings were wearing Feltte Six enforcer uniforms under hospital garments. They carried credentials which identified them as enforcers. We sent this information plus DNA samples to Feltte Six, but they have yet to respond. In fact, they have yet to acknowledge the receipt of our communication. Our security personnel believe the Feltte Six officials are ignoring our inquiry. There's a good chance these two were on a rogue mission. These two also brought weapons onto the depot."

The doctor took a long sip of energy fluids from an overhead gravity feeder. "The next two beings you see are hospital doctors. Or, I should say, they were hospital doctors. Both are dead. The name of the first one was ...."

"Doctor, I don't need the bio information on the doctors. Continue with the remaining beings."

How rude of the Lead Trifect. Two of his best doctors were dead and not one word of condolence from the Yandan. The doctor debated whether to shut off the halo-screen in protest or finish his presentation. He took a deep breath, gritted his teeth, and continued.

"The next six halo-visions are security officers. Four worked in the hospital and two were on the docking platform. Of the four in the hospital, three are dead. The fourth one has minor injuries. The two patrolling the docking platform are dead. Do you want their bio information?"

"No, but do you know who killed the two on the platform?"

"Lead Trifect, all we know is they were put down by a Verasiun. In the docking bay recording, a Verasiun comes out of nowhere and puts a hole in the head of each officer."

"Then where does he go?"

"He walks to the other end of the docking bay and gets on a ship which blasts off five minutes later. This is the same ship which two patients got on as the firefight raged in the hospital."

"What are their names, doctor?"

"Let's see. One was Joseph Conway and the other one was an Officer Morg. Both were being treated for...."

"Doctor send me a copy of the docking bay recording immediately. Also, tighten up your security procedures. There are too damn many weapons brought onto your depot. A depot is supposed to cure the sick and injured, not be a firing range for lunatics."

The Lead Trifect broke the halo-screen communication and turned to his underlings. "Gentlemen, it appears that Morg and the Earthling left Alpha 30 with a stowaway aboard their ship. We need to know everything about this Verasiun. When you get the recording run him through the facial identifier. Also, identify the ship they left on. We need to stop that ship before it gets to Earth. I need to talk with Officer Morg."

"Well, why are you two hanging around here? You've got assignments, so go." The Lead Trifect shooed them away with a swipe of a back-hand and started reviewing a month's worth of messages and data reports.

"There's something you need to know, Lead Trifect. In the past two days, we've lost five interceptors."

"What do you mean, lost?"

"I guess we mean they exploded for no clear reason. Every one of them was on a normal, routine mission when they disintegrated. There were no other ships within firing range. They were completely alone in deep space. It was as though they hit a brick wall."

"Could it be due to equipment failure?"

"We asked the command engineers and they assured us that wasn't possible. Maybe one ship but impossible for five ships to explode within two days due to equipment failure."

"How about sabotage by an enemy?"

"Possible, but unlikely. The five Interceptors were stationed and took off from different military bases located anywhere from a half to two light years from each other."

"So, let me see if I understand this. Five Interceptors are out on patrol, minding their own business and whamo, they blow up. Is that correct?"

"From what we know, that's exactly what happened."

The Lead Trifect closed his eyes hoping this would help him understand the exploding Interceptors. "Okay. You can go now."

He watched the underlings leave the military campaign room. There was something about this room which made him a bit more patriotic. It was the historical focal point for so many strategic battles and campaigns. He could almost hear the battle plans of yesteryear debated and finalized by prior Trifects. The voices of great Yandan military minds from the past encouraged him to think deeper about what the underlings said about exploding Interceptors. And then a couple other pieces of the puzzle entered his mind. The Shooting Star disappears and can't be found. Morg communicates coordinates for a service planet which doesn't exist on any stellar chart. Commander Fritase witnesses a transport instantly materialize out of nowhere. And now, exploding Interceptors.

The Lead Trifect wondered, "What do these incidents have in common?" He was energized by the riddle. There had to be a common denominator. There was only one thing that could explain all these things; cloaking. But, cloaking of what?

Back on Alpha 30, Dr. Molusko put his chair into the fetal position. He needed to get some sleep after working thirty-six straight hours. Four or five sound hours would renew his energy and forget the pithy conversation he had with the Lead Trifect. He couldn't get over how disrespectful and condescending the Yandan was. There was no excuse for his attitude. He might be under a lot of stress but who wasn't? He should try being on the front lines fighting a major epidemic which was on the verge of turning into a plague.

As his eyes grew heavy, he wondered if he should waste time reconnecting with the Lead Trifect. He didn't want to withhold information, but it wasn't his fault the Yandan rudely ended their communication. If he hadn't been so short-tempered, the doctor would have told him about the other being who boarded Officer Morg's ship. Also, he was sure the Lead Trifect would be interested in the vap pistol rounds fired into Morg's ship by the Verasiun. The doctor's last thought before falling asleep was, "The Lead Trifect can go screw himself."

33

The Verasiun and kid were thrown to the floor as the transport was pummeled with wave after wave of Locomites. The tiny creatures thrived in the sub-zero temperature of deep space. Individually they were harmless. But, when they swarmed together in the millions, they created a juggernaut of death and destruction. Yandan folklore contained epic stories about Locomite swarms devastating everything in their path. Even military launch platforms and ship armadas were overwhelmed.

The kid bounced along the floor until he found and clung on to a support post. Out of the corner of his eye, he watched the Verasiun hit another support post head-first and lose consciousness. His vap pistol hop-scotched across the floor to the Earthling's waiting grasp. The Verasiun was now easy prey if the transport survived the Locomite swarm.

The Earthling hung on with all his might. He could feel the ship bouncing up and down and from side to side. The thumping and creaking of the ship's hull was getting louder. The bridge viewing port was covered with layer after layer of Locomite guts and body parts. If the ship survived this holocaust there was only one way to clean the viewing port. Someone would have to don a survival suit, go out into space and chip-off the frozen Locomite remains. He let out a weak chuckle thinking about Morg doing this job. He could already hear the Yandan bitching about such a nasty task.

He wanted to fall asleep. Between the energy needed to hold on for dear life and the toll the epidemic wreck on his body, he was fading fast. He wished he was in sickbay with Morg strapped onto an operating cot. Then all he'd have to do is pray to a higher being if there was one. His father didn't think so, but he knew a couple kids from childhood who believed in a Master of all life and destiny. If there was ever a time to become a believer, it was now. In fact, he might consider becoming a better human if the higher being answered his survival prayer.

He could feel the transport slowing down. It was inevitable as the Locomite cloud blocked the destination star's light. As the target light faded, the transport's shadow drive system lost propulsion. It could only lock on to so many secondary light sources before everything was blocked by the swarm.

The Earthling woke up twenty minutes later. He was still hanging on to the support post. Somehow, he willed himself to stay glued to the post. The transport was quiet and stable. The hum of the shadow drive system was silent. The system would need to be re-calibrated to get the ship moving again. Thankfully, he read how this was done and wouldn't have to wait until Morg regained consciousness. He bit his lower lip to make sure he wasn't dreaming. The taste of blood reassured him that the transport survived the Locomite onslaught.

He hung on to the post in case this was a lull in the storm. There was always the possibility another wave of the slimy creatures would hit the ship. He listened for any unusual sounds as he surveyed the bridge area. The Verasiun was about twenty feet from the support post he hit. The gash in his head was still oozing blood or some type of Verasiun body fluid. The wound left a liquid trail across the floor.

From what the kid could see, the Verasiun slid back and forth across the floor like a pinball.

He let go of the post and stood. He was light-headed with shaky legs. He wanted to sit back down but knew if he did, he might stay on the floor for days. The thought of dragging the Verasiun back to lock-up was too draining. It would be easier to get restraining bracelets and lock him to the support post he hit. The kid didn't care if the Verasiun sat on his ass and bled all the way to Earth.

After ten minutes of wobbling and stumbling down the hallway, he made it to sick-bay. Morg was still strapped on the operating cot and motionless. The Yandan was precisely as he left him. No new injuries and the old ones seemed to be healing properly.

The kid leaned over the cot to make sure Morg was breathing. He was two inches away when Morg's eyes popped open.

"Holy crap, Morg. You scared the shit out of me."

Morg blinked a couple times but didn't say anything. Finally, his eyes shifted to look at the kid.

"Where am I, Earthling?"

"You're on the transport. Do you remember boarding the transport?"

Morg gave a slight nod. "What happened to me?"

"You took a vap round in the shoulder."

"When can you get me to a doctor?"

"You won't need a doctor. I patched you together. We had all the medical supplies needed for your surgery in the cargo bay."

"Thanks, Joseph Conway." Morg's eyes closed and he fell back to sleep.

The kid couldn't take his eyes off the Yandan. After eight light years of bickering, arguing, and stabbing each other in the back, the Yandan called him by his given name. Was it a slip of the tongue due to his groggy state or a sign of respect? He wanted to think the Yandan was finally beginning to like him.

He stood up and started back to the bridge. There was no use wasting more time trying to figure out what a Yandan was thinking.

Especially one that was unconscious. As he passed the security lock-up, he grabbed a pair of anklet and bracelet restrictors. The Verasiun was going to have an uncomfortable ride to Earth. It might teach him a lesson about working for that louse, Prefect Conway.

The walk back to the bridge seemed like it took twice as long as it should. The kid stopped three times to catch his breath. During two of those stops, he thought he heard footsteps or some type of movement coming from the cargo area at the back of the ship. Each time he wrote it off to a creative imagination tainted by the epidemic. Even if there was something moving around in the cargo bay, he wasn't in any condition to investigate it.

The Verasiun was moaning and groaning and making a valiant attempt to wake-up. The kid didn't have enough energy to nurse the assassin back to health. He would have to make it on his own. The kid wrapped the Verasiun's legs around the support post and locked them together with an ankle restrictor. Whether the Verasiun liked it or not, he was going to spend the rest of the voyage on his back.

The kid put a couple deep-wound cleansing packets and surgical putty on the Verasiun's stomach. These medical supplies were adequate for the Verasiun to nurse himself. That was assuming, of course, he awoke from the semi-coma. The kid didn't care one way or another.

When he got to the control bridge, he flopped into the captain's gyro chair. It would have been easy putting the chair in the rest position to take a nap, but he had to get the transport moving again. Plus, falling asleep would be the worst thing he could do if there was another stowaway on the ship.

The Earthling pushed a couple buttons on the control panel and spoke. "Shadow drive, system acknowledge."

"Yes, co-pilot Conway. What is your command?"

"Re-calibration. Destination Earth. In the quadrant of ......"

It took close to ten minutes for the kid to give the shadow drive system the correct re-calibration codes. It would be another one to two hours for the system to gin up and go into the launch sequence.

There wasn't much for the Earthling to do while the system reset itself.

His gaze shifted to the viewing port window. He couldn't get over what a mess it was. It was an opaque slate of Locomite body parts. If he didn't know better, he could swear there were a couple smiling Locomite faces squished on the window. Those had to be optical illusions. As far as he knew, Locomites didn't have faces.

Gazing at the viewing port weighed heavy on his eyes. They closed a couple times. They snapped open again when he caught his head falling forward. He was about ready to lay back for a much-needed nap when the ship's eavesdropping system alerted him to an intruder.

He switched the bug system over to a viewing screen. On an outline of the transport's interior, there were four beings highlighted in green. One was Morg in the operating bay. The Verasiun was near the entrance to the bridge and the Earthling was sitting at the bridge control panel. The fourth being was moving out of the cargo bay toward the mess hall. Apparently, the unknown intruder was hungry.

The kid checked the Verasiun's vap pistol to make sure it was loaded and ready for use. He put it in his lap and sat back to watch the intruder move through the transport. This was the lazy man's way to track an intruder. It was a hundred times easier than stalking an assailant who didn't want to be found or was dangerous.

The kid congratulated himself again for thinking ahead and outside the box. Having the Ziptowtheon technicians put in the eavesdropping system was a damn smart move on his part.

34

"Mentat, get your ass in here."

"Yes, Prefect Conway."

Conway watched the Mentat walk into his office. The truthsayer, which he paid handsomely for each month, walked like a robot. His six-and-half-foot, slender frame was stiff as his Johnson before he did Beth. Nothing, other than his legs, moved when he walked. His arms were locked in place at his sides and his head stayed rigid. He looked like a new automaton spit from a mold. His ash-colored skin was flawless. Every hair on his head and face laid perfectly in place. He was the only being Prefect Conway ever met with a hundred percent uniformity from one side of his face to the other. There were times when Conway wanted to slice him open to see what was inside. The only thing which stopped him was the huge deposit he would lose by not returning the Mentat to the planet Mentattis in perfect condition.

"Mentat, have you ever arranged a party?"

The Mentat stood before Conway's desk and stared. "I don't know what a party is, Prefect."

"That's what I was afraid of. A party is a social gathering for select beings to celebrate a specific event. Do you understand?"

"I don't think so, sir."

Prefect Conway rubbed his face in frustration. "Okay, let me explain it this way. When your service is over here on Earth and you go back to planet Mentattis, your friends will have a party for you. They'll be happy you are home. Everyone will get together and celebrate your homecoming. Do you understand now?"

The Mentat knew exactly what the Prefect was describing but wasn't about to give in so quick. He was having too much fun watching his jerk boss get irritated.

"We don't do that, sir. When a Mentat's contract expires, he immediately goes back to school for more training in preparation for the next assignment. Besides, Mentats don't have friends."

Prefect Conway rolled his eyes. "Forget it. You are going to manage a homecoming party for my son. Besides the homecoming celebration, you will supervise a demonstration at Mount Mikilopii for the Florid ambassador. We will be showing the ambassador and guests how our new toxic gas condensator works."

"When is this to take place, Prefect?"

"Here's all the information you'll need. The date, who is invited, where they are staying, blah, blah, blah. Beth will help you. Now hit the road, I've got a ton of work to do."

The Mentat scanned the celebration-demonstration documents as he walked to the door. Halfway there he stopped and turned back to the Prefect. "Sir, this says you are inviting the Lead Trifect from Yanda. Is that correct or a mistake?"

"Of course, it's correct. I'm not a sore loser and I don't think the Lead Trifect is either." Prefect Conway started laughing. Even outside of the office, the Prefect's laughter could be heard echoing throughout the complex. The Mentat wasn't an expert in Earth comedy, but he knew this laughter wasn't humor-based. It was diabolical.

THREE HOURS LATER MILLER, Beth, and the Mentat reviewed Conway's homecoming party and demonstration folder. They were dumbfounded by the itemized specifics in the documents. Every event was planned to the minute. The menus for each day and special dietary meals were set. Great care was given to the accommodations for each guest. The attendee list for each event included those invited as well as those not invited. From what Miller could see, every member of Earth's Global Union Assembly was invited. The Floridians would bring an entourage of fifteen beings to the ceremonies. The Yandan Trifect had an open invitation even though the distance to Earth prevented them from attending. They could watch the proceedings on a special broadcast arranged and transmitted by Prefect Conway's staff.

"Beth, who the hell prepared this? There's no way Conway did this by himself."

Beth shook her head in disbelief. "I don't know. You're right, Conway didn't do this. He's a generalist. Whoever did this is a person who loves detail. I can't think of anyone on his staff capable of this."

"Sir, do you know who put this together?"

The Mentat loved the title, *sir*. It was so respectful compared to the way Prefect Conway addressed him. "I do not, Secretary-General Miller. I agree with both of you. Prefect Conway is very clever but not capable of something like this."

Beth and Miller continued discussing the ceremony information packet. Most of their discussions centered on the motives Conway had for each event. Nothing Conway ever did could be taken at face value. There was always a hidden, surprise agenda for everything he did. And, the real motive usually meant death or destruction for someone or something.

"Why does he want to take everyone to the Mikilopii volcano? I know it says for a demonstration of the toxic gas condensator, but that doesn't make a lot of sense to me. It would be a lot easier if everyone sat in the comfort of the assembly hall and watched the demonstration on a halovision telecast. Dragging everyone out to the volcano is expensive and a pain in the ass."

"Did you see this comment under his son's homecoming celebration. He plans to make a surprise announcement about his son, Joseph."

"God only knows what he has up his sleeve. Beth, maybe he's going to announce your engagement to his son."

Miller couldn't help himself. He started laughing as soon as the last word left his mouth.

"Millard, that's not funny. I'd rather die than marry that jerk."

The Mentat sat and watched Beth and Miller spar back and forth. It was in fun with a slight hint of seriousness. He was jealous of their close relationship which could withstand such sarcastic quips. He wondered if one day he would be close enough to some beings to joke around with them. The thought of going through life without this experience was depressing.

He learned another thing from their good-natured jousting. Neither of them had any idea who was the mastermind behind the ceremony agenda. He didn't detect one bit of deception from them.

Beth dropped her copy of the packet. Her mood changed from light-hearted to grave importance. "I think I know who put this together." The smile on Miller's face vanished.

"It was Conway's son. I don't know how or when he did it, but he's a strategic genius. This would be child's play for him."

35

THE KID WAS GETTING TIRED WATCHING THE UNKNOWN intruder make his way through the transport. He spent forty-five minutes alone in the mess hall. He must have prepared and eaten a complete dinner. His next stop was sickbay. He went over to Morg's cot and stood there for a minute or two. Morg's blimp continued to flash green so the intruder didn't kill the Yandan. Most likely, he wanted to make sure the Yandan couldn't hinder his plans, whatever they were.

The intruder moved through the main hallway leading to the bridge. The kid estimated he would see the Verasiun locked to the support pole within two minutes. He would then become very cautious and creep at a snail's pace to the bridge.

The Earthling was ready for him. It was irritating that the intruder wasted so much time. Time that could be put to better use, like sleeping. The kid thought about going after the intruder to end the cat-and-mouse game. He knew the transport better than the intruder. It would be easy setting an ambush and either take him alive or put a vap round in his back. But he reminded himself several times that a basic rule of victory was letting the enemy travel to the battle. That principle along with possessing the element of surprise ensured triumph in war. At least that's what Sun Tzu, an ancient Chinese military theorist, claimed in his work, "The Art of War".

The kid could hear the intruder bend over the Verasiun and examine him. He was exactly fifteen yards from the kid's gyro chair. As the kid predicted, the intruder crept toward the bridge, staying low and hugging a wall.

"Turn your chair and identify yourself. Do it, or I'll put a round through the gyro chair."

The kid could tell from the intruder's accent he was an Earthling. Most likely from the eastern part of the European continent. He was cautious and deliberate with every move he made. He was skirting the wall over the kid's left shoulder which meant he held the vap pistol in his right hand.

The kid pretended he was taken by surprise. "Okay, okay, calm down. I'm turning around. Don't shoot."

The kid turned to face a forty-something Earthling with a bold scar running down his left cheek. He looked to be around six-feet-tall with a barrel-chest and long, greasy black hair. His vap pistol pointed in the general direction of the kid. He was either very confident in his ability to target or stupid for not using the laser sights.

"Ah, if it isn't Master Joseph Conway. You look exactly like the halovision your old man showed me."

"And, you might be who?"

"You can call me Omar. I'm here to escort you safely to Earth."

His name was of little consequence to the kid. It was an obvious alias. He was more concerned about the vap pistol aimed in his direction and who this being worked for. The intruder definitely fit the mold of the type of being his old man hired. Addressing him as Master Joseph Conway was typical for a Prefect Conway hired-gun. Overconfident to the point of being a smart-ass. But, if he was telling the truth, then who did the Verasiun work for?

"Do you usually hold a vap pistol on beings you are hired to escort?"

A cocky smile crossed the intruder's face as he looked away from the kid and scanned the bridge.

That's all the time the kid needed. In a millisecond he pulled his vap pistol from under his thigh and shot. The pistol flew from the intruder's hand. It landed fifteen feet behind the intruder and skidded along the floor for another ten feet.

"Dammit, what the hell did you do that for?"

The kid watched the intruder dance around in pain, examining his right hand to make sure it was still attached to his arm. The kid knew he had third-degree burns which needed medical attention.

"I'm not crazy about looking down the barrel of a vap pistol. Now, who do you work for, bucko?"

"Your father hired me." Omar kept blowing on his hand trying to cool the burning. "Shit, man. Put something on this to kill the pain."

"That's interesting. The Verasiun lying over there claims he works for my father too."

"Well, maybe he does. Who the hell knows? I don't. All I know is your old man paid me very well to get your ass and bring it to Earth."

The kid considered interrogating the intruder to verify his claim but decided to wait. The intruder couldn't concentrate because of his injury. And, the kid needed some sleep or risk slipping back into an epidemic-induced coma. He could ask all the questions he wanted later.

"Okay, I'm going to take care of your hand. You try anything, and I'll kill you. Understand?"

"Yeah, yeah, yeah. Just hurry up."

The kid led Omar to the same support pole the Verasiun was locked to. When his arms were wrapped around the post, the kid put a restrictor bracelet on him. He grabbed a deep wound cleansing packet from the Verasiun's stockpile and gave it to Omar.

"Do you know how to use this?"

The intruder didn't bother answering. He was too busy ripping the packet open and applying the pad to his injured hand. The opiate derived drug in the pad entered the intruder's bloodstream through skin pores and rushed to his brain. Within thirty seconds, Omar was glassy-eyed and in La-La Land. The burning pain in his hand was gone. He fell to one side and started to dream about happy times from his past.

The kid looked at the two stowaways. “I’ll talk to you two clowns later.” He stumbled back to the gyro chair and put it in full rest position. He closed his eyes and started to nod off.

“Co-pilot Conway. The shadow drive system is re-calibrated. Awaiting your approval to start launch sequence.”

“Son-of-a-bitch. Am I ever going to get some sleep?”

SEVEN HOURS later the kid awoke to an alarm going off on the bridge control panel. It was coming from the eavesdropping viewing screen. The green light in sickbay turned to red and moved from the operating cot to the personal waste collection closet. It was a good sign. Morg was getting better if he could make his way through the sickbay to relieve himself in the waste closet. The kid flipped on the audio and video to take a look.

“Officer Morg. You look better. How do you feel?”

“Like shit, but I’ll survive. Where are we?”

“About one light year from Earth. We would have been there already but hit a Locomite storm.”

Morg began to open the waste closet door but stopped. He looked up to where a transceiver might be located. “Is there any chance I can get you to delay docking on Earth?”

“Why?”

Morg was too tired and feverish to make up fictitious reason. “To be honest, I’d like to check in with the Lead Trifect before landing on Earth.”

“Well, I’m getting pressured by my old man to get to Earth. Plus, I have some personal business to take care of there. So, I don’t want to stop the ship.”

"Yeah, I didn't think so."

"Morg, let's do this. Get a couple more hours of sleep and then come to the bridge and place a communication to the Lead Trifect. You or both of us can talk to him and find out if he has any last-minute instructions. Fair enough?"

Morg thought about the kid's offer. He wasn't in a position to argue or negotiate. "Yeah, that sounds fair. I'll see you in a couple of hours. Wake me if you I don't come up there in three hours."

The kid turned off the eavesdropping system and sat back in the captain's gyro chair. He stretched and took in a deep breath which he let out very slow. The seven hours of sleep had done wonders. The last thing he remembered before falling asleep was the drone of the shadow drive system kicking-in at launch. It was a hard sleep which left him refreshed and feeling close to normal. If he took care of himself, he should be close to epidemic-free by the time the transport landed on Earth.

The Verasiun and Earthling chained to the support pole were starting to regain consciousness. They moaned and groaned and opened their eyes occasionally to look around. In a couple hours they would be awake and complaining about their accommodations. Of course, they would be hungry, so the kid would have to serve something. He had a lot to do before his uninvited guests started making demands.

He got up from the gyro chair and headed to sickbay. It was time for Morg and him to take their epidemic medicine. By the time he got there, Morg was sound asleep again. He opened a packet containing the medicine and rubbed the pad across his arm. He did the same thing for Morg. Like the deep wound cleansing pad, the epidemic medicine entered through body pores and openings. It then went to work attacking the virus, bacteria or whatever was causing the illness.

The kid took a quick peek at Morg's wounds before leaving sickbay. They seemed to be healing correctly and there was no evidence of infection. He pulled down the optic enhancer from over the operating cot to get a magnified image of the wounds. He was surprised to see new scales sprouting on the circumference of each wound. At this rate, new scales would cover the wound holes within a couple weeks.

The Verasiun was awake by the time the kid got back to the bridge area. He was examining the gash on his head using the reflective back on the deep wound cleansing packet.

"How do you feel?"

"I've had better days. How about taking off the ankle bracelets? You've got my vap pistol, so there's not much I can do."

"You're fine exactly where you are. You might have noticed the other jerk-off lying on the other side of the post. You and he have a lot in common. Neither of you were invited on this ship. Both of you thought it'd be fun to point a vap pistol at me and he claims to be working for my old man too."

"What's that got to do with me and getting these bracelets off?"

"I can't trust either of you and I don't have the time or desire to babysit you. So, lay back and enjoy the ride to Earth. By the way, I recommend you use the cleansing pad and wound putty as soon as possible. I'm not going to doctor you if that gash gets infected."

The kid turned and headed for the captain's gyro chair. Halfway there, the Verasiun started throwing a fit. "Thanks, buddy. I'll remember this, turd. Your old man won't like the way you're treating me. Hey, I'm hungry; when do we eat? How am I supposed to take a leak and ...?"

The kid gave the Verasiun the universal sign for "don't care what you have to say" and kept walking. He had just learned something important; the Verasiun had a short temper. It wouldn't take long for him and his post-mate to go at each other's throats. That might reveal what their real missions were and who they worked for.

"Communicator on. Private comm channel 45-879032."

The kid sat back and waited for the communication to be answered on Ziptowtheon. He needed to get an update from his co-conspirators. It had been several days since he spoke to his war-council. He expected unanticipated news which would change his invasion plan. If there was one thing he had learned, it was that life revolved around the unexpected, not the expected.

"First Comrade Joseph. Good to see you again."

The four members of the war-council appeared on the halo-screen. They were sitting around the executive chamber table. It was a lucky coincidence he called when they were all together.

"Gentlemen. I'm surprised I caught you together. What's the occasion?"

The Crelon spoke for the group. "We were discussing a minor problem. Trying to decide what to do about it."

"I'm listening. What's the problem?"

The Crelon hesitated. The Earthling could tell he didn't want to talk about it."

"Well, a couple of our cloaked planets and weapon platforms were hit by objects."

"What kind of objects?"

"Yandan Interceptors, First Comrade."

The kid wanted to explode and start yelling. He grabbed the small finger on his left hand and yanked it out of joint. The pain was searing and gave him something else to think about. Inflicting pain on himself was the easiest and quickest way he knew to calm down and not make stupid comments and decisions.

"How many and what was the damage?"

"Five Interceptors hit five different planets and weapon platforms. Our damages were minimal. Our frontal shields absorbed almost all of the explosions. All five Interceptors were destroyed."

"What do you plan to do about this?"

"We haven't got that far, First Comrade. Any suggestions?"

For the first time in years, he didn't have an immediate answer. He was almost ecstatic that he pulled his finger out of joint to keep quiet.

"Let's think about this. The Yandans know they lost five Interceptors; all within a brief period of time. They also know mechanical failure and enemy attack wasn't involved. By now, they realize their ships exploded like hitting a brick wall. So, what are they going to do?"

The Earthling co-conspirator spoke for the first time. "They'll send out other Interceptors to investigate and look for physical evidence. I'm sure they have a sizable number of military technicians and physicists looking for explanations."

"You're absolutely right. So, what do we do? How can we turn this to our advantage?"

There was dead silence. First Comrade Joseph and his four henchmen sat quietly in deep thought. They needed a solution which didn't turn their invasion plans upside-down.

The kid spoke after five minutes. "Gentlemen, I think we have only two choices. We can either...."

The kid stopped talking when he saw someone burst into the executive chamber on Ziptowtheon. This unknown being was dressed in lab technician coveralls. Two guards ran into the room and tried to restrain the technician. Each of them grabbed an arm and started to drag him from the room. The technician kicked and squirmed, trying to break free of their grasp. When he realized he was losing the tug-of-war, he started yelling at the four co-conspirators. The tone of his voice wasn't hate-filled or angry. It sounded like someone trying to warn others about a dangerous situation. The guards stopped pulling the technician when the Crelon said something to them.

After a minute of back-and-forth with the technician, the Crelon turned back to the halo-screen. "First Comrade Joseph, this technician claims there is a hidden explosive on the experimental Interceptor we hi-jacked. It's the Interceptor the Yandans call the Shooting Star."

"So, what's the big deal?"

"Our techs can't figure out how to disarm it and think it's set to go off at ...."

That was the last thing the Crelon and his co-conspirators said to First Comrade Joseph Conway. Ziptowtheon collapsed upon itself and then burst outward in a shower of sub-atomic particles. The remains of Ziptowtheon flew in every direction. They didn't stop until they hit something light years later.

The kid's halo-screen turned from yellow to red and then black. Something told him the unexpected just happened and his life would never be the same.

36

"Lead Trifect, we received an invitation to attend a demonstration of Earth's toxic gas condensator. And, there's going to be a homecoming celebration for his son."

The Lead Trifect was still in deep thought pondering the mysterious appearances, disappearances, and unexplained Interceptor explosions. He hadn't reached a theory to explain all these events. Yet, he couldn't shake the idea they were all tied together by cloaking, but what else was involved? There had to be a common denominator. It was this wild card which could mean the difference between a secure and safe Yandan empire and disaster.

"What did you say?"

The underling looked at his boss quizzically. It had been fifteen minutes since anything was said in the room. It took him a while to remember the invitation.

"Oh, I said we're invited to attend Earth's demonstration of its toxic gas condensator."

"Yeah, but wasn't there something else?"

"Ah, yes. Prefect Conway is also having a homecoming party for his son."

"When?"

"Three days from now."

The Lead Trifect smiled even though he was disgusted. He had been bested by Prefect Conway. The Earthling was either on Earth or arriving there soon. If only Morg had stopped the transport before it arrived on Earth. The kid could have been a bargaining chip to push through the CASETA Agreement. At least he was valuable enough to trade for a piece of Earth's toxic gas reserves. Now it was clear that wasn't going to happen. Yanda would have to search the universe for another source of toxic gases of the correct mixture. It was either that or invade Earth and take by force what it needed.

"Well, we certainly aren't going to the demonstration or festivities."

"A special halo-screen vision is being made available for anyone who can't attend. To get the feed, you have to sign up for it. Should we ignore Prefect Conway and his invitation?"

The Lead Trifect wanted to say "yes" but knew that was a mistake. He had to swallow his pride and ignore Prefect Conway's ridicule. He needed to know what the enemy was doing. It might point to a weakness in the Prefect's plans which could be taken advantage of.

The underling was surprised when his boss said, "Sign up for the halo-screen feed."

"Has anyone heard from Officer Morg and do we know where the transport is?"

"Nothing from Officer Morg. The last we heard was when he left Alpha 30. If the transport is moving at normal shadow drive speed, it's within six hours of docking on Earth."

The Lead Trifect began to ask another question. He stopped when a courier entered the room and handed a recorder chip to one of the underling Trifect. The chip went into his transceiver and scrolled a coded message across the screen.

"Well?"

The Trifect looked up with a puzzled look on his face. "Lead

Trifect, the Shooting Star 38 has vaporized. The destiny explosive went off approximately twenty-four minutes ago."

"How do we know it was the destiny explosive from the Shooting Star?"

"The destiny explosive has a very unique formula of chemicals and metals. When it goes off, this formula is evident in the explosion signature. There is no question this was the destiny explosive from the Shooting Star."

"How close was the explosion to the quadrant where the Shooting Star disappeared?"

The underlings didn't know the answer. They hurriedly pulled up coordinates and stellar charts to get the answer.

"The Shooting Star vaporized approximately one light year from where it disappeared."

"Which was closer to Yanda? The quadrant where it disappeared or the quadrant where it vaporized?"

"Where it vaporized, Lead Trifect."

"Brothers let me take a wild guess at something. The magnitude of the explosion was far greater than the maximum output for a destiny explosive?"

The underlings checked the statistics provided by the physicists who analyzed the explosion.

"You're right, Lead Trifect. The explosion was three times greater than what a destiny explosive can produce."

"This is too easy, brothers. Let me take another wild guess. There are no planets or satellites where the explosion took place?"

Again, the underling Trifect did a quick search of the stellar charts. "Yes, that's correct. How do you know these things, Lead Trifect?"

The Lead Trifect shook his head from side to side. He got up from the meeting table and went to the Cannis dispenser for a snort of the intoxicating drug.

"Brothers, I apologize. I've been negligent in my duties as a Lead Trifect. I should have seen what is going on days or weeks ago. But, I didn't. Brothers, Yanda and our allies are under attack. Let's hope it's not too late."

For the next two hours, the Lead Trifect gave his brother Trifect a detailed explanation of the invisible threat approaching Yanda. Much of his explanation was guesswork but it all made sense. Cloaked planets and weapon platforms moving toward the Yandan empire explained every strange occurrence in the last couple weeks. The mysterious appearance of the transport out of nowhere and the disappearance of the Shooting Star were explained. Five Interceptors crashing for no apparent reason made sense now.

"Brothers, we have to find out three things and do it fast. First, how big is this enemy armada? Second, where are they? And last, who is the enemy? We may have bought some time when the Shooting Star blew up. It's reasonable to believe our Shooting Star was hijacked to one of the larger and more important cloaked planets to be reverse engineered. I'm sure losing that planet hurt the enemy quite a bit. Thank the heavens one of our physicists had enough forethought to load the Shooting Star with the destiny explosive. He may have saved the empire."

The Trifect was ready to end their meeting and begin working on a plan to defend the empire when a communication was passed through to the meeting room.

"Sir, it's Officer Morg."

"It's about time. Put it on visual."

A roughed-up, bruised, and sickly Morg appeared on the halo-screen. His shoulder was bound in bandages. He was sitting slightly tilted to the right favoring his left shoulder. To his side was the Earthling looking a little under the weather but a lot better than Morg.

"Officer Morg, what the hell happened to you?"

"I took a vap round in the shoulder, Lead Trifect. It's healing well. The Earthling... I mean, Joseph Conway patched my wounds and is taking care of me."

"Who shot you?"

The kid jumped into the conversation to answer the Lead Trifect's question. "One of those losers cuffed to the support post behind us. Can you see them?"

Morg's head swung around as quick as his shoulder allowed. The Trifect strained to see the would-be assassin in the murky background. It was the first time Morg heard that his assailant was on board the transport and bound by restrictor cuffs. He meant to ask the kid about the two beings locked to the support post but thought the communication to Yanda was more important.

"Good, I'm glad you captured him. Where are you two?"

"We are on our final approach to Earth. Roboland is in control of the ship."

"So, you got to Earth ahead of schedule. Too bad."

"Why is that, Lead Trifect?"

The Lead Trifect paused and debated with himself. As much as he wanted to say something about the break-down of the CASETA negotiations and using the kid as a bargaining chip, it was too late. Nothing would be accomplished by bringing up this information in front of the Earthling.

"Forget I said that, Officer Morg. It doesn't matter now. I want to congratulate you on completing your mission. I know you two have been subjected to several harrowing events. I commend you for working together to overcome every obstacle."

"Thank you, sir." The kid and Morg sat at attention and stifled their real thoughts. The kid wanted to laugh at the Lead Trifect's naiveté. And, Morg wanted to strangle the Lead Trifect for sending him on such an insane and dangerous mission.

"Son, I understand your father is planning a homecoming celebration for you. It should be enjoyable seeing your friends and family again."

"It will be, sir." The kid couldn't wait to get off the transport and start making his old man's life miserable. He wouldn't do it in the open. Rather, every manipulative and destructive act would be done in secret, behind the Prefect's back. The only thing more important than toppling the old man was taking back Beth. The sooner she joined him, and they deposed the Prefect, the better.

"Sir, how long should I stay on Earth before coming home?"

"Officer Morg, stay on Earth for a few days. Get better and enjoy yourself. By the way, there's a demonstration of Earth's toxic gas condensator system. I want you to attend that demonstration as the official Yandan representative. Contact my brother Trifect tomorrow for instructions. Gentlemen have a safe docking."

The halo-screen went blank. The Lead Trifect looked at his underlings. "Tomorrow, put Officer Morg on a private comm number. I need to give him instructions on how he can stop the pending disaster facing Yanda."

37

"Welcome home son. You look great. Just as handsome as your old man."

The kid avoided his father's hug and simply shook his hand. "Sorry sir, I'm still sick so I don't want to get too close to you."

"Hey, that's okay. After eight years I'm not going to let a little bug come between us."

Prefect Conway embraced his son for a couple minutes. He then turned to face the crowd of dignitaries and reporters milling around on the docking platform.

"Welcome guests. First, I'm pleased to present my son, Joseph Conway." The Prefect waited for the reporters to take hundreds of halovisions before going on with his announcement. "He has been gone for almost nine years representing Earth on a very important secret mission. My office will be releasing a detailed brief explaining that mission. I cannot tell you how great it is to have him back on Earth. To celebrate his homecoming, I will be hosting an informal reception...."

The kid's mind was elsewhere. He didn't care what his old man was saying. Who cared if there was going to be a homecoming party, festivities, and formal dinner? The kid had only one thing on his mind. Find Beth and make his old man's life miserable.

He scanned the crowds looking for the innocent, young lady he left almost nine years before. Every time he saw someone who looked like her, he wanted to bolt through the crowd to embrace her. But she wasn't in the crowd. It was unlikely she would intentionally miss his arrival. There were only two possible explanations. Either she was working or gone.

The Prefect watched his son in his peripheral vision as he spoke to the crowd. He knew exactly why the kid was scanning the crowd. He sought the love of his life. The romantic fool would rush to her and hold her in his loving arms if he could. His son was a genius but terribly naïve when it came to women. Did he believe things were exactly the same as when he left Earth years before? The Prefect couldn't help wondering how his son became so stupid when it came to this woman. Yes, she was good in bed but not any better than thousands of other women. Well, that was the kid's error in judgement. Beth would stay hidden until he used her up as a bargaining chip. If his son wanted to see her again, he would do everything the future Prefect of the Universe wanted from him.

The kid could feel the old man's stare, but he didn't dare look at him. If he did, he would likely attack and try to kill him. His crafty father had most likely out-maneuvered him again and spirited Beth away. He would never find her. He needed to calm down and not let the old man know her absence was driving him crazy. It would come out eventually what he did with her and why.

He caught a glimpse of the two assassins being led from the transport by Earth authorities. The kid knew he made a huge mistake by not ejecting these two agents into space before landing the transport on Earth.

Two-deep in the crowd, Millard Miller stood trying to think of a way to reach his agent before the Prefect's men went to work on him. He also wondered why his agent hadn't committed suicide by taking a death capsule. The only being pleased to see the two agents alive was Prefect Conway.

Morg still didn't know a thing about the agents other than the Verasiun put a vap pistol round through his shoulder. Why he did this and where the one called Omar came from was a mystery. Between sleeping for hours and communicating with the Lead Trifect there wasn't time to hear the Earthling's account of how these two losers got on the transport. If he could get the kid alone in the next day or two, he might find out who these two assassins worked for.

Morg stood at the top of the transport ramp watching and listening. He was still in tough shape. The illness had tapered off, so he was no longer delirious. However, his shoulder was still in the initial stages of healing. Every movement was painful. If he moved too fast or awkwardly the pain was extreme. If it wasn't for pain-abatement drugs and several hits from the Cannis dispenser, he would most likely pass out.

His immediate concern was what Prefect Conway just announced to the crowd. Had he heard the Prefect correctly? His son was supposedly on an important and secretive mission for the past nine years? That didn't jibe with what he and the Trifect knew about the kid. Or, what they thought they knew about the kid. If the Prefect was telling the truth, what the hell mission was the kid on? The obvious answer was that he was spying on Yanda. But, what information did he gather and for who? He would tell the Lead Trifect tomorrow what the Prefect said about his son's secret mission. Most likely it wouldn't be necessary. He was sure Yandan comm technicians were monitoring every public broadcast from Earth and Florid.

"I don't know anymore. I've told you everything I know."

The victim slumped over in his chair bleeding from every orifice in his body. His torturers were masters at their trade. They had years of experience working for Prefect Conway. Their methods were fool-proof. The mental and physical torture they used always resulted in complete and accurate confessions.

"Okay, tell us again."

"First, water or a hit of Cannis."

"When you get done Verasiun; not before."

The Verasiun mustered his remaining energy, forced some saliva to his throat and began.

"I overheard the Prefect's son confess to Officer Morg."

"What was Officer Morg doing during this confession?"

The Verasiun wanted to scream his answer but knew he didn't have enough energy in reserve. "I already told you. Morg was passed out on an operating cot in sickbay."

"So, Joseph Conway was talking to himself?"

"Yeah, I guess you could say that. He talked to himself while he patched Morg's wounds."

"Go on."

"The Prefect's son said he was leading an army of ten thousand warriors against the Yandan empire. I think he called himself an Exalted Comrade or something like that."

"You said First Comrade before."

"That's right, he called himself a First Comrade."

The Verasiun waited for another pulse shock to his testicles. When it didn't come, he blabbered on before his torturers thought he needed more prodding.

"His army is approaching Yanda and their allies on cloaked planets and weapon platforms."

"The entire planet is cloaked? For how long?"

"I don't know. He didn't say. All I remember was that once the Yandan empire was overthrown he would do the same to his father. He would then become King of the Universe."

"What else?"

The Verasiun knew he had forgotten something but was having a tough time remembering his prior confessions. "Ah, Ah, oh yeah. He talked about making someone named Betha his queen."

"Do you mean Beth?"

"Maybe. It might have been. I don't know. I really need something to drink."

"Soon, Verasiun. Did you believe what Joseph Conway said."

"When I confronted him, he tried to deny it. But, yes, I believed every word. Morg was passed out and he didn't know I was listening. There was no reason for him to lie to himself."

The inquisition of the Verasiun went on for hours. He was given only enough drugs and liquid to keep conscious and talking. The interrogation method used on him was quite simple. Twist, turn, verify, repeat, and go over his story a hundred different ways. After hours of questioning, the only story remaining was the truth. No one, including the Verasiun, had a good enough memory to remember every lie after extensive torture.

In a room not far from the Verasiun's interrogation, the second assassin taken off the transport was interviewed by members of the Prefect's secret militia. The interrogation method used on him was completely different. It was a friendly interview often referred to as a debriefing. Anything the agent asked for he got. Food, Cannis, and plenty of rest were the tools of his interrogators. The Prefect's men were his pals. He did anything he could to make them happy.

"Omar, can I call you Omar?"

"Sure, go ahead."

"First, I want to tell you that Prefect Conway is very pleased with the results of your mission. He has authorized a bonus which you will receive in a few days. How does that sound?"

"That's great."

"You understand how important it is for the Prefect to know everything you saw and heard on his son's ship? It's the only way he can make sound decisions as the leader of Earth. So, don't hold back on anything. Tell us everything no matter how difficult it might be to repeat or how trivial you believe it is. The future of Earth depends on your truthful testimony. Do you understand?"

"Sure. I'll tell you exactly what happened."

"Great! You mentioned earlier that Joseph locked you to a support post and gave you a deep wound cleansing pad for your vap pistol burns. In your own words, what happened after that? Don't leave out anything, Omar."

"Well, let's see. After Joseph gave me the pad, I rubbed it over my injured hand and fell asleep. When I regained consciousness, I heard Joseph and the Verasiun arguing about something. The Verasiun wanted his restrictor bracelet taken off which Joseph wouldn't do. I pretended to be asleep. I remembered the amplifier bud concealed in my wristband, so I snuck it into my ear. Before long, Joseph placed a communication to a private comm channel."

"Do you remember the private channel number?"

Omar shook his head trying in earnest to remember the number. "Sorry, I don't"

"That's okay. What happened next?"

"It was kind of hard hearing exactly what was said because the Verasiun was shouting smart-ass comments at Joseph. But whoever answered the communication referred to Joseph as a First Comrade, whatever that is. It seemed like Joseph was this being's superior. Anyhow, they talked about some Yandan Interceptors destroyed by hitting cloaked planets. Joseph was worried and spent a lot of time trying to figure out how they should respond. If I remember correctly, he said something like, "how can we turn this situation to our favor?"

"Do you remember how many Interceptors and what did he mean by cloaked planets?"

"I think he said five or six Interceptors. I haven't got any idea what he meant by cloaked planets. I've never heard of such a thing. Have you?"

"No, Omar, I haven't. What happened then?"

"There was some type of commotion on the receiving end of the communication. Whoever Joseph was talking to got more and more excited."

"Why did he do that, Omar?"

"He kept referring to an explosive found on something called a Shooting Star. He was afraid his technicians couldn't disarm it."

"What did Joseph say to that?"

Omar looked up sheepishly at his pals and shrugged. "Nothing. Absolutely nothing. He ended the communication."

The two militia interviewers looked at each other and wondered what the sudden end to Joseph's communication meant. One thought Omar must be mistaken and missed a critical piece of Joseph's communication. The other began to wonder if Omar was intentionally misleading them. Over the next several hours the interviewers questioned Omar, filling in the blanks in his story. They were as non-confrontational and agreeable as possible. It wasn't easy. With their military background and use of harsh tactics, it was difficult not grabbing Omar and beating the information out of him.

Joseph's communication to an unknown being somewhere in the universe consumed the interviewers. They were so focused on this conversation and its ramifications, they forgot to ask Omar if he heard anything else. Omar followed their lead and used all his brain power to remember what was said during Joseph's communication to a private comm number.

After a wonderful dinner, Omar went to bed satisfied he told his pals everything he heard and saw on the transport. He dreamed about the bonus coming his way. Everything that happened on the transport flashed through his dreams. The only thing missing was the communication Officer Morg and Joseph had with the Lead Trifect.

"So, let me see if I have this right. The Verasiun claims he heard my son say he was leading an invasion force against Yanda and her allies. His army is sneaking up on Yanda using cloaked planets and weapon platforms. And, when they're done winning that war, he's turning his army on Earth. And, after that victory, he will crown himself King of the Universe. Is that accurate?"

The supervisor of the militia interrogation team sat upright in the chair across from Prefect Conway. The stoic expression on his face was normal. In over twenty years, Prefect Conway hadn't seen the man display any sort of emotion. At times, he comically wondered if the militia supervisor and Mentat were relatives. But now, there was nothing funny about what his man reported.

"That's correct, Prefect."

Conway fought to keep his anger in check. He could throw a fit later. But for now, it was important not to let the militiaman know what he thought about his double-crossing son. The son who was just added to his enemy list. The son whose life meant nothing more than a piece of dung. And, the son who would suffer the consequences.

"The other agent I hired said what?"

"His name is Omar, sir. He claims to have overheard a communication between your son and an unknown being somewhere in the universe. Omar believes the unknown being is an important supervisor in Joseph's army. He told Joseph about the Yandan Interceptors crashing into their cloaked planets and weapon platforms. He also said they found an explosive on something called a Shooting Star and didn't know how to deactivate it. We've been able to confirm that the Yandans have an experimental Interceptor called the Shooting Star."

"Was that all they talked about?"

"Apparently, Joseph spent a lot of time thinking about how to deal with the crashing Interceptor problem. Omar said he was about to explain how to deal with the problem when the communication mysteriously ended."

"Who ended it?"

"Prefect, Omar doesn't know who or why."

There wasn't any question in the Prefect's mind that his son was a back-stabbing, son-of-a-bitch. The kid had an army and planned to use it to overthrow Yanda and his dictatorship. He admired the kid's initiative and creativity, but he had gone too far. He would have to pay the ultimate price for disloyalty.

After accepting his son as a traitor, Conway mellowed and began thinking about the technical piece of this new information. Was it true a large planet could cloak long enough to creep up on its enemy undetected? What an incredible piece of military hardware permanent cloaking could be. The more he thought about it, the more he relished the thought of having this knowledge. He had to think of a way to provoke his worthless son into turning over this technology.

"Should I have the Mentat question these two? As you know, he can tell when someone is lying."

"I don't think that's necessary, sir. I'm very confident we got the truth out of both of them."

"Very good. Excellent job. Here's what I want you to do. Send your interrogators on vacation to a remote planet. I don't want them on Earth for a couple days. And, make sure they keep their mouths shut. Anything they heard from Omar and the Verasiun is top-secret, confidential, not to be repeated."

"No problem, Prefect."

Conway got up from the conference table and started for the door. At the last second, he stopped and added, "Get rid of Omar and the Verasiun."

The militia supervisor knew exactly what that meant. The Verasiun had collected his last bit of useful information to sell and Omar wasn't getting a bonus from The Prefect.

38

The homecoming gala for Joseph Conway started at 10 a.m. and was still going strong at midnight. Everywhere Officer Morg looked there was entertainment and festivities. Cannis dispensers were plentiful for those who wanted to get and stay high. Kirrleon warriors gave demonstrations of jousting combat while riding Serian hawks. Three theaters on the perimeter of the government campus performed non-stop plays. The most popular thespians in the universe played the lead roles. Every type of old or popular music could be heard. Games of skill, trickery, and dexterity challenged the old, young, quick, and dim-witted.

Prefect Conway spared no expense to bring the best entertainers to Earth from the four corners of the universe. Joseph's homecoming was equal to any royal celebration.

Miller Millard and most of Earth's Global Union Assembly didn't share the Prefect's enthusiasm. They saw his extravagance as frivolous spending. It served no purpose other than welcoming back to Earth a royal pain-in-the-ass.

In the early afternoon, Morg snuck off to place a communication to the Lead Trifect. The communication only lasted ten minutes.

The Lead Trifect had a prepared plan for Morg to follow during the homecoming celebration and toxic gas condensator demo at Mikilopii volcano.

"Lead Trifect, did you see the broadcast of Prefect Conway welcoming his son home?"

"Yes, all of us watched it. Quite touching, wasn't it?"

"I don't know about touching, but did you hear him say his son spent the last eight years on a secret mission for Earth?"

"Officer Morg, we knew Joseph Conway was sent to Yanda as a spy. We watched every move and communication he made while he was here. His mission was to evaluate our military preparedness and health of the planet. He reported back to his father how long our atmosphere would last without an infusion of toxic gases. There was no sense trying to hide the condition of our atmosphere. It's widely known and can be found out through any number of different sources."

"Then, why did you allow him to stay on Yanda?"

"Because we fed him misinformation about our military. His old man bought most of it. Anyhow, when he outlived his usefulness, we tactfully sent him back to Earth on the transport. Someday, after things calm down, I'll tell you exactly how we used Joseph."

"Thank you, Lead Trifect. I look forward to that day."

"So do I, Officer. But, in the meantime be cautious and don't go anywhere unarmed. The Prefect is up to something, so be on your guard at all times. And, no matter what happens, keep the Prefect alive. He holds the key to Yanda's survival."

Morg signed off and rejoined the homecoming party. He tried to hide the troubling news the Lead Trifect shared with him.

"Officer Morg, you look upset. Do you feel okay?"

"Oh, hello, Joseph. I still don't feel very well. The vap pistol wounds plus the bug took more out of me than I thought." Morg grimaced in imaginary pain. He wanted the kid to think his ailment was physical rather than what he just learned communicating with the Lead Trifect.

"Joseph, you don't look very well either. What's wrong?"

"I guess the bug still has me by the balls. Great party, huh?"

"Yeah, your father spared no expense for your homecoming. He must think a lot of you."

"I'm sure he does. I'm sure he does."

Morg could tell the kid was lying. After spending ten light years of travel time with the kid on a small transport, Morg learned when he told the truth versus a lie. Repeating himself was the first clue the kid was lying. That combined with fluctuations in his voice tone and non-eye-contact confirmed a falsehood. There was no question the kid had a problem with his father. Morg didn't know what it was, but something was irritating him.

Morg was ready to continue the conversation but the kid's mind was elsewhere. His eyes darted every which way, surveying the crowd for something or someone.

"What are you looking for?" Morg's question went unanswered. The kid hadn't heard a word Morg said. He grabbed Joseph's arm and repeated, "Joseph, what are you looking for?"

"What? What, did you say Morg?"

"I've asked you a couple times what you're looking for?"

"Sorry, Morg. I'm supposed to meet someone tonight and I thought she might be in the crowd."

"Joseph, welcome home. It's been a long time."

Morg looked to his right to see the two strangers who joined the kid and himself. One was tall and lanky, with a pasty complexion and deep-set, narrow eyes. His jet-black hair and eyebrows blended well with the black outfit he wore. Morg immediately recognized this being as a Mentat. He ran into these creatures several times during his military career. All Mentats dressed entirely in black and had the same vacant look on their faces.

The other being who welcomed Joseph home was an Earthling. Morg guessed he was in his fifties. His clothes were modest yet custom-tailored from exquisite and expensive linens. The man had a deep tan which looked like it was spray-painted on his skin. He was groomed meticulously. Every strawberry-blonde hair had its place and Morg doubted that even a strong wind could move them from their assigned positions. When he opened his mouth, Morg couldn't take his eyes off the man's teeth. They sparkled a white which Morg didn't think was possible. They made Jimmy Washington's beautiful teeth look dingy.

"Oh, hello, Secretary-General Miller. Thanks for coming tonight. May I present Officer Morg. He and I flew the transport from Yanda to Earth."

"Hello, Officer. I've heard a lot about you. All good and very heroic, I might add. This gentleman is your father's Mentat." The Mentat gave Morg and the kid a slight nod.

For the next five minutes, the kid and Millard Miller bantered back and forth meaningless topics. Neither of them spoke of the meaningful topics on their minds. Morg and the Mentat stayed silent and listened to the verbal volley between the two Earthlings. It was evident they hated each other.

Morg lost interest and was ready to excuse himself when the kid asked Miller, "Have you seen Beth tonight?"

"Actually, Joseph, that's why I came over. I wondered the same thing. Have you seen her?"

"No, but answer this, Mr. Miller. Why would you be looking for a lowly assistant to the Prefect?"

Miller debated whether to say anything about Beth being the Prefect's concubine for several years. It was obvious that Joseph didn't know about their seedy liaison. He decided to keep that information to himself and not push his luck. If the kid found out about Beth's sexual prowess it was a short step to her espionage effort to bring down the Prefect. And then, the kid would find out about his hired Verasiun assassin.

"Nothing more than we've become friends over the past couple years, Joseph. She's a wonderful woman."

Joseph looked hard at Miller attempting to decide if he believed him or not. He opted to believe Miller, but it was what he didn't say that concerned him.

"When was the last time you saw her?"

"About six hours before your transport docked."

"Why don't we spread out and see if we can find her. Officer Morg, would you like to come with me?"

"Joseph, I'm going to retire for the night. In fact, I'm going to stop at the medical depot before turning in."

"That's a good idea, Officer. Get those wounds looked at and take some more bug medicine."

"Officer Morg, will I see you at the condensator demo tomorrow?"

"I plan on it, Mr. Miller. But I'll see how I feel in the morning."

"Brothers, have you made any progress identifying our cloaked enemies?"

The Lead Trifect only had to look at their faces to know what the answer was.

"Have any more of our Interceptors run into a cloaked planet?"

"Not one Lead Trifect."

"Can't our physicists identify some type of trail left by these cloaked invaders? There has to be some type of disturbance or residue left by a planet or weapon platform moving through space. It shouldn't matter whether they are cloaked or not. There should be something left behind in their wake."

"I'm sorry Lead Trifect. Our physicists haven't found a thing. They think the cloaked planets have either stopped or, or, or...."

"Or what?"

"Maybe they don't exist, sir."

The Lead Trifect was close to throwing a fit but caught himself. He began to question his logic. Had he created an incorrect theory from indisputable facts? Was his deductive reasoning flawed? As much as he didn't want to entertain the thought of being wrong, he had to consider it. What other theory could explain ships appearing and disappearing out of nowhere? And, what could explain five Interceptors bursting into atomic particles for no reason?

"Brothers, I understand why you and our physicists may not think there is an invisible enemy creeping toward Yanda. You are entitled to your opinion, but I still think my theory is right. Not only do the facts support my theory, but I can feel the enemy coming toward us. Yes, I can feel them."

The two underling Trifect looked at each other. They wondered if their boss was losing his mind. Since when was military strategy based on feelings?

"Brothers, I know what you are thinking. I would think the same if I was in your position. I'm not sure what else we can do now. Keep our Interceptors in a crisscross search pattern. Maybe one of them will stumble upon something. Otherwise, it's up to Officer Morg. I believe Prefect Conway is behind the cloaked armada preparing to invade Yanda. If Morg follows my plan, we have a chance. If he doesn't, we are doomed."

39

"Honored guests. Welcome to the Mount Mikilopii volcano. This morning, you will witness one of the greatest technological breakthroughs in the last thousand years. Behind me is Earth's toxic gas condensator. It captures over ninety percent of the toxic gases released by volcanos. The gases are reduced to their basic elements and compacted into secure shipping containers. These lightweight containers can then be sent economically to customers throughout the universe. Here on Earth, we have an overabundance of the toxic gases discharged from volcanos. However, many planets lack these basic elements which are vital to maintaining a healthy atmosphere for their inhabitants. When our condensator vessels arrive on these planets, the gases are recombined back to their original state and released into the atmosphere. It's a win-win. Earth gets rid of the toxic gases it doesn't need and the planets in need of these elements have their atmospheres restored."

"What a load of crap! If that were only true. This speaker, whoever he is, has obviously never heard of the CASETA Agreement which his exalted leader, the Prefect, reneged on. The Prefect is using this technology for political blackmail and advancing his military schemes."

While the Trifect underlings waited for the Lead Trifect to cool down, they intently watched and listened to the condensator demonstration ten light years away. On the lip of the volcano was a massive piece of equipment which towered five stories in height and a quarter-mile in length. It sat on a perfectly cut ledge twenty-five feet from the summit. The back side of the condensator hung over the volcano lip so its input ducts could suck in the toxic gases released from within the earth. In front of the condensator was a viewing stadium chiseled into the mountainside. It held a maximum of three thousand beings. The ships which brought attendees to Mikilopii hover-docked in a semi-circle around the volcano.

Everywhere the Trifect looked, Earth technicians watched, adjusted, and minded the condensator equipment. They estimated the crowd on Mount Mikilopii to be several hundred. The demo attendees consisted of dignitaries from the most influential and powerful planets in the universe. Their fancy clothes and uniforms were the norm rather than the exception.

"Lead Trifect, I see the Earthling. There he is!"

The Lead Trifect looked to where his brother Trifect pointed on the halo-screen. Standing on the presentation stage, approximately ten yards from the speaker, was Joseph Conway. It was easy to see the kid wasn't interested in what the speaker had to say. His head swiveled right and left repeatedly. The Lead Trifect wondered what he was looking for.

"I wonder where Officer Morg is? Shouldn't he be on the stage with the Earthling?"

"Brother, I hope he isn't. In fact, he better not be anywhere near that presentation. He should still be in sickbay."

The Trifect underlings looked at each other and wondered how their boss knew Officer Morg was receiving medical attention at that moment.

"Most of you don't know this, but Mount Mikilopii has a minor eruption every three years. The eruption is as predictable as the sun rising in the east and setting in the west. We are in luck, for today is exactly three years since its last eruption. So, in approximately forty-eight minutes, the gods who live within Mikilopii will once again rumble awake from their long slumber and vomit lava and gases."

The speaker was proud of his cutesy description of the upcoming eruption. He thought how clever he was referencing the Polynesian gods who lived within the volcano. The broad smile on his face vanished when he realized the crowd didn't share his sentiments. Anxiety ran through the crowd. There was an undertow of comments racing back and forth. People looked at each other with apprehension and wondered about their safety. Many started to file out of the viewing stadium and headed for the docking platform to make a hurried departure.

"Honored guests, there's nothing to be afraid of. The condensator equipment will control the eruption. It will moderate the energy given off by the mountain. Rather than one or two huge blasts, the volcano's energy will be released in many minor explosions. You'll feel a slight trembling underfoot but that's all...."

The speaker's pleas didn't convince the crowd. When they heard the word "explosions", pandemonium broke out. The guests ran, crawled, and battled their way to the stadium exits. Joseph Conway and Miller Millard stood their ground on the stage and watched the confusion below. They didn't notice the speaker hauled off the stage by militia goons and replaced by Prefect Conway and Beth.

The Prefect and Beth ascended the podium like heads-of-state. His entire wardrobe was a rich purple. Even his shoes were the color of royalty. The only non-purple items were six ten-carat diamonds which served as buttons running in a vertical line down the middle of his waistcoat.

He held Beth's right arm high to escort her to the podium. The tiara on her head and the full-length cape draped around her shoulders shimmered gold, silver, and platinum in the mid-morning sun.

The expression on her face was one of a reluctant participant in an elaborate scam.

Thunderous horns erupted from the audio system and filled the stadium. Their collective blast overwhelmed every other sound. The fleeing guests, stadium marshals, and laborers froze in place. The simple melody the horns played announced something great. Everyone's attention refocused to the stage where they beheld Prefect Conway and a beautiful young lady dressed as a princess.

Joseph Conway didn't recognize Beth at first. The heavy layers of colored makeup around her eyes and smeared on the lips hid her natural beauty. The tiara and jewels hanging from her ears and hair were ornaments a make-believe goddess would wear. The girl from his youth would never make a spectacle of herself with such gaudy accessories.

His eyes bulged from his head when he realized who was standing next to his father. Without thinking of why or what it meant, he yelled to his former love and headed for the podium. Miller Millard grabbed him from behind and held him in place with a bear-hug. The horns stifled his call so only a weak "Beth" reached the Prefect and his concubine. Neither of them looked in his direction. Prefect Conway needed to get the crowd under control and Beth was too embarrassed to look in his direction.

The Prefect stood motionless and stared into the crowd. Each guest felt like he was the object of his piercing gaze. The horns stopped. No one spoke to each other. Like scolded children, the guests filed back to their seats and waited to hear what the Prefect had to say.

"Isn't this a beautiful morning?"

When the crowd stayed quiet, the Prefect asked again, "I said, isn't this a beautiful morning?"

The crowd didn't understand why the Prefect was asking such an odd question when a volcanic eruption was less than a half-hour away. Half the crowd wondered if he was crazy. The other half hoped he wasn't. Everyone in the crowd replied with a weak "yes".

"Ladies and gentlemen let me welcome you to Earth's first-ever demonstration of the toxic gas condensator. You have my word that you are as safe here as anywhere in the universe. That includes your home planet. Frankly, I wouldn't be here if I thought there was any chance of endangering my life or the life of Queen Beth."

The Prefect looked at Beth and smiled. Three men rushed onto the stage with an ornate throne and helped the bejeweled Beth into it.

"Isn't she beautiful?" Again, the guests responded with a feeble approval.

"Yes, she is a beautiful creature." The Prefect stopped and leaned toward the crowd. He cupped his ear straining to hear an imaginary question from someone in the crowd. "What's that? You don't know who she is? We have a few minutes before the demonstration so let me tell you about the stunning Queen Beth."

Prefect Conway went over to Beth and kissed her on the forehead. Joseph went rigid with anger.

"Queen Beth has a humble history. She grew up in a dirt-poor family. Her father was a drunkard and her mother a Jessabelle. I graciously took her out of this pathetic existence and gave her everything. Food, clothes, a beautiful home; anything her heart desired. And, all she had to do in exchange was be faithful and put-out occasionally. You might say she is a high-priced concubine."

Beth's fingernails dug into the chair's wood arms. Her face turned crimson and sweat ran down her forehead. The crowd loved the trashy story told by the Prefect. They forgot about the up-coming volcanic eruption. Joseph Conway tried to break free from Millard's grasp. Miller had no love for the kid, but they did share one thing; they both hated Prefect Conway. If he let go, the kid would be cut down before he got within ten feet of his father.

"And, how did Queen Beth repay me for this life of luxury? She became a traitor. She joined the rebel faction who plots daily to overthrow my administration. She and her friends want to end my reign and turn Earth into a Yandan colony. And, when that's done, Earth's

Global Union Assembly will be squashed. Earth will no longer determine its own destiny. We will no longer own the rights or profits from our condensator technology. All toxic gases will be sent to the thieves on Yanda. Our friends on Florid will be suffocated out of existence. The swine on Yanda will be our masters."

The Prefect's accusations had the desired effect. The Floridians in the crowd called out for the execution of Beth, the whore queen. Most of the Earthlings backed the Prefect and screamed out their allegiance to him. Rulers and powerful guests from other planets cast their doubts aside and fell in line with the pro-Prefect fervor in the stadium. The only opposition within the stadium came from Millard and Joseph Conway. They stood on stage trying to out-scream the crowd. Their effort to tell the crowd about the lunatic Prefect got drowned out. Ten light years away, the Lead Trifect swore to kill the Prefect if he got the opportunity.

When the shouting and swearing subsided, the Prefect started again. "But.... but, let me tell you the rest of what's been going on. That man, over there, is the leader of the rebels." Prefect Conway pointed and shook his finger at Miller. "I'm speaking of the Millard Miller, the Secretary-General of the Assembly. He's the mastermind who wants to turn Earth over to the Yandans. He and some fellow rebels in the Assembly want you to be slaves to the Yandans."

"That's not true. The Prefect lies. He's a lunatic who...." Miller went down hard onto the stage when a militiaman slammed the butt of his assault rife against his head.

"That's what all traitors deserve." The crowd erupted in applause and yells of support.

Prefect Conway raised both arms above his head to quiet the crowd. "My fellow beings, there's more. I saved the most despicable piece of information for last. I'm sorry to say, my only son, Joseph, is also a conspirator and Yandan spy." There was dead silence in the stadium. The crowd was shocked by this revelation. How could a son betray his father? Wasn't this the same son who received a lavish homecoming party?

Two militiamen put Joseph in restraints and gagged him.

"My son has assembled a massive army whose mission is to overthrow Earth, Florid and our allies. His wave of death is moving toward Earth as I speak. He is working hand-in-hand with the Yandans who have promised him riches and power to overthrow Earth. Fortunately, my Mentat uncovered the plot against Earth and brought it to my attention. I am so embarrassed... embarrassed that the son I showered with love is a traitor to his family and planet."

A disappointed Prefect hung his head and wiped fake tears from his cheeks. His portrayal of a dejected parent was flawless. He let the crowd sympathize with his despair and build a hatred for the treacherous, good-for-nothing son. The Mentat who was at the rear of the stage looked on in disbelief. He didn't warn the Prefect about an invading army led by his son. Was this a joke or fable created to enrage the crowd? Or, could it be the Prefect knew of his association with Millard, Beth, and the rebels within the Assembly? This had to be Conway's way of driving a wedge of suspicion between them. He knew his days of being a trusted Mentat were over. From this day forward he was a disgraced, rogue Mentat.

The Prefect raised his head slowly and looked to the crowd with grim determination. He reached toward the heavens and screamed, "No....no, I will not allow these traitors to destroy the good folks of Earth and Florid. That will not happen."

He shook his finger at the crowd so violently his entire upper body shuddered in rage. "I make you this promise. I will get to the bottom of this treachery and put an end to it. I don't care what methods I use, even if I have to torture my own flesh and blood. The Yandan army led by my son will be destroyed. That is my promise to you. We will persevere."

The crowd erupted in cheering and cat-calls. A few of the more enraged guests tried to rush the stage to attack Miller, Joseph Conway, and Beth. The militiamen guarding the stage made a half-hearted effort to push them back.

Prefect Conway took a satin cloth from his waistband and wiped the perspiration and spittle from his face. The carotid artery in his neck throbbed with less intensity. The overflow of blood to his face started to drain. His beet-red complexion returned to normal.

"The end to this menace will start now. Bring Millard Miller over here."

The Secretary-General was dragged to the podium. A trail of his blood smeared the stage floor.

"Millard Miller, why are you an enemy of Earth?"

Miller stayed on his knees trying to catch his breath and avoid another butt-end of an assault rife. "I...I don't know what you're talking about."

"Why do you lie? Do you deny that you conspired with members of the Assembly to overthrow the rightful government of Earth? Do you deny that you wanted to give condensator technology to Yanda? Do you deny that you did everything possible to push through the CASETA Agreement with Yanda? Were you opposed to a toxic gas agreement with Florid?"

"Yes, I did those things for the betterment of Earth. Anything to ...."

"You lie, dog. You did those things for your own self-interest and enrichment. You had a vested interest in having the CASETA Agreement signed with Yanda. You would profit handsomely from Yandan kick-backs. Unlucky for you, I found out about your plot to cheat the people of Earth."

"That's not true. I did everything for..."

The Prefect nodded his head and one of the militia goons gave Miller a quick kick to his kidneys. Miller rolled on his side and gasped for air. As the Prefect prepared to accuse Miller of another crime, the ground trembled. A few boulders dislodged from the mountainside and rolled onto the demonstration platform. Everyone in the stadium either fell to the ground or latched on to something to keep their footing.

"Ah, the Mikilopii gods have awakened."

Prefect Conway looked to the lead technician for the condensator equipment. "How soon before the volcano spews its gases and lava?"

"Two minutes, Prefect."

"Wonderful. The gods are going to be very satisfied this eruption." He turned back to Miller. "One last question, dog. Do you deny that you conspired with the whore over there?"

Miller looked at Beth who was held in the royal throne by two militiamen. Her face paint ran down her cheeks in a rainbow of colors. There was no sense responding to the Prefect's question. No matter how he answered the Prefect, it would be use it as evidence in a trumped-up conspiracy.

"Take this dog away. Feed him to Mikilopii."

Miller struggled the best he could. Years of physical exercise tested the militia goons. The crowd watched as he fought the entire way to the top of the condensator. When the volcano rumbled again, the Prefect gave a thumbs down. Miller went head-first into the erupting volcano. The only sound heard was a scream from the militia goon who couldn't break free from Miller's grasp and went over the lip of the volcano to a fiery death. The crowd applauded and screamed their approval.

"Now, my son, it's your turn. Are you going to cooperate or join your buddy, Miller?"

"You, pathetic piece of dung. You can kiss my ass. The only regret I have in life is you were my sperm donor. You certainly weren't a father."

"That's not nice to say, Joseph. And, after all the nice things I did for you. I sent an agent to Alpha 30 to make sure you got safely back to Earth. I gave you a great homecoming party. And, I slept with your girlfriend for years. If that isn't the description of a good father, I don't know what is."

Most of the crowd laughed at the Prefect's quip about bedding his son's girlfriend. Beth and Joseph fought to break free of their captors. They wanted to get their hands around the Prefect's neck and strangle the life out of him. The more they struggled, the more Prefect Conway laughed at them.

"Kid, you have something I want. Earth needs your cloaking technology."

The Prefect waited for his son to think about what he was demanding. "I'm sure you're wondering how I know about the cloaking technology. Do you remember the Verasiun agent on your transport? He was sent to Alpha 30 by Miller to kill you, but a strange thing happened. The Verasiun overheard you talking about your army's use of cloaked planets and weapon platforms. And, instead of killing you, he decided to make a deal with you. Well, he never got the chance to cash in on what he knew. However, he was nice enough to tell me about your cloaking technology."

The Prefect laughed deviously to himself. "So, the question my dear boy is this. Are you going to help your old man or be an obstinate brat and refuse to cough-up how this technology works?"

Joseph knew his father would use the cloaking technology to overrun any planet that stood in his way to rule the universe. Planets would be given a choice. Either become an Earth colony or be destroyed by an invisible invasion force. As long as he withheld the secret of this technology from his old man, he had a chance to live. Giving up the information was signing his own death warrant.

"I have no idea what you are talking about, old man. Have you finally lost your mind? What cloaking technology?"

Prefect Conway grinned and shook his head. He had reached his limit of patience and didn't have the time or energy to play mind games with his son.

"I really wish you hadn't said that." He turned and swaggered toward the lyft which would take him to the top of the condensator unit. "Bring the whore."

Between the restrictor bracelets and militia goons, Joseph was locked in place. His gag was removed but the only part of his body he could move was his head. He watched his father, Mentat and two goons escort Beth into the lyft and ascend to the top of the condensator. When the doors opened, they dragged her by the hair onto the same viewing platform Miller was thrown from.

The Prefect turned on the audio system which amplified everything spoken at the top of the condensator and on the stage below. "Hello, down there, boy. Now I'm going to ask you only once. Are you willing to trade this whore's life for your cloaking technology? Yes or no?"

The kid knew he was screwed. No matter what he decided was wrong. There was no negotiating with a psychotic like his father. There was nothing he could counter-offer to keep the old man in check. The final question was simple. Should he and Beth die now or try to delay the inevitable and hope for a miracle?

"I'm waiting, son. You have ten seconds and then your love goes into the belly of Mikilopii."

The crowd below screamed for her execution. Few of them understood what was at stake. They had no idea what the Prefect was talking about when he described a cloaked army, Alpha 30 and a Verasiun assassin.

"Okay, okay. I'll tell you. Just leave her alone. Let her go and I'll tell you."

"Boy, when will you learn your old man is smarter than you? You come up here and place a communication to your lead physicist. As soon as he makes the specifications transfer to my physicists, I'll let Beth go."

"How do I know you'll keep your end of the bargain?"

"You don't. You have exactly thirty seconds to get your ass up here or watch her go into the volcano. Hear that rumble? The Mikilopii gods are hungry, again."

"Then tell these monkeys to take off my restrictor bracelets so I can walk and use my hands."

The Prefect nodded to the goons below. The guards led the kid to the lyft for the fifteen-second ride to the top of the condensator. It was the shortest fifteen seconds of the kid's life. He racked his brain trying to think of a way to turn the tables on his old man.

When the lyft stopped at the summit he was still groping for a solution.

"Beth are you okay? Don't cry, darling." Joseph tried to hug her but was shoved toward the communications control panel.

"You can play with her later, Joseph. Place the communication and let's get this over with."

Everyone listened as Joseph placed a communication to a private comm number. Whoever answered on the other end was frantic. The destruction of Ziptowtheon had left the armada leaderless. They didn't know whether to go forward with the assault on Yanda, retreat or wait for new instructions.

"First Comrade Joseph, what are we to do?"

Joseph stalled for more time trying to think of a way out of his predicament. There wasn't one. He was in a corner with no escape.

"Soldier, your orders are to stand-down. The authorization code is State Street 64. Also, I want you to have the cloaking specs transferred to this sender unit immediately. The authorization code for this is Old Hickory 99. Do you understand?"

"Yes, First Comrade. Stand down and transfer cloaking specs. Anything else, sir?"

"No, only verify the authorization codes and pass on my instructions to everyone in the armada. Also, thank everyone for a job well done. Take care, soldier."

"That was very touching, Joseph. I didn't know you were such a savvy leader. Another thing you picked up from me." The Prefect laughed at his sarcastic remark. Anything he could do or say to belittle his son's competency was worth a good laugh.

The transfer of cloaking technology took less than four minutes. Earth's physicists did a flash verification of all the formulas to ensure they were correct and made sense. Mikilopii started to rumble again as the physicists pour over the data.

"Prefect, the data looks correct and the underlying theory is very plausible. In fact, the theory is simple. I can't believe no one else thought of it."

"Excellent. You have done well Joseph. Now, here is your reward."

The Prefect nodded to the militia goons who took Beth by the arms and threw her over the observation platform railing. "That's for calling me Honey Nuts, you bitch."

"No. No." Joseph ran to the railing, hoping to save his love. He never got there. The two goons beat him about the head and back with enforcement batons. When he was nearly unconscious, the goons looked to the Prefect for his approval to toss the kid over the railing. The Prefect gave a thumbs down. The crowd below roared with approval and delight. The real-life drama unfolding before them was better than most fictional plays and stories.

The goons bent over to pick up the kid. They didn't make it. One was sliced in half and the other was lifted into the air and thrown over the railing like a rag doll. A quarter-mile from Mikilopii, Morg locked-in the transport's laser cannons on targets and opened-up. After the two militia goons, he swept the mountainside taking out anyone who looked like he might be associated with Prefect Conway.

Joseph struggled to move along the platform floor. The beating left him with a cracked skull, shattered vertebrae, and many broken bones. He found one of the goon's vap pistol and pointed it at his father.

"Son, you don't want to do that. I'll give you anything you want. Miller and Beth deserved..."

Morg watched the Prefect beg for his life. As much as he wanted to see the Prefect's reign end, he needed to follow the Lead Trifect's instructions. He opened up the transport's external audio and spoke to the kid.

"Joseph don't kill the Prefect. The Trifect needs to know about his cloaking technology."

The kid took in a deep breath and mumbled, "It was me, Morg. It was my technology." That was all he said before passing out.

Prefect Conway went for the vap pistol. Morg locked-in on him but didn't know whether to fire or not. Should he believe the kid or consider this another one of his egotistic lies? He had milliseconds to decide. Either let him pick up the vap pistol or kill him. He hesitated too long. The Mentat walked up behind the Prefect, lifted him into the air and tossed him over the railing. The being who was trained as a truth detector had made Morg's decision.

There was dead silence in the conference room. The three Trifect continued to stare at the halo-screen long after the broadcast stopped.

"Brothers, I think we just averted a major catastrophe."

40

"Who's that heading our way in the land cruisers?"

Morg squinted toward the horizon shielding his eyes from the two suns orbiting Feltte Six. His parabolic shaped ears heard the cruisers long before seeing them in the distance. From the reverberating sounds, Morg estimated their distance at roughly ten miles.

"Help me up, Morg. Damn, I hate these prosthetics. I feel like a marionette puppet.

Before Morg could turn around and help the kid, the Mentat lifted Joseph to a standing position. The kid was relieved to finally get out of the custom-built chair designed for patients recovering from spinal injuries. In the past two years, the kid's skull fused back together, and his leg and arm bones mended as well as possible. He would never be a star athlete but that wasn't a problem. He wasn't known for his physical dexterity before being beaten silly by his father's goons. The next year would tell the story of whether he could walk again without robotic prosthetics.

"Why don't we call it a day. I don't know about you guys, but this heat zaps the hell out of me. Let's clean up for our guests."

The kid, Jimmy Washington, and Mentat went into a mobile

cleaning unit. They emerged five minutes later in fresh clothes and scrubbed clean from head to foot. Morg had his own mobile cleaning unit which used a custom-formulated, acidic wash rather than water. They relished the end of each day when the fine-grit pumice and sand washed down the drain.

None of them imagined they would end up as Molum crystal miners. Each day was ten hours of drudgery. Blast away to uncover new deposits of crystals. Load the ore into separators which extracted the valuable crystals. Then make sure every hauler transport was at maximum capacity before flying off to the Precious Mineral Exchange. On a good day, their crystals netted a fortune. On a bad day, they took in a smaller fortune.

Morg went to the mess hall and put enough dinners in the auto cooker to feed ten beings. That left a couple extra dinners in case neighbor miners dropped in for a visit. It was a rare evening when unexpected guests didn't show up for camaraderie and Cannis laced drinks. For some reason, the two earthlings, Mentat and Yandan attracted other miners in the area. At first, Morg thought it was because they were celebrities. After all, they took down the criminal regime of Prefect Conway. But, after two years he changed his mind. They were no longer considered celebrities but rather, the good guys who operated the Honey Nuts mining company.

Morg looked out of the mess hall at his partners. Each day he marveled at how four beings with such extreme and diverse backgrounds could become close friends. Somehow, a cab driver, truth detector, career military officer, and egomaniacal genius got along. In a rare instance of Yandan emotion, he smiled to himself and thanked his ancestors for the three pals who sat around the outdoor enviropit.

Morg had just enough time to pour himself a Cannis drink before the two land cruisers arrived. He wasn't surprised to see Luna and Samantha, but the third guest was a shock. He took a large gulp of the Cannis drink and watched in amazement as the Lead Trifect disembarked.

"Lead Trifect, what are you doing here?"

"Well, officer Morg, I thought I'd better come out here to deliver this message in person. It seems your discharge from the military was never approved. Yandi, you are still on active duty."

The normal gray and green of Morg's face drained away. His pulse doubled and the repulsion glands behind his knees and elbows began to open to discharge their noxious smelling odor. The Lead Trifect knew what was coming so he quickly corrected his sarcastic remark.

"I'm kidding, Morg. Luna and Sam put me up to it. They thought it would be funny. It's what the Earthlings call a joke. You should know Yanda doesn't want an old fart like you in their modern military."

Everyone around the enviropit started laughing. Even the Mentat broke a smile. Morg was still frozen in place, fearful there might be something more to the Lead Trifect's antic.

"Son, I'm here for a visit. I'm on an inspection tour of ally planets and thought it would be good to see you again. Trust me, you are not in the military. Why don't you show me around your Molum crystal mine?"

Morg and the Lead Trifect spent close to an hour going through a few excavated caves which produced load after load of Molum crystals. If the mining engineers were right, the rich veins in the Honey Nuts mine would continue to produce high-grade crystals for another two-hundred years.

The questions the Lead Trifect asked were thoughtful and detailed. It was obvious he had a genuine interest and curiosity about the mining operation. Each time Morg tried to change the subject to current conditions on Yanda, the Lead Trifect deflected his questions.

"Morg, why is it so damn hot down here? I would think it should be cooler than the planet surface because it's underground."

"The reason is because the mine is between two ancient lava fields. Believe it or not, the lava, thousands of feet below, is still liquid and very hot. That heat rises and collects in our caves. If we didn't have these huge exhaust fans, working in here would be impossible."

"Interesting. By the way, how did you find these Molum crystals? None of you are mining engineers, so how did you find this deposit?"

"Lead Trifect, it would take me hours to tell you the entire story. The short version is that a dying Trikian shared the secret with me."

"So, you were in the right place at the right time?"

"That's very close to the truth, Lead Trifect. I had to spend some time piecing together the Trikian's clues, but he provided enough information to figure out the location of this deposit."

"Is this your only mine?"

"For now, yes. If we decide to expand, we'll open another mine about twenty clicks from here. We know there's another rich deposit in that area. We've already picked out a name for it. We're going to name it after Luna's mother who was the Yandan agent killed on Alpha 30. Do you remember her?"

The Lead Trifect thought for a moment trying to recall every event which took place on Alpha 30 during the epidemic. "Do you mean the female Landan who was found dead in a closet?" Before Morg answered, the Lead Trifect continued. "She was Luna's mother? The Luna I came out here with today?"

"That's right, sir."

"It's certainly a small universe, Morg. Very small."

Morg and the Lead Trifect left the mine and headed back to the base camp.

"Morg, I don't know if I should bring this up, but do you want to know about your offspring?"

"I don't think so, sir. I have a feeling you would tell me nothing but bad news."

"You know your offspring well. They have pissed away all your estate and pension. Do you want to set up a minor trust for them?"

"Absolutely not. It's about time they get off their lazy asses and fend for themselves."

"I understand. Sometimes the best thing you can do for someone is make them take responsibility. I've been doing the same thing at the palace. It hasn't been easy getting rid of the dead weight. I'm amazed by how many freeloaders we had working for the government."

"Otherwise, how are things on Yanda?"

"Actually, pretty good. After signing the CASETA Agreement with Earth we started to retoxify the atmosphere. There's been a remarkable change in the health of our citizens. We also figured out Joseph Conway's cloaking technology, so we'll never be surprised again by a rogue army who wants to destroy us."

"That's great, Lead Trifect. With everything going so well, you should be able to retire soon."

Morg waited for an answer but none came. The debacle of sending Joseph Conway to Earth taught the Lead Trifect many lessons. First, he made too many mistakes and had a lot to learn. He was still reeling from misjudging Prefect Conway as the brains behind the cloaking technology and its army. But, the most important lesson was the realization that he enjoyed being the Lead Trifect for the Yandan empire. He wasn't going to kid himself any longer. He desired and thrived on the power of the position. He had no intention of turning over this power until he died or was too ill to perform the duties.

When they got back to the base camp, everyone was sitting around the enviropit. The constant mild temperature plus bug-and-animal-free condition created by the enviropit was perfect for outdoor get-togethers.

The first thing Morg noticed was Luna and Joseph holding hands and sneaking a kiss every so often. He didn't understand their attraction to each other, but when it came to love and affection, he was far from an expert. All he could hope for was that the trip from Yanda to Earth had matured Joseph into a decent being. He thought it had, but when it came to the kid it was smart to hope for the best but expect the unexpected. Regardless, Luna deserved the best in life.

"Can I have everyone's attention? I have an announcement, so everyone grab a drink and listen up."

It was Samantha, Jimmy's girlfriend, calling the group to order. It was obvious from Jimmy's expression that he didn't have a clue what her announcement was about.

"Everyone. On the way here, something very unusual happened. I'm not going to give you all the details, but the bottom line is that the Lead Trifect asked me if I wanted to be the next Yandan Director for Feltte Six. For those of you who don't know, the job is being the Feltte Six ambassador to Yanda. I agreed to take the position providing Jimmy agrees."

Jimmy was the first to respond. He stood up with his Cannis drink and said, "Here's to my best friend, Sam, the next Director for Feltte Six. Everyone saluted her and took a healthy gulp as Jimmy and Sam kissed.

And, the being who enjoyed the evening the most was the Mentat. He finally learned what having friends was all about.

DEAR READER

Dear reader,

We hope you enjoyed reading *Ten Light-Years to Insanity*. If you have a moment, please leave us a review - even if it's a short one. We want to hear from you.

Want to get notified when one of Creativia's books is free to download? Join our spam-free newsletter at http://www.creativia.org.

Best regards,

C.M. Dancha and the Creativia Team

NOTES

CHAPTER 1

1. Apparatus used for sitting, relaxation, and sleeping. It is balanced independently of the ship's direction and motion.
2. A device which captures and translates words and some thoughts from one language to another.
3. A hollowed-out tube made of synthetic drugs. User blows into one end of stick to create plume of hallucinogenic gas or breathes in on the other end to inhale hallucinogenic drugs.
4. One stralock equals approximately fifty pounds.
5. Ruling military body on planet Yanda. Consists of three members; the Lead Trifect and two underlings known as brother Trifect.
6. Propulsion system used by spacecraft. The ship locks onto a distant light source near its intended destination. When the light source is eliminated, a vacuum is created which pulls the ship through space at a fraction of the speed of light.
7. Containers located throughout spacecrafts which provide liquid nourishment, medicine, and hallucinogenic drugs to the passengers. Contents are gravity fed from the containers mounted at ceiling level.
8. Small, oval glands on the exterior of a Yandan's bony, exoskeletal membrane. They glow aqua and chartreuse when excited by good news. Not to be confused with displeasure pods which glow red when a Yandan is angered.
9. A plant grown on Yanda which emits a hallucinogenic sap three times per year. Very rare and difficult to cultivate. Used by Yandans of higher rank to boost libido and courage.

CHAPTER 3

1. A weapon used by elite Yandan invasion troopers. It is lightweight, reliable, and very accurate. A rife can discharge either 'sound' or 'hard' ammunition.
2. A six-legged, pig size animal used by Yandan invasion troopers to root out enemy troops hiding in subterranean tunnels and caves.
3. An illegal and unlicensed party establishment open from sunset to sunrise. Serves all types of drugs and alcoholic beverages. Some blind pigs double as prostitution and gambling dens.

CHAPTER 6

1. Large holographic screen used to project images and transmit dialogue. Used often by planets, ships and outposts when communicating over long distances.
2. A being from the planet Mentattis. All Mentats are male and are trained to identify beings who are lying and withholding information. Mentats are leased to planetary governments throughout the universe. The lease amount is high but well worth the expense. A good Mentat will pay for himself many times over.

ABOUT THE AUTHOR

C. "Mike" Dancha retired five years ago and immediately began pursuing his life-long dream of writing fictional novels. Story plots and characters collected for nearly fifty years are being "put to paper" as quickly as his passion for golf will allow. He and his lovely wife live in sunny Florida after escaping the arctic tundra known as Minnesota. His greatest compliment is when a reader asks, "Wow! How did you think of that?"

CPSIA information can be obtained
at www.ICGtesting.com
Printed in the USA
LVHW090838150920
666052LV00013B/251